6

GARRETT LEIGH

Riptide Publishing
PO Box 1537
Burnsville, NC 28714
www.riptidepublishing.com

What Remains

Cover art: Garrett Leigh, blackjazzdesign.com
Editor: Carole-ann Galloway
Layout: L.C. Chase, lcchase.com/design.htm

ISBN: 978-1-62649-398-8

First edition
July, 2016

Also available in ebook:
ISBN: 978-1-62649-397-1

What
REMAINS

GARRETT LEIGH

RIPTIDE
PUBLISHING

For my Foxes, with love . . .

Table of CONTENTS

Prologue

The remnants of their broken dreams lay scattered all around . . . but what remained was something beautiful.

July 24, 2014

"**D**on't go." Jodi tugged playfully on Rupert's coat. "Come on. You had that big warehouse fire yesterday, and the gas leak. Take the rest of the week off."

Rupert grinned and allowed Jodi to reel him in with the dark, cajoling eyes he'd been unable to resist since that damp December night four years ago. Not that Rupert often tried that hard. Jodi was an addiction he had no interest in quitting. Now, though, he needed to pull away. "I gotta go, boyo. I'm late already."

Jodi scowled. "Late for what? Sitting around watching football with a bunch of old men?"

"I'd imagine so, until a call comes in. It's Saturday night. Whatever happens, it ain't gonna be quiet."

"Wish it was—" Jodi's grumble was cut off by his phone. He retrieved it from his back pocket, glanced at the screen, then tossed it onto the couch. "Sophie's bitching. Would you believe I'm late too?"

Rupert chuckled. Jodi's tardy timekeeping was legendary. "We'd both better go, then. You're hitting the town, remember? Come on."

"It's only dinner at Sophie's." Jodi planted his feet stubbornly on the shiny wooden floor—kept so dust-free by his unnatural obsession with his elderly Henry hoover—still gripping Rupert's coat. "I'm not even hungry. I just want to stay here with you."

Rupert's heart ached. He'd wanted to be a firefighter since he was six years old, but as much as he loved his job, he loved Jodi more. "You're always hungry, and you know I'd stay if I could."

"Hmm. Perhaps I can persuade you."

Jodi dropped to his knees, taking Rupert's tracksuit bottoms with him. He hooked his thumbs around Rupert's underwear and dispensed with that too, then lifted Rupert's feet out of it and tossed it away.

He pushed Rupert against the nearby living room wall and traced Rupert's balls with his tongue. The gesture should've felt devilish and filthy, but Jodi's touch was gentle and hypnotic, so much so that it was hard for Rupert to remember why he'd ever tell him no. Reluctantly, he stilled Jodi's hands. "I've gotta *go*."

Jodi sighed and pressed his forehead into Rupert's thigh. It was about as close to admitting defeat as he ever got, and Rupert's tenuous grasp on his self-control broke. He hauled Jodi to his feet. Jodi let out a grunt of surprise, but responded almost instantly, crushing their lips together and growling into Rupert's mouth.

Rupert groaned. Jodi was smaller than him, slighter, leaner, but when it came to sex, he was all the man Rupert could take, even now—especially now—with his hands, tongue, and teeth everywhere. Blunt nails raking over his skin. They stumbled to the bedroom. Jodi pushed Rupert onto the bed, stripping his own scruffy T-shirt and tossing it over his shoulder. He straddled Rupert's waist. "I need you."

The gravelly confession lit Rupert on fire. He grasped Jodi's slender hips and rolled over, pinning Jodi beneath his broader frame. "You don't ever have to need me. I'm always here."

Jodi's dark gaze flashed. *No, you're not.*

Rupert growled and wrestled with Jodi's belt buckle. The silent accusation was true, but far from fair. Rupert worked long shifts, often leaving Jodi for twenty-four hours or more, but Jodi had an engrossing occupation of his own and rarely had nothing to do when Rupert was gone. Rupert fixed Jodi with a glare. *I'm here when it matters.*

He yanked Jodi's skinny jeans down his legs and threw them on the floor, then reached for the lube in the bedside drawer.

Jodi claimed it with a devilish smirk and shoved him onto his back. "Like this."

As if Rupert would argue. Jodi was a dominant lover. People often said he had an ethereal look about him, but his fragile form was a wonderful deception. Despite his long limbs and slim bones, there was nothing delicate about Jodi. He loved Rupert fiercely and demanded it back in return.

Jodi tore open a condom and rolled it onto Rupert. "I *need* you, Rupe."

"You have me." Rupert gritted his teeth, hardly able to contain himself as Jodi rubbed lube into himself, stretching and teasing. "I'm right here."

"Show me."

Rupert drove up into Jodi in one slow slide. Smooth, tight heat enveloped him, and his vision blurred, obscuring Jodi's beautiful form. He thrust his hips, softly at first, but as Jodi pushed down, meeting Rupert's every move, Rupert's caution faded away. Fucking Jodi was like breathing, he didn't need to think about it, just closed his eyes and felt, letting Jodi fall apart around him, rushing him to a heady climax that made his head spin.

He came fast and hard with a low roar, mindful of their nosy downstairs neighbours. Jodi wasn't so considerate. He yelled out and came all over Rupert's chest, then collapsed to one side in a sweaty heap.

Rupert chuckled and tossed the condom into the bin by the bed. "Wanna shift over? I've got time for a quick spoon."

"I wanna reverse spoon."

"Come on then."

Jodi grunted drowsily, and they crawled under the covers, Jodi curled against Rupert's chest. Rupert wrapped his arms around Jodi and held him tight, absorbing every twitch and breath as Jodi drifted off. Jodi wasn't much of a sleeper—too busy with work and keeping the flat to his eccentric standards—and Rupert rarely got to hold him like this, wide-awake while Jodi's dreams made his eyelids flutter and his tongue dance over his bottom lip.

It was entrancing, until he glanced at the clock. *Damn it.* Time had slipped away from him, leaving him twenty minutes to dash south to the fire station in Brixton.

Fuck. Rupert disentangled himself from Jodi, mourning the loss of his warmth. Who wanted to tramp around bloody Brixton when they could hold Jodi close and doze all night, waking up from time to time to love each other a little bit more? God, Rupert's heart wanted so desperately to stay.

Stop it. Rupert retrieved his scattered clothes, dressed, and got ready to leave again. In his coat and shoes, he crept back into the bedroom and gazed at Jodi, still sleeping soundly. He kissed Jodi's forehead, his cheek, his lips.

"I love you, boyo. See you in the morning. Be safe."

Jodi awoke with a shiver. He reached for Rupert, but his heart already knew he was alone. He rolled over and stared at the ceiling. Waking up without Rupert's comforting bulk wrapped around him was always hard, but it felt particularly depressing when it happened to be dark and cold outside. He searched for a word to suit his mood. "Bleak" . . . yeah, that would do. He preferred "desolate," but applying it to himself made him feel like a twat.

A twat who'd fallen asleep, despite plans to be on the other side of London more than an hour ago.

Jodi forced himself out of bed and shuffled to the bathroom. He was a little sore, but he took pleasure in the pain. Without the dull ache at the base of his spine, he would have wondered if he'd dreamt his snatched encounter with Rupert.

He took a shower, then wandered, nude, through the Tottenham flat he shared with Rupert. It was a small maisonette—poky and cramped when they were both home—but in Rupert's absence it seemed empty and cavernous. His gaze fell on a photograph of them, taken last Christmas, cuddled up on the sofa with Rupert's daughter, Indie. Jodi absorbed the warmth of the image. Rupert had the best smile. It was infectious and lit up his whole face. With his warm hazel eyes gleaming like embers in the fire, Jodi couldn't look away. The only thing he'd ever change was Rupert's haircut. He hadn't known him before he'd cut the shaggy blond mop he'd sported in his younger days, but Jodi had dreamed about what it would feel like to run his fingers through those curls.

Give me something to tug on.

Jodi's black mood began to dissipate. He felt bad for making Rupert late, but the guilt was almost worth it for the fuck-awesome sex. Closing his eyes, he pictured it: Rupert thrusting up into him, his cheeks flushed, every muscle strained—

The phone interrupted his dirty daydreams. He retrieved it from the couch and read another cheesed-off message from Sophie—his best friend—wondering where the fuck he'd got to. Cringing, he checked the time. Oops. He should've rocked up in Primrose Hill hours ago.

He erased the messages and hit Rupert's speed dial, waiting for his voice mail to kick in as he stamped into his shoes, grabbed his coat, and headed for the door. The message tone on Rupert's voice mail beeped. Jodi jogged down the stairs and let the heavy exterior door slam shut behind him before he spoke. "Hey. So . . . I'm sorry if I made you late. I was feeling a little needy, but in my defence, that new software is driving me round the fucking bend *and* Henry tried to kill me this morning. Ran over my foot, bloody dick-splash. Can you believe that?" Jodi manoeuvred his way through Tottenham's bustling streets. He reached the zebra crossing and stepped off the pavement. "Anyway, I'll see you in the morning, yeah? Bring your helmet home. I want to fuck you while you're wearing it. Be safe, Rupe. I love you."

Part
ONE

Chapter ONE

July 26, 2014

Drip, *beep, drip, beep, drip, beep.* Rupert counted the drops of blood as they passed through the device monitoring the pressure in Jodi's brain. The doctors said clear fluid would mean an improvement. For two days now, there had only been blood.

A nurse appeared at Jodi's bedside. She placed a plastic cup of grey tea beside Rupert, then sanitised her hands with the gel dispenser on the wall. "Do you need anything, love?"

Rupert shook his head. It seemed to be the only thing people said to him anymore. Didn't they know that all he needed was for Jodi to live? To wake up, get better, and chase this nightmare away? Didn't they know there was nothing else?

The nurse let him be and got on with Jodi's fifteen-minute observations. Rupert watched her for a while, scrutinising her face for any sign of change, but eventually, his gaze returned to Jodi: his coal-dark hair and scruffy hipster beard. The geometric tattoo on his neck. The tiny mole on his cheek, just visible beneath the wide bandage around his skull.

Rupert shuddered. The accident had been like a perfect storm. Eyewitnesses said Jodi had stepped onto the zebra crossing, eyes down, his phone tucked under his chin. He'd never looked up, even when the stolen car had come roaring round the corner, sending other pedestrians scrambling for safety. It had hit him at fifty-four miles an hour. The impact had hurled him twenty feet and thrown him facedown in the middle of the road. Two cracked ribs. His left arm fractured in three places. Rupert closed his eyes. *And his brain so badly damaged he might never wake up.*

Nausea ran through Rupert. He forced himself to open his eyes, and ran his gaze over Jodi again, tracking every wire and machine, absorbing every bruise and scrape, but nothing changed. He couldn't count the tubes jammed into Jodi's body, wouldn't count them, because if he did, he'd have to accept that they were the only thing keeping Jodi alive. That without them, he'd be dead.

Rupert took Jodi's hand. A familiar warmth tickled the chill in his bones. Jodi had always made him feel warm inside, from the heady heat of their first, tentative naked encounters, to the comforting acceptance that had cloaked him the moment he'd realised Jodi loved him too.

But the warmth felt different now, marred by the sickening dread that their dream had been cut short. Rupert closed his eyes and found himself at the fire station, jogging down the front steps to come home, only to be intercepted by two police officers he knew well.

"Rupert, there's been an accident. Get in the car. We need to take you to King's."

Rupert blinked. King's College Hospital was in Camberwell, barely a stone's throw from the station. Why the fuck would anyone need to drive him there? Besides, it had been a quiet night in South London— no major incidents, and all the crews were safely inside, or on their way home, like him. Perhaps they had come to the wrong station. "Karen—"

Karen touched his arm. "Rupert, I'm sorry, love. Jodi's been in an RTC. He's been airlifted to King's. You need to come with us so we can take you to him."

They rushed Rupert to King's in a blur of blue lights and sirens. Minutes later, he found himself at sea in the bustling efficiency of London's busiest trauma centre, searching desperately for any sign of Jodi. It was half an hour before a nurse told him he'd already been transferred to intensive care.

The doctor up there had been blunt. "Jodi was brought in by helimed at nine o'clock last night. He'd been hit by a car as he crossed the road outside what I believe to be your home. The impact cracked his ribs and broke his arm in three places, but the severe head injury he sustained when he hit the road is causing us the most concern . . ."

Bleeding, pressure, coma. Death. The doctor had said then—and still said now—that Jodi might not survive, but she was wrong. Jodi wouldn't die. He couldn't, because aside from his propensity for anarchy, Rupert wouldn't bloody let him.

December 26, 2009

Jodi stumbled out of Tottenham's dodgiest gay bar. He tripped over the kerb and dropped his wallet and phone straight into a murky puddle. *Oops.* Lurching, he retrieved them. His wallet looked salvageable—not that there was much in it after tonight—but his phone was butt-fucked. He sniggered. "Butt-fucked" was the name of the sparkly pink powder he'd been snorting all night, a legal high, apparently, though it hadn't had a big effect on him, save his wobbly legs and a bad case of the giggles.

Still swaying, he stuffed the wallet in his pocket and considered his phone. The screen was waterlogged. He swiped it a couple of times, but nothing happened. Damn it. He'd dropped three phones in the last year, and the death of number four was probably a sign that it was time to go home.

Luckily for him, home was a five-minute walk away. He left the dodgy bar behind and drifted along the pavement, weaving between the revellers who'd come out to party on a frosty Boxing Day night. He crossed the road outside the chicken shop, in a world of his own until a commotion ahead startled him.

A fight had broken out in front of the pub the footie boys favoured. Three blokes on one. Jodi winced. Shit like that never ended well. He bypassed the commotion, looping a bus stop, letting the curses and screams wash over him. Trouble in Tottenham was nothing new, but as he left it behind with half a mind to mention it to the next pub's security team, a shout rang out above the others and made him look round in time to see a doorman enter the fray—a tall, blond doorman who was just about the hottest bloke Jodi had ever seen.

Dressed in black, he waded into the fight and seized two men by their collars. "All right, all right. Pack it in."

He sent the first two men flying, launching them in separate directions. The altercation seemed abruptly over, both men stayed by the doorman's fierce glare, but the third man was less obliging—or more stupid. Either way, the doorman appeared unmoved as the remaining attacker picked up a bottle and charged him.

With good reason, it seemed. The bottle was gone before Jodi could blink, and the third man facedown on the wet pavement, the doorman's foot on the back of his neck. "Stay there, shit-tits. The coppers are coming for you."

Wow. Jodi's pulse quickened as the fourth man scrambled to his feet and scarpered. The man melted into the crowd, and Jodi turned his attention back to the doorman, hoping he'd say something else in the Irish brogue that was rough enough to make Jodi shiver. Approaching sirens should've moved him on too, considering the state he was in, but he couldn't look away. Bathed in the orange glow of a nearby streetlight, the doorman was enthralling. Though powerful and strong, he wasn't as big as Jodi had first thought. Yet his strength was striking, enticing, and Jodi's breath caught in his throat.

The police arrived and cleared the scene. Jodi took a seat in the bus stop and lit a fag, blowing smoke to the moon as he watched the doorman turn the third man into their custody and give his account of events. Jodi thought about going home when the doorman went back into the pub, but garbled signs of life from his half-drowned phone distracted him.

He was still poking at it when a shadow blocked out the light of the bus stop.

"Lost your Oyster card, mate?"

"Hmm?"

The doorman raised an eyebrow. "You've been sat out here for hours. Must be time to go home, eh? You need anything?"

"Um . . ." Jodi rarely found himself lost for words, but the power of speech evaded him now. Instead, he held up his phone, showing the doorman the buggered screen.

"Ah, dropped it in the bog, did ya?"

"Puddle, actually," Jodi said. "I think it's fucked."

The doorman took the phone and held it up to the light. "Nah. Bury it in a bowl of rice and stick it in the airing cupboard. Be right as rain in a few days."

"Really? Sounds like witchcraft to me."

"Suit yourself. Anyway, you didn't answer my question. Do you need anything? We're all closed up here. Probably time you went home. Got far to go?"

Jodi ran his gaze over the doorman and saw that his earpiece was gone and he had a bag slung over his shoulder. "I live round the corner. Where are *you* going?"

"Bedsit in Harringay. It's a heap of shit, but I need my bed, so come on, off you fuck. Get your arse home so I can rest knowing I've done my job for the night."

"What are you? Some kind of social worker?" Jodi stood and absorbed the drunken buzz that washed over him. Damn. He'd forgotten how wasted he was. "I'm just sitting here, mate. Minding my own business. Didn't ask for no help."

He said the words with a smile, but the doorman frowned. "You're fucking twatted. Can I walk you home?"

"Not a serial killer, are you?"

"No, I'm Rupert."

"Rupert?" Jodi covered a treacherous, buzz-fuelled giggle with a cough. "Like the bear?"

"If you say so. Far as I know, Rupert Bear never killed anyone, so I guess it fits."

"Bet he did. Let's google that shit." Jodi reclaimed his phone and peered at the frozen screen. "Balls. Forgot it was broken."

Rupert rolled his eyes. "Come on, hooligan. Let's get you home."

He took Jodi's arm and steered him out of the bus stop. Jodi allowed himself to be led, distracted from the bizarre situation by Rupert's commanding grip on his arm. For some reason, it didn't feel odd. Hmm. Perhaps the sparkly powder had scrambled his inhibitions. Ha. Not that he'd had many to start with. The neon body paint smeared all over his torso was testament to that.

"Where are we going?"

"Eh?" Jodi glanced up to find they'd come to a stop at a junction. He glanced both ways, then turned left. "Oh, erm, it's this way, I think."

"You think?"

"I *know*." Jodi pulled his arm from Rupert and grabbed his hand. "Come on. I'll show you."

Rupert let Jodi drag him to the zebra crossing, but he stayed Jodi before he stepped into the road. "Oi, look both ways, mate. You gotta death wish, or something?"

A series of black cabs rumbled past. Jodi's coat blew up in the backdraft. He shivered and instinctively moved closer to Rupert, seeking warmth. "Sorry."

"It's okay." Rupert smiled, showing Jodi a set of teeth that had clearly never seen a cigarette. "How about you tell me where to go and I'll do the driving? You haven't even got your laces done up."

Jodi looked down at his scruffy, untied boots. "Yeah . . . let's do that." He took Rupert's arm again and, despite an embarrassing lack of control over his own feet, navigated the remaining twenty metres to his first-floor maisonette. "This is me."

"Nice. Figured you for one of those horrible yuppie apartment blocks."

"Piss off. I ain't no yuppie."

"Fucking hipster, though, aren't ya?"

Jodi couldn't argue with that. His skinny jeans and obligatory beard gave him away. "Nothing wrong with hipsters."

Rupert snorted. "If you say so. My ma warned me about city boys like you."

"Yeah?"

"Well, no. She actually warned me about slutty city girls with loose morals, but she didn't know any better."

Jodi's heart skipped a beat. "Does she know now?"

"Yeah." Rupert's tone turned flat and his endearing grin faded. "Think it's safe to say I'm off her Christmas card list."

"But it's Boxing Day," Jodi said. "Who did you spend Christmas with?"

Rupert slid Jodi a sideways glance. "What do you care?"

Jodi shrugged. "I guess in the same way you *care* enough to walk me home."

"Unless I'm a serial killer."

"You're not, though, are you?"

Rupert grinned again, and the cloud that had descended on them lifted. "Not in the slightest. Just don't want you to come to any harm. I'll sleep easier knowing you're safe in your bed."

Jodi let that hang for a moment while he fished around in his pockets for his keys. Retrieving them proved simple. Finding the right key and aiming it at the lock, not so much.

Rupert took the keys from him and unlocked the door. He pushed it open and eyed the steep stairs that led to Jodi's maisonette. "You gonna be okay getting up there, mate?"

"Hmm?"

Rupert sighed. "Come on. Let's get you in."

He offered Jodi his arm. Jodi took it and was once more drawn to the comforting warmth of Rupert's larger frame as they tackled the stairs.

Jodi stumbled onto the landing. "This is me."

"Yeah, you said that downstairs. Which door is yours?"

"The blue one. Silver key."

Rupert unlocked Jodi's front door and stood back. Jodi ducked under his arm. He sensed Rupert turn away, and reached for him before he knew what he was doing. "Don't go."

"Why? Do you need help with something?"

"No, I, er . . ." Jodi stared at his hand, wrapped around Rupert's wrist like a limpet. "I've got coffee. Want some?"

It wasn't his best chat-up line, though he'd got laid behind the weight of far worse in the past, but after a protracted pause, Rupert shrugged. "Reckon I could bang a cuppa down before I head home. Got any tea?"

Turned out Jodi hadn't, but Rupert settled for a mug of dubious-looking decaf while Jodi brewed himself a pot of nuclear Colombian espresso. "So," Jodi said when he'd coaxed Rupert into taking a seat on his tatty living room couch. "Do you often walk pisshead gay boys home?"

Rupert spluttered into his drink. "What? Fuck, no. Shit. Sorry. I didn't come over to you because I thought you were gay."

"No?" Jodi frowned. He wasn't getting come-on vibes from Rupert, but there was no denying the bloke was gay, even without his vague admission. "Why did you, then?"

It was Rupert's turn to stumble over his words. "Um . . . I s'pose I couldn't stop myself. I saw you sitting out there after I put that bloke on his arse. After that, shit, I couldn't look away." Rupert cringed and briefly covered his face with his hands. "It didn't cross my mind that you were gay, though, mate. I swear. I just got worried when you didn't move on. Young lad got mugged by that bus stop a few weeks ago. Bastards left him for dead."

Jodi's disappointment warred with an overwhelming sense of endearment. Rupert was bloody gorgeous, and Jodi wouldn't have minded in the slightest if his insistence on walking him home had been a ploy to get him into bed, but the fact that it wasn't? Damn. Jodi could fall in love with a man that fucking sweet. "Did he die?"

"As good as. Think he's still in a coma."

"Fuck that." Jodi shuddered. "My cousin had a diving accident when we were kids. Took them weeks to turn him off, even though the doctors said he was already dead."

"I'm sorry."

"Don't be. I hardly remember him."

"Stays with you, though, doesn't it? When you lose someone?"

Jodi shrugged and picked up his coffee. Talking about death wasn't good for his buzz. "So how often *do* you pick up waifs and drunks and take them home for whatever reason?"

Rupert chuckled. "Actually, you're the first. I usually call them a cab."

"I'm privileged, then?"

"If you say so. I'm the one getting a cuppa instead of a cold walk home."

Jodi could think of better ways to keep warm. He shifted on the couch and let his leg brush against Rupert's. Rupert jumped. Jodi grinned. "Jesus, you're like a stray cat."

Rupert looked away. "I'm not used to people—blokes, touching me. It's a little new."

"How new?"

Silence. Jodi chanced another nudge with his leg. "It's okay. You can tell me. We've all been there."

Rupert glanced up, and the sadness in his gaze broke Jodi's heart. "Too new for me to stay here much longer. I should get going."

"Don't go." Jodi sat up. Something told him that if he let Rupert slink away, he'd probably never see him again. "We don't have to do anything. I didn't ask you in for that, honest."

"No? Shame, eh? I could've freaked out on you properly, then."

Jodi set his coffee aside. The urge to put a comforting hand on Rupert was strong, but the very real fear that it would make things worse stopped him. "Everyone freaks out when they first touch another man. It's a rite of passage."

"Yeah? Did you?"

"Yup." Jodi pictured his first disastrous dalliance with a bloke after he'd realised his bisexuality. "Ran off like a scalded cat. Was halfway down the garden with my pants round my ankles before he caught up with me."

Rupert chuckled his deep, warming chuckle again. "Another cat metaphor? I'm sensing a theme."

"I have a limited imagination."

"I don't believe that."

It was on the tip of Jodi's tongue to invite Rupert to find out, but Rupert leaned forward before he could speak, and put his hand on Jodi's leg, hesitantly at first, then his grip strengthened, and it was all Jodi could do not to moan.

He settled for sucking in a shaky breath. Bloody hell. What was it about this bloke? A touch, a brush of skin, a stare that went on just a beat too long; tiny gestures that lit Jodi on fire. He stared at Rupert's hand and then covered it with his own, entwining his fingers with Rupert's until their hands were clasped, bound together like lovers, rather than two souls who'd met less than an hour ago.

Rupert squeezed Jodi's hand. Jodi squeezed back and tugged gently, coaxing Rupert closer until their faces were inches apart.

Rupert's nerves were tangible. His beautiful, gold-flecked eyes had widened, and he swallowed thickly. But it was him who leaned in first. Him who ghosted his lips over Jodi's. Him who tentatively pushed his tongue into Jodi's mouth and kissed him as the room began to spin.

Jodi gasped and wrapped his arms around Rupert, clutching at the dark shirt he was wearing under his unzipped doorman's jacket. The shirt came loose from Rupert's waistband. Jodi pushed it up until his hands found the hard, unyielding flesh of Rupert's abdomen.

He dug his nails in. Rupert groaned and bit Jodi's lip, so Jodi did it again and again, until he suddenly found himself on the floor.

"Ow! Jesus."

Rupert lurched up like he'd been burned. "Oh God, I'm so sorry. Are you okay?"

"I'll live." Jodi walked on his knees to where Rupert stood and accepted his proffered hands. Rupert hauled him up like he was made of feathers. "Let me guess. You had an epiphany, realised my dick is probably as big as yours, and lost your shit?"

"Something like that?" Rupert winced. "I'm so sorry. I told you. I'm new at this."

"It's okay." And it was. Who the hell was Jodi to judge a man flying blind in his sexuality? Accepting his own bisexuality had been a journey fraught with denial and false starts. It was only in the last year he'd truly grown into it, and it wasn't so long ago he'd been toppling blokes off the end of the bed himself. He squeezed Rupert's hands. "But tell me, have you ever—"

"Nope. Never put my hands on a fella . . . like this, until tonight. Oh God, I'm so sorry. You must think I'm such a twat."

Jodi shook his head slowly. "No, not at all. I'll tell you exactly what I think, *Rupert*. I think you should calm the fuck down, go home, get some sleep, then come back tomorrow so I can teach you how to make this shit awesome."

Chapter TWO

August 26, 2014

Drip, beep, drip, beep, drip, beep. Rupert counted the drops of clear fluid as they passed through the pressure-measuring device in Jodi's brain. That's right, they were clear now. The blood had faded away one evening nearly two weeks ago. Rupert recalled his surge of elation like it was yesterday, remembered every minute of the twenty-four-hour vigil he'd mounted after, waiting on tenterhooks for the moment when Jodi would surely wake up. But he hadn't woken up. Not then, and not now, a month and two days since that damn fucking speeding car had catapulted him across the streets of Tottenham.

Rupert tore his gaze from the drip and focussed on Jodi. He touched his cheek with the pad of his thumb, and smoothed the scruffy beard that, despite the nurse's diligent efforts, was now slightly longer than he'd ever seen on Jodi before. Rupert liked it. It would suit Jodi's brown eyes, if Rupert was lucky enough to ever see them again.

Lucky. Ha. Rupert clenched his teeth and turned his attention to Jodi's shattered arm. It had been operated on again in recent days. The surgeons had inserted metal rods to keep the bones' original realignment in place, but they wouldn't know if Jodi had retained full function until he woke up.

If he woke up.

Rupert took Jodi's good hand and squeezed, trying to remember what life had been like before the cramped ICU bay had become their home. But it was so fucking hard. Most of Jodi's outward wounds had healed, but the ominous shadow on his brain remained, dark and deadly, and the doctors reminded Rupert every day that even if Jodi did wake up, there was every chance he wouldn't be the Jodi that Rupert had loved—still loved so much he could barely breathe.

But he'd run out of time to grieve today. It was midday, and he was due back at work in ten minutes. He closed his eyes, still clutching Jodi's hand. The brigade had been patient with him so far, but with Jodi's business not earning, someone had to pay the bills—

Jodi's hand squeezed his. Rupert jumped a mile, his heart in his throat. His eyes flew open, and he stared down at Jodi's hand, his own suddenly red hot. *It moved.* But had it? It didn't seem any different.

Don't be a dick. You haven't got time for imaginary drama. Rupert counted to ten, praying he'd feel that brief pressure on his palm again, but nothing happened, because it was all in his damn fucking head.

Twat. He looked down at Jodi one last time. For a moment, he dared to dream Jodi really had returned the death grip he had on his hand, but their grim reality wouldn't quit. Jodi remained slack and lifeless, and Rupert had to go to work.

January 26, 2010

Rupert didn't come back the next day or the day after that. In fact, it was nearly a month before his name flashed up on Jodi's phone. The message was short, sweet, and perfectly timed. *Fancy a late night cuppa?*

Hell yeah.

Jodi tapped out a reply, inviting Rupert to come over whenever he was ready, then shut down his computer and drifted to the bathroom to take a much-needed shower. He'd been on a deadline for the last few days, and things like eating, sleeping, and washing had fallen by the wayside.

Dressed in trackies, hair still dripping, he emerged from the bathroom to another text. *Twenty minutes.* He glanced at the clock: 2 a.m. Jesus. How had that happened? Last time he'd checked, it had been nine o'clock and he'd been considering ordering pizza. Or was that yesterday? Shamefully, he had no idea.

He padded barefoot through the flat to the kitchen and opened the fridge. The contents were uninspiring, but he had enough bacon left for sarnies. Poaching about in his neglected salad drawer revealed some tired mushrooms too. He was tipping them into the sizzling bacon fat when the doorbell rang.

Jodi turned the hob down and went to the intercom. He buzzed the exterior door open, put the front door on the latch, and returned to the kitchen. Rupert's shadow appeared in the doorway a few moments later.

"Bloody hell. Are you trying to kill me?"

Jodi laid bacon rashers on slices of thickly buttered white toast without looking up. "Don't tell me you're one of those gym freaks who only eats nuts and organic spinach smoothies?"

"Fuck no. That's not what I meant."

"Then what did you—" Jodi's words died on his lips as he turned around to find Rupert leaning on the doorframe, dressed in softly worn tracksuit bottoms and a hoodie—a far cry from the all-black bouncer attire he'd been sporting last time—and totally fucking gorgeous. "What did you mean?"

Rupert stepped forward and touched Jodi's damp hair. "I meant *you*. I've spent the last week or so trying to convince myself you weren't as fit as I remembered. Then I find you like *this*." Rupert shook his head. "Not cool, mate. Not cool."

Jodi snorted. "I never claimed to be cool, but if it's any consolation, you're pretty fit yourself."

Rupert flushed and looked away. The bloke was beautiful, but it was clear he wasn't used to people—to *men*—telling him so. Jodi took pity on him and let it go. "Wanna bacon sarnie, then? And I bought a box of PG Tips the other day. It's around here somewhere."

"Sounds great. Can I help?"

"You can put the kettle on." Jodi rummaged in the cupboards for the tea bags while Rupert filled the kettle and flicked the switch. They didn't speak, but the silence was comfortable, familiar, like they'd muddled through such domesticity a thousand times over.

Jodi put two plates on the breakfast bar. Rupert placed two mugs beside them and folded his tall frame onto a stool.

"So tell me," he said. "What are you doing tucked up in your PJs on a Saturday night? Thought you were a raver?"

Jodi yawned. "Not this weekend. I had to work. And in my defence, you caught me on a particularly mad one when we met."

"Where do you work?"

"Here. I'm a web designer."

"Nice," Rupert said. "What does that involve? All that coding and shit?"

"Yup. That's me. Keeps me out of trouble."

Rupert grinned. "I don't believe that, but it's nice to see you sober. You were right the other way last time I saw you."

"Yeah, sorry about that. I don't usually get that wasted. Just get a little cabin fever crazy when I've been stuck indoors working too much."

Rupert picked up his sandwich. His silence told Jodi he knew exactly how hard Jodi had partied that night and that he perhaps didn't approve. And he had a point. Jodi had given up party drugs years ago, and the week-long comedown he'd endured after his Boxing Day blowout had reminded him why.

Time for a subject change. "So how was work for you tonight? Was the club busy?"

"I wasn't at the club. I was at my real job."

"Which is?"

"I'm a firefighter."

Jodi choked on his tea. "Seriously? You're a fireman?"

"Aye."

Something about the way Rupert's gentle Irish brogue wrapped around that word made Jodi feel warm all over, but it was nothing compared to the image of Rupert decked out in full fireman's kit. Jesus. If he hadn't fancied the arse off Rupert before . . . "What were you doing at that wanky club, then? Moonlighting?"

"Something like that, though it's not called moonlighting anymore. We're allowed second jobs now. They prefer it to paying us properly."

Jodi swallowed the last bite of his sandwich and reached for his tea. "How the hell do you find the time? Don't you work shifts?"

"Four days on, four days off. Working at the club helps me keep my sleep cycle when I'm on nights. Besides, I need the cash."

"Why?"

Rupert sighed. "Because firefighter pay is shite, especially when you have London rent to pay and an ex-wife crawling up your arse for maintenance."

Jodi blinked. "Whoa. There's a backstory if I ever heard one. You have kids?"

"A daughter, Indie."

"How old is she?"

"Three. I split up with her mum last year."

Jodi tried to picture a miniature, feminine version of Rupert. "Does she look like you?"

"See for yourself."

Rupert retrieved his wallet from his back pocket and held up a photo of a tiny, fair-haired toddler. Jodi wasn't much for screaming kids, but he had to admit the little girl was beautiful. "Sounds like her mum gives you grief."

"Whenever she can," Rupert said. "She's never forgiven me for leaving her, which is ironic, because she never wanted me in the first place."

"Ah, one of those." Jodi stood and dumped their empty plates in the sink. "Let me guess: she kept you in a box and kicked you every time you tried to get out?"

"Kinda. She had a way of making me believe everything was my fault because she said so."

Jodi touched Rupert's arm. Hearing about his ex wasn't easy, but it was plain to see that it wasn't something he talked about often. That it still hurt. "My first-ever girlfriend cheated on me . . . like, not just physically, she had another boyfriend up north where her dad lived. Everyone knew, except me."

Rupert winced. "Girlfriend? Bet that was messy."

"Not in the way you're probably thinking. I bounce both ways. It's just taken me a while to figure out that's as valid as being straight or gay. My other ex-girlfriend is my best mate. I love her to bits."

"Then you're lucky. Jen is a bitch. I've tried not to hate her, but it's hard when she does everything she can to make my life miserable. Shit, why am I even talking about this?"

Rupert covered Jodi's hand with his own, and, like the first time they'd been alone in Jodi's flat like this, their fingers entwined with little conscious thought, on Jodi's part at least. Something about Rupert made Jodi want to wrap himself around him and hold him tight until the hurt in his eyes went away.

"Do you want to come through to the living room?"

"Hmm?" Rupert's distant gaze refocussed. "Oh, what time is it?"

"A little after three."

"Damn. I should chip off home, then. I'm back on shift at eight."

Disappointment flickered through Jodi. "Where do you live? I remember something about a bedsit."

Rupert snorted. "I'm surprised you remember me at all, considering your eyes were pointing in different directions, but yeah, I've got a bedsit in Harringay."

Jodi frowned. Harringay was a half hour night-bus journey, and Rupert seemed exhausted. "Kip here, if you want? Where's your fire station?"

"Brixton, so it's about the same whichever way you look at it. But, as much as I'd love to stay with you, couch or otherwise, my stuff is at home."

Couch or otherwise. Jodi's breath caught in his throat, but Rupert was already getting ready to leave.

Jodi walked him to the door. "It was really nice to see you again."

"Yeah? Even though I chewed your ear off about my ex-wife?"

"Of course. Seriously, mate. I don't mind. Just wish you hadn't had to go through all that."

Rupert smiled, and the fatigue in his face seemed to fade. "You're the first person to give a shit in quite some time. Question is: why do you?"

Jodi shrugged. "Dunno. I just do."

And it was true. Rupert had been on his mind a lot since they'd first met. Their second meeting had proved nothing like his dirty, late-night fantasies, but in the dim light of the hallway, it felt right. Perhaps they'd never revisit that fuck-hot kiss, perhaps they weren't meant to, but Jodi could live with being friends—

Jodi's back hit the door. He sucked in a breath and suddenly found himself caged in Rupert's arms, their faces—like that night—

inches apart. They stared at each other, teetering on the precipice of something explosive, until Jodi remembered the distress in Rupert's gaze when he'd accidentally shoved Jodi to the floor.

Slow. Don't push him. Even if I think he wants me to.

Yeah, 'cause some days even Jodi was still learning. He took Rupert's face in his hands and kissed him, lightly at first, but then deep . . . *slow* and deep, like he could calm his own hammering heart with the brush of his lips against Rupert's. Like he didn't know better. Like he didn't know that Rupert's touch, however hesitant, would light him on fire.

Rupert gasped and pressed his body into Jodi's. Jodi lifted his leg and hooked it over Rupert's hip, grinding them together until his every nerve was ready to combust. *Pull away, pull away.* But he couldn't. Backed against the door, he had nowhere to go, nowhere he *wanted* to go, and his good intentions edged toward the proverbial window, ready to jump.

Just one more kiss . . .

Rupert withdrew. He laid his forehead against Jodi's and inhaled a deep, shaky breath. "Jesus Christ, you get under my skin."

Jodi shuddered and closed his eyes, absorbing the warmth of Rupert's body, which was still keeping him upright. "Come back soon, yeah? We can get under the duvet instead."

Chapter THREE

September 26, 2014

Turned out Rupert hadn't imagined the twitch in Jodi's hand. After that first time, it happened every day, but the neurologist had flatly confirmed it was nothing more than a muscle spasm. Rupert absorbed the news with little emotion. Jodi had been in a coma for weeks, and he'd grown used to any sign of recovery turning out to be a symptom of Jodi's prolonged vegetative state.

Vegetative state. Jesus fucking Christ. It was a term Rupert had only seen on TV before, and despite the doctor's reassurances that it wasn't necessarily permanent, the phrase haunted him as he kept his vigil at Jodi's bedside, went to work, and lay awake at home, counting the hours until the hospital let him in again.

The only break in the torture was when the physical therapist came in to manipulate Jodi's body to combat the muscle wastage ravaging his already slight frame. Rupert liked to think Jodi enjoyed the young Asian man's attention. The therapist was good-looking with the kind of easy smile Jodi loved, and the thought of Jodi opening his eyes to that grin was oddly comforting. It was a shame the therapist hadn't smiled today, a week after Jodi's hand first moved. Instead, he'd discovered a blood clot in Jodi's injured arm and alerted the ICU doctors. Jodi had been rushed to surgery in the blink of an eye, and he'd yet to return.

Rupert stood and walked to the waiting room's wide window. Outside, the hospital car park seemed to go on forever. He counted every car he could see—sixty-eight—and wondered if the window's placement had been deliberate in the hospital's design.

If the architects had known the distraction of counting cars would be far more soothing than the blandness of some pretty flowers.

"Rupert?"

Rupert turned. Caz, Jodi's primary nurse, stood in the doorway. "He's back. You can come and see him now."

"Thank you." Rupert followed Caz to Jodi's bedside. She scribbled on the fat wad of notes at the end of the bed, touched Rupert's arm, and disappeared, leaving Rupert alone with Jodi.

He took in Jodi's prone form—the wires, the tubes—then peered closer at his pale face, losing himself in the dark circles under Jodi's eyes. How was it possible for him to look so tired when he'd done nothing but sleep for sixty-three days? As Rupert claimed Jodi's hand and dropped into a chair, it struck him darkly ironic that Jodi had spent the day pumped full of anaesthetic when he was already so deeply unconscious that he was practically dead.

Stop it.

Rupert silenced the demon on his shoulder, the harsh adversary that kept him awake almost as much as his constant fear that Jodi would never come back to him. He squeezed Jodi's good hand. There was no response. Defeated, he closed his eyes and let his head drop, breathing in the stale antiseptic scent of the hospital. The ICU ward was stifling and claustrophobic and in the harsh light of the early morning, it was unbearable. His heart quickened, his skin prickled, and for the first time in the four years since he'd met Jodi, he felt uncomfortable in his own skin, a feeling that was exacerbated by the creeping sensation of someone watching him.

Seriously? Rupert beat his irritation back and pressed his fist into his forehead, but it wouldn't quit. He sighed and opened his eyes. Madness had threatened to overcome him so often since Jodi's accident that it had begun to feel like an old friend, like a droll antidote to the pessimistic monster in his mind. Sometimes he welcomed the distraction, but not today. Today he craved the distressing gravity of his reality, something—anything—to tie him down to the world. He returned his attention to Jodi, seeking out the bitter reassurance of his serene, sleeping face. Instead, an unseeing dark gaze staring back nearly sent him to his knees.

February 26, 2010

> *Are you working tonight?*
> *10-10, but maybe later if something goes tits up*
> *Fancy a drink after? At Dorothy's?*
> *I'll do my best — R x*

Jodi slipped in the side door of Dorothy's and scanned the faces already sitting at the bar. None were Rupert, and he tried to reason with the wave of disappointment that tickled his belly. *I'll do my best*, Rupert had said. Chances were he wouldn't make it at all, let alone be waiting for Jodi an hour before his shift finished.

In need of distraction, Jodi got himself a pint of stupidly pricey hipster ale and took a seat at the end of the bar, half an eye on the West Ham game replaying on the big screen. Not that he cared much who was winning. Football was for overpaid douche bags and lagered-up wankers. His first pint slipped down like a dream. He bought another two while he scrolled through a few stock sites on his phone, searching for vectors to use on his current project—a full rebrand for a tattoo studio. The shop was an old-school ink parlour, awash with flaming skulls and biker paraphernalia, but it had been recently bought out by a younger artist, and Jodi was hoping she'd be game for something a little more modern.

He bookmarked some images and logged out just as the lights dimmed to signal that the bar was about to get hot and heady. A bottle of WKD appeared beside his empty glass. He glanced up to find a thirtyish redhead grinning at him.

"Can I buy you a drink?"

Jodi smirked. "Looks like you already have."

"Nah, I bought it for the twink over there, but he turned me down."

Jodi followed the man's gaze to a slinky young figure tearing up the dance floor. "That's a woman."

"Really?" The man's eyebrows shot up. "Fuck. You'd never tell."

Dick. Jodi started to turn away.

"I was only joking, mate. I bought it for you."

Jodi regarded the man and considered his options. Boozy pop wasn't his bag, but Rupert's shift had ended ages ago and it appeared he wasn't coming. *Fuck it.* Jodi lifted the bottle to his lips. He felt like another drink, or three, and the sickeningly sweet WKD was the closest thing, even if he had to make small talk with an idiot who was clearly after a cloak-and-dagger handjob in a nearby alley.

On cue, the man leaned closer. "Have you been here before? I've never seen you. I'm Dean, by the way, in case you were wondering?"

"I wasn't."

"What's your name?"

"Jodi."

"Jodi, eh? Isn't that a girl's name?"

"If you say so." Jodi rolled his eyes. Like he hadn't heard that before. Like he gave a shit that his name made people assume he was either a girl or a little bit gay. Besides, they were half right. He *was* a little bit gay, perhaps gay enough, drunk enough, and stupid enough to give Dean the Dick a second glance.

At least until Dean encroached too far into Jodi's personal space and belched stale smoke-laced beer breath across his face. "Want to ditch this place and come back to mine?"

Fuck no. Jodi downed the WKD and slid the empty bottle along the bar. "Nice try, mate, but if you're after a shag, it'll take more than a bottle of pop and some shite small talk. See ya."

Jodi left Dean to it and wandered through the crowded bar. A few blokes made eye contact, but he didn't stop. By his body clock, it was early, but despite Rupert's warning that he might not make it to the Tottenham bar, Jodi had counted on seeing him and him alone. Didn't seem much point staying out.

He edged around the dance floor and headed for the side door, his mind on the bottle of Sailor Jerry and teensy bag of weed he had stashed at home. A few shots and a jazz fag would mellow him enough to sleep—

"Leaving already?"

Jodi jumped and stumbled into the tall frame blocking his path.

Rupert steadied him. "Whoa. Easy now. Didn't think you'd be falling over your feet just yet."

Jodi stared at Rupert's hands on his arms. "I didn't think you were coming."

"Isn't much that would keep me away." Rupert put two fingers under Jodi's chin and tilted his face until their eyes met. Jodi's world narrowed to Rupert's tired grin, his warm, gold-flecked gaze, and the crazy heat blooming where they touched. "Do you want to get a drink?"

"No. I want to go back to mine."

Rupert didn't take much persuading. They ditched the bar and walked to Jodi's flat. Before long, they were camped out on the couch with tumblers of spiced rum and Nutella on toast, a late-night snack that seemed to make Rupert's day.

"I make this with bananas for Indie. It's her special treat when she stays with me."

Jodi licked chocolate off his fingers. "How often is that?"

"Once a month if I'm lucky. My ex likes me to babysit, but she's not keen on my place. Says it's minging."

"She really does sound like a bitch." Jodi sipped his rum. "She must know you wouldn't let Indie come to any harm. You're a fireman, for God's sake. How much more responsible can you be?"

"It's not a good night to ask me that, mate. We lost three to a house fire. That's why I was late. Had a lot to sort before we clocked out."

Rupert said the words like such horrors happened to him every shift. Perhaps they did. Jodi didn't know much about the day-to-day life of a firefighter. "Bet that shit stays with you."

"Sometimes," Rupert said. "You get used to it, though, even the scary stuff."

Jodi wasn't sure he wanted to know just how scary Rupert's job could be. He chanced a change of subject. "So, have you been seeing anyone since I saw you last?"

"As in going out with someone?" Rupert cringed and rubbed his palms on his thighs. "Fat chance. I wasn't taking the piss when I said I was new to this. Tonight was only the second time I've ever been in a gay bar."

Jodi chuckled. "That's not something to be ashamed of. Being gay isn't all about shagging and raving, you know."

"That's just it, though, isn't it? I *don't* know. I don't know fuck all about how to be who I am. You're the only gay bloke I've ever spoken to."

"So? You don't have to be like every other gay bloke, mate. You've just got to . . . be, I guess. Be *you*. Fuck anyone else."

"Chance would be a fine thing." Rupert grinned. "Not that I'm propositioning you, or anything."

Jodi winked and poured them both another rum. "Never say never."

A little while later, he was quite happily, and quietly, drunk. Rupert seemed to be in a similar state, slouched on the couch, one hand behind his head, the other resting idly on Jodi's legs that were sprawled in his lap. Jodi wasn't sure how they'd ended up entangled on the couch, but he had no desire to question it. Relaxing with Rupert felt right. He didn't need to know any more than that.

"So," Rupert said. "You've heard all about my sordid past. What have you been up to the last year or so?"

Jodi shrugged. "Not much. I left my job in the city eighteen months ago and set up my own company. I've only had time for a few friends with benefits. Nothing serious."

"Benefits, eh? Sounds interesting."

"If you say so," Jodi said. "I went through a phase of whoring it up when I split with Sophie, trying to out-gay my imagination, you know? But I settled down when I moved in here. Found my own company more fun than I thought."

Rupert smirked and waggled his fingers. "Even I'm familiar with my own company, mate."

"Ha-ha." The idea of Rupert having a wank was enough to derail Jodi's train of thought. He lost himself in the tickle of Rupert tracing absent patterns on his jean-clad thigh until the bellyful of rum got the better of him, and he yawned so hard his jaw cracked.

Rupert stirred and looked at his phone. "Jesus. It's nearly three. I should go."

"Go where? Home?"

"Yup. I'm off for a couple of days now." Rupert lifted Jodi's legs and stood. "Shit, fucking Tube's shut, isn't it? I need to catch the bus."

"The night bus? Fuck that. Do you have anywhere to be tomorrow?"

Rupert shrugged. "Not really. Just the gym and getting my barnet chopped."

"Screw it, then. Stay here."

"On the couch?"

"If you like." Jodi stood too and held out his hand. "Or you can kip in with me."

Rupert didn't strike Jodi as a man who made rash decisions. Perhaps it was the rum, but it wasn't long before he abandoned his plans to leave and followed Jodi to his bedroom. He stared at the minimalist decor and neatly ordered shelves that contained nothing but alphabetised DVDs.

"Jesus. It's like an IKEA showroom in here. Where's all your stuff?"

"Where it should be. I can't sleep in clutter," Jodi said. "It's gotta be neat, or I lose my fucking marbles. Do you want something to sleep in?"

Rupert shot Jodi a smirk that made it clear he thought it was too late for Jodi to be worrying about his sanity. "I've got about a foot on you. I reckon your skids are gonna look pretty bloody daft on me. How about I sleep in my T-shirt and boxers?"

Getting Rupert out of his jeans was all kinds of okay with Jodi, but he silenced the horny devil dancing in the back of his mind. *He's new to this, remember?* "Fine by me, mate. Wanna pick a DVD?"

He gestured to the categorised collections at the end of the bed, then turned his back to change his clothes, leaving Rupert to ditch his jeans and socks in peace. When he looked again, Rupert was crouched by the shelf, in his boxers, as promised, running a finger along the titles. "You like epics, eh? *The Last of the Mohicans*, *Braveheart*, *The Last Samurai*."

"I don't like *The Last Samurai*." Jodi crawled onto the bed in a pair of worn tracksuit bottoms and stretched out on his stomach to peer at Rupert's selection. "Tom Cruise is a dick."

"I know. It's a shame. The film would be awesome without him. What about *Gladiator*? I've never seen it all the way through."

Jodi nodded. "Russell Crowe and Djimon Hounsou? Sold."

Rupert slipped the disk into the DVD player, then joined Jodi on the bed. In spite of his hesitance earlier, he seemed at ease now, and Jodi was glad of it. Seeing Rupert mirror the contentment in his own soul was beautiful. Like Rupert.

Jodi scooted back and held up the duvet. "Get in, mate. I don't bite."

"Never mind, eh?" Rupert smirked, warm and wonderful.

They wriggled under the covers. Jodi turned off the lamp, and the TV came to life, bathing the room in blue light. He lay back. Rupert did the same, and it felt so familiar Jodi almost cried. Huh. Perhaps it was *him* who'd been craving the company of a man—real company . . . companionship, not just a bedmate to roll around with, then kick to the kerb before the sun rose.

The film opened with the Germanic battle scene. Rupert rolled onto his side, facing Jodi. "I've seen this bit, and the end. It's the middle I keep missing. I've never quite worked out how Maximus gets to Rome."

Jodi mirrored Rupert. "The buildup to that is the best part. It's all a bit melodramatic after he takes his mask off."

Rupert looked mystified. Jodi made a mental note to divert his attention back to the film by the time Maximus was bought by Proximo. He opened his mouth to ask Rupert what he wanted for breakfast in the morning, but Rupert's hand on his face silenced him. The touch was light, just his palm on Jodi's cheek, but Jodi was mesmerised.

"Thanks for this." Rupert smiled shyly, like he had no idea of the effect he was having on Jodi. "It sounds strange, but being with you makes me feel so much better about myself, about everything. I feel normal."

Most folk would probably reckon there was nothing normal about spending the night in the bed of a man you hardly knew, but it made sense to Jodi. "I'm glad you're comfortable here. For what it's worth, I don't find you strange at all."

Rupert dragged his palm softly down Jodi's cheek, brushing his scruffy jaw with his fingertips. He hesitated at Jodi's neck, before continuing his gentle exploration, drawing invisible pictures on Jodi's bare chest.

Jodi sucked in a subtle breath. The sensation of Rupert's fingers was maddening, reminding him how caught he was between his charged attraction to Rupert, and the very real desire to be his friend. Dressed and drinking on the couch, the distinction had been clear, but huddled up in bed, face-to-face, toes touching, it was hard to ignore the urge to put his lips on Rupert.

It turned out not to matter, because, as had become their routine, Rupert kissed him first. The kiss was gentle and sweet, a brush of a kiss like the ghost of a feather. A ghost that sent Jodi reeling, had him gasping for air and desperate for more. He let Rupert draw him closer, and they kissed again, harder this time, reigniting the fervour of the night they'd met, but instead of the crazy heat of before, a slow, smouldering burn began, like they both knew there was no need to rush, that they had all the time in the world to stoke this fire.

Rupert pushed his tongue into Jodi's mouth, teasing and dancing, like a cat with a string, and *nothing* like a man who was new to the art of snogging blokes. He put his hands on Jodi's chest, palms flat at first, until his devilish fingers went to work on Jodi's nipples.

Jodi broke away with a low groan. "Fuck yeah. I like that."

"Yeah? I'm not hurting you?"

"You are, but I like it. Do it harder."

"Like this?"

"More."

Rupert tightened his grip, twisting until the stinging pain became almost too pleasurable to bear. He watched Jodi gasp and writhe with a curious gaze. Jodi took the hint and returned the favour, lightly, testing the waters.

But there was no need for caution. Rupert's eyes rolled the moment Jodi pinched the sensitive flesh, and his gravelly moan went straight to Jodi's cock. "God, I see what you mean."

"Good, eh?" Jodi squeezed a little harder, studying every facet of expression on Rupert's beautiful face. "It goes well with a fuck-hot blowjob too."

Rupert smiled wryly. "I'll bear that in mind."

"Don't think on it too much. You'll drive yourself mad, second-guessing yourself."

"You sound like my mate Briggs at the station. Only fella who doesn't think I'm after his nuts. Total pisshead, but salt of the earth. He keeps telling me to go get a fucking shag and be done with it."

Jodi chuckled. "He's kinda right, though it's better with someone you've got some kind of bond with. This life gets lonely, sometimes, you know? Sex is easy to come by, but it's hard to make it mean something."

"Does this mean something?" Rupert stilled Jodi's twisting fingers and entwined their hands. "To you? Or do you feel sorry for me?"

"I don't feel sorry for you. I'd shag you in a heartbeat, but to be honest, mate, tonight, I just want to put my arms around you."

Rupert squeezed Jodi's hand. "I'd like that."

Chapter FOUR

October 26, 2014

"I brought your iPod from home today. It's got a full battery, and I downloaded that Blur album you thought you'd lost." Rupert waited for a response, but as usual, there was none. Jodi stared blankly for a moment, before his gaze drifted back to the TV, the only thing that seemed to hold his attention for any length of time.

Rupert sighed and dropped the iPod on the table with a clatter, letting his frustration get the better of him for a moment. Jodi had been "awake" for a month now, but he'd yet to utter a word, or focus on the world around him with any real cognisance. He obeyed commands—sit up, hold this, rest your head—but his actions were robotic, like he'd been preprogrammed before the accident to come back and subject Rupert to the world's cruellest trick.

"Rupert?"

Rupert glanced around. Sophie hovered by the curtain rail, biting her lip. Rupert schooled his features and raised a half smile from the pit of his stomach, beckoning her forward. Sophie had found it even harder than him to reconcile herself with what remained of the eccentric, witty man she'd called her best friend. Some days, it was all Rupert could do to persuade her to hold his hand.

"But he's so cold, Rupert."

"Then help me warm him up."

Sophie touched his arm. "Sorry, Rupe. Have I come at a bad time?"

Rupe. Only Jodi called him that. Rupert's slowly crumbling heart fractured again. For months, he'd believed he wanted nothing more than for Jodi to be awake and alive, but fuck, it wasn't enough. It was nowhere near enough, and Rupert couldn't bear it.

"Rupert?"

Rupert stared at Sophie's pretty blue eyes and flaxen curls. At her kind smile and honest gaze. It was easy to see why Jodi had loved her for so long, and why he continued to love her, long after their relationship had come to an amicable end. "Yeah?"

"Have you eaten today?"

"Erm . . ." He honestly couldn't remember. His days had fallen into a routine of working, sleeping, and sitting at Jodi's bedside while Jodi fixated on the TV.

Sylvester, the physical therapist who coaxed Jodi from the bed three times a day, teaching him to stand and walk again, appeared around the curtain. "Evening, Jodi. Are you ready to go back to bed and do some work on your arm?"

Jodi held out his hands without looking at Sylvester, even when Sylvester took them to help him stand.

Rupert had to turn away. Watching Jodi struggle to perform such simple tasks was too much on the best of days, but today it hurt more than ever.

Sophie tugged his arm. "Come on. You need a dirty burger."

Rupert let her drag him across the street to the dodgiest McDonald's in South London. She parked him at a sticky table and went to the counter. She returned with four Big Macs and enough nuggets to feed an engine crew.

"Eat." She stuck a straw in a large milkshake and slid it across the table. "I don't care how much, just humour me, yeah?"

Rupert knew better than to argue. Sophie reminded him of his long-dead gran back in Dublin—gentle, sweet, and thoroughly terrifying. He picked up a burger and peeled away the greasy paper, swallowing his apprehension as the scent of fat and spooky processed meat invaded his senses. The first bite tasted far better than it should have. He took another, and another, until the burger was gone.

Sophie passed him a second and the stern worry in her gaze faded a touch. "Should we get something for Jodi?"

Rupert shook his head. "They're still weaning him on soup and toast, not that he's eating much. I don't think he understands why he has to."

"Or maybe he does, and he can't make his body do what they're asking him to do?"

Pain lanced Rupert's heart. Though Jodi's gaze had remained hollow since he'd opened his eyes, the thought of the real Jodi—the Jodi from before—trapped behind that blank stare, haunted Rupert every moment he wasn't worrying that Jodi still might die. "I don't know . . . I don't know anything about anything. Just gotta take each day at a time, eh? Trust him to get better."

Sophie said nothing for a moment, her expression distant. "What's going to happen to him, Rupe? If he doesn't get better? How are we going to look after him?"

The junk food in Rupert's mouth turned to dust. The answer to Sophie's bleak question was complicated; Jodi's physical recovery was slow, but tangible. Despite Rupert's pessimism, there was no denying the daily improvements—improvements that left Jodi's damaged brain far behind. What would happen if he became too well for the hospital, but too vulnerable to come home?

Rupert squeezed his eyes shut. He hadn't believed there could be anything worse than what they'd lived—*ha*—through already, but that would be a whole new nightmare, and his grotty dinner had long gone cold by the time he found the words to answer Sophie. He opened his eyes and glared at her like *she* was the one who'd mowed Jodi down with a stolen car. "I'm taking him home. Whatever happens, he's coming home with me."

March 26, 2010

Jodi did put his arms around Rupert that first night, and the one after, and it wasn't long before they fell into a comfortable routine. Rupert stayed over three or four nights a week, sometimes more, and, eventually, Jodi found himself unable to sleep when Rupert went home to his bedsit.

One morning, a few weeks after their bar date, Jodi awoke just before dawn to find him still sleeping. He rolled over and studied his companion, stretched out on his front, naked, because they'd ditched their clothes the night before and slept bare and open, facing each other, hardly daring to touch. Rupert's body had seemed perfect in the darkness, his pale skin flawless in the shadows, but now, with the sun rising through the blinds they'd forgotten to close, Jodi saw that what he'd glimpsed the night before hadn't done Rupert justice. Jesus fucking Christ, the bloke was beautiful. Skin, muscle, and bone, all melded together with a wry, warm innocence that made Jodi's heart ache.

"Stop staring. You'll give me a complex."

Jodi came back to earth to find Rupert wide-awake and grinning. "Caught me, eh? Sorry, can't help it. You're too cute."

"Cute?" Rupert pulled a face that made him look like a young boy. "That wasn't the effect I was hoping for, lying here in my birthday suit."

"You don't want to know the effect your birthday suit is having on me."

"Wouldn't bet on that, mate."

"That right?" Jodi leaned in and kissed Rupert full on the lips, letting Rupert's strong arms engulf him in the embrace he'd come to crave when Rupert wasn't around. The kiss deepened, and it wasn't long before they were pressed together and gasping for breath, the point where Jodi usually put the brakes on, mindful of pushing Rupert too hard and too fast.

The wait for Rupert to make the next move had seemed endless, but Jodi forgot all about it as Rupert took Jodi's cock in his hand and brushed his thumb along the length, his lips still fused to Jodi's. Jodi jumped and let out a strangled groan, breaking their kiss. "Bloody hell. Do that again."

Rupert repeated the gesture. "I don't really know what I'm doing."

Jodi begged to differ, but rather than scoff, he passed on the best nugget of wisdom he'd ever been given about pleasuring another man. "Treat my dick like your own and we'll be just fine."

"Yeah?" Rupert laughed and the nervous tension in his face eased. "Makes sense. I've had plenty of experience making *myself* come."

Jodi found Rupert's hand, which had drifted away while they'd been talking, and moved it back to his cock. "Haven't we all. Now, show me what you do to yourself when you're alone in bed."

"That hasn't happened much recently." But Rupert gripped Jodi's weeping cock all the same, squeezing and twisting, building up to a teasing rhythm that barely scratched the surface of the simmering heat between them.

Jodi bit his shoulder. "More."

"More?"

"*More.*"

Rupert hesitated a moment, then threw the duvet aside, exposing them both to the early morning draft. But Jodi barely felt the chill in the air as Rupert scooted down the bed and took his cock in his mouth, enveloping it in a firm, hot suction that sent Jodi's eyes into a rolling spin.

"*Fuck.*"

Rupert sucked harder and grazed his teeth along the underside with just a little too much pressure. Jodi hissed. Rupert adjusted himself with a gentle lick, and Jodi's back arched from the sweetly subtle pleasure. He took note of the gesture and filed it away, ready for when they switched roles, something he couldn't contemplate while Rupert was blowing him like this. Fuck no. This couldn't end. Ever.

But it seemed Rupert had other ideas. After a few more false starts, he found his rhythm and picked up the pace, using his hand for extra friction, and tickling Jodi's balls with the other. Jodi cried out again and fisted the sheets beneath him. *Damn it.* He was the one supposed to be giving the lessons, and now he was about to blow his load in ten seconds flat. How the fuck had that happened?

Orgasm crept up on him, rushing through him and spilling out into Rupert's mouth before he had a chance to warn him. Rupert's eyes widened, and for a moment Jodi feared he'd gag, but he didn't. He swallowed with a smirk and then continued to tease until Jodi begged him to stop.

"You sneaky bastard." Jodi heaved for breath and wiped away the sweat that had trickled down his face and chest. "You're supposed to be a fucking amateur."

Rupert shrugged, clearly trying to hide his glee. "I did what you said, and it worked. Can't believe I never thought of it that way before. Perhaps if I had, I wouldn't have been so shit-scared of it all."

That theory held a host of conflict for Jodi. A Rupert who'd been at peace with his sexuality might not have found his way to Jodi's bed.

Stop being a selfish dick.

He stopped, distracted by Rupert crawling back up the bed, still naked, hard, and outrageously beautiful. Jodi tugged him down on top of him. "I wanna blow you too."

Rupert laughed. "Sure about that? 'Cause you look near enough asleep to me."

"Do I?"

Rupert's answering chuckle sounded distant, growing fainter as Jodi slipped into that magical trance between sleep and consciousness, his favourite phase of sleep. As a child, he'd often wondered if it felt like that when you were dead.

It was midmorning when he woke for a second time, sprawled on his back like he'd had the best orgasm ever.

Rupert smirked down at him from his position propped up on the pillows. "All right?"

Jodi nodded slowly as his faculties returned to him, and he remembered that it was Friday, the day he left free for admin, or doing sweet fuck all, and Rupert wasn't working either, leaving them both naked with nothing to do and nowhere to be. *And I owe him a blowjob.*

He sat up and pounced on Rupert, swallowing his gasp with a crazed kiss, covering Rupert with his body and pressing him into the mattress. Rupert was bigger than Jodi, taller, stronger, but he put up no fight as Jodi pinned his arms above his head.

"Don't move . . . unless I tell you to."

Rupert raised an eyebrow, but said nothing. Jodi took his cue and moved down Rupert's body, pausing at each sensitive zone—his neck, the curve of his chest, the trail of chestnut hair that led to his cock—to acquaint himself with the body he'd been craving to explore from the moment they'd met. And it was worth the wait. Hard, smooth, and lean, Rupert was everything Jodi had dreamed of and more. He reached Rupert's dick and teased it with the tip of his tongue. Rupert jumped. Jodi grinned and did it again. He'd planned on giving Rupert the blowjob of his life, bringing him to the brink over and over until Rupert begged to be allowed to come, but watching Rupert fight to stay still beneath him, fists clenched, jaw set, his eyes a heady mixture of curiosity and desire, Jodi had another idea.

He gave Rupert's cock a gentle tap. "Wanna fuck?"

"What?" Rupert's eyes widened. "I've never—"

Jodi crawled quickly up the bed. "I don't mean any heavy shit. Trust me, yeah? I'll do it all."

Rupert sucked in a shaky breath. "What do you mean, all of it? I don't want to play the v-card, but I've never . . . and I don't think I want to—"

Jodi silenced him. "I'm going to ride you. Fuck you from the bottom, if you're comfortable with that. The stuff you're talking about can come later, or not. You don't have to do anything like that if you don't want to."

"No? Thought it came with the territory?"

"Hell no." Jodi shook his head. "Being gay isn't about getting fucked. I do it because I like it—more than like it—but plenty of men don't. It's not obligatory."

Rupert nodded slowly. "I've thought about it a lot, even before I really *knew*, you know? And I don't want to. I've tried it on myself, and it doesn't feel right, which is kinda weird, because I think about you in that way all the time, and it doesn't feel wrong at all."

"That's because there is no right or wrong, Rupe." Jodi touched Rupert's cheek. "Just us."

Rupert covered Jodi's hands with his own. "'Rupe'? No one's ever called me that before."

"Does it feel wrong?"

"No, nothing about you ever does." Rupert raised his hands again, returning them to where Jodi had placed them. "Do what you want with me. I'm yours."

His warm, comfortable smirk let Jodi know Rupert was ready for whatever he threw at him, and his choice of words stirred something in Jodi. He kissed Rupert with a softness that belied the rising heat between them. "I'm yours too, you know, if you want me."

He pulled back before Rupert could respond, sitting up and grinding down on Rupert's cock. "This is what I'm going to do. Think you can handle it?"

Rupert swallowed. "I can try."

Jodi chuckled and reached across Rupert to the bedside table, retrieving his long-neglected stash of johnnies and lube. "Babe, you don't have to try to do anything. You're fucking perfect."

"Can I touch you?"

"Please."

Rupert brought his arms around Jodi, kissing him in a frenzy that made Jodi's head spin. Jodi let him have his way for a moment, then grasped Rupert's face in his hands, breaking the kiss so that he could return to Rupert's cock.

He took Rupert in his mouth, and Rupert jumped again and let out a strangled moan. "Jesus fucking Christ."

Jodi smiled and sucked Rupert harder, taking him as far into his throat as he could, straining his gag reflex. Deep-throating was uncomfortable, but he'd always got a kick out of choking on another man's cock. The suffocating thrill made his heart beat faster and his blood rush through his veins to the point where he could hardly see straight. And being with Rupert, the effect was tenfold. Jodi's senses came alive as Rupert wove his fingers into his hair, and he felt every groan and shudder like they were his own.

"You're gonna make me come," Rupert gasped. "If you want to ride me . . ."

Jodi got the message and reluctantly eased off. The urge to let Rupert shoot down his throat was strong, but the throb in his dick reminded him that he'd had a plan, a fucking awesome plan, and it was time to see it through.

He sat up and reached for the condoms. "Wanna do the honours?"

"Me? Fuck no. This is your show. Do what you will. I'm ready."

That was good enough for Jodi. He tore the condom wrapper open with his teeth, rolled it onto Rupert, and lubed up, then cast the paraphernalia aside. They'd ticked all the boxes; what came next was about them and chasing down the current that had simmered between them for so long Jodi couldn't imagine life without it.

He kissed Rupert deeply, prying his hands from behind his head, and guiding them to his cock. Having Rupert at his mercy had its appeal, but not right now. Rupert needed to feel this, all of it. "Hold it still so I don't have to wriggle around trying to find it."

"Can I touch yours too?"

"You can touch whatever you like."

Jodi leaned back as Rupert held his cock still, his other hand closing tentatively around Jodi's dick.

"*Fuck.*" Jodi groaned, and his eyes fluttered shut. Rupert had the lightest touch, but it was just enough to set Jodi on fire. Rupert's fingertips grazed his cock and merged with the burn of taking Rupert inside him. Suddenly, he found himself on the edge, fighting off an orgasm that threatened to derail them before they'd even got started.

Beneath him, Rupert threw his head back and panted out a moan. "Jesus. It's only halfway in."

Is it? Dear God. Jodi steeled himself and eased down the rest of the way, batting Rupert's hands aside. He placed his own hands on Rupert's hips, breathing deeply, and reacquainting himself with the sting of having another man's dick—and Rupert had a *big* dick—crammed inside him, a sensation that had never felt so good.

He opened his eyes. Rupert was watching him, gaze wide, chest heaving. Jodi circled his hips, absorbing the tiny shocks of pleasure that jolted through him, growing in magnitude with every movement. He grasped the headboard. The growing furnace in his belly told him that they didn't have long, and there was no way he was leaving Rupert behind. Jodi used the headboard for balance and fucked himself on Rupert's cock in a rhythm he fast lost control of. He dropped his head, feeling Rupert's touch all over him—strong hands that belied the quivering in Rupert's thighs.

Rupert gasped. "Shit, I'm gonna—" And he came with a low cry, sudden and hard, the force of it sending his eyes rolling into the back of his head.

Jodi slowed his pace, awed. He'd pictured this moment many times since he'd caught sight of Rupert outside that dodgy club on Boxing Day. Beautiful, beautiful Rupert. Jaw clenched, pale skin flushed and shimmering with sweat, he was breathtaking.

A few long, drawn-out moments later, Rupert stirred and reached for Jodi's cock. Jodi shook his head and let go of the headboard, leaning back and jutting his pelvis forward. "Don't worry about that. Ever come without touching your dick at all?"

"Er . . . no?" Rupert raised a bemused eyebrow. He put his hands on Jodi's thighs and squeezed. "Show me?"

Jodi had slowed his movements when Rupert had come, lost in it. Buoyed by Rupert's grip on his legs, he picked up the pace, slamming down again and again until the coil of pleasure inside him snapped.

He sucked in a harsh breath, then yelled out, spilling over Rupert's belly as Rupert looked on, his face a conflicting mix of confusion and wonder.

"How is that even possible?"

"Prostate, baby." Jodi slowed, drawing out every last shudder and gasp, but eventually, they were both spent. Holding the condom in place, lifted himself from Rupert's body, and collapsed in a heap beside him.

Rupert tossed the condom and rolled over, wrapping himself around Jodi from behind. "That was amazing. Are you okay?"

"Yeah, I'm okay." Jodi raised his head, then let it drop again, absorbing the drowsiness that came from an awesome fuck as it washed over him. "Was it good for you? I mean, did you like it?"

Rupert laughed, though, like before, it sounded distant. If not for the warming cage of his arms, moulding their bodies together, Jodi would've thought he'd left the room. That, and the gentle brush of Rupert's kiss on his cheek, and the soft whisper of words that felt like a dream. "Like it? Boyo, you blew my damn mind. Now go back to sleep. I've got you."

Chapter FIVE

November 26, 2014

Rupert dropped down low and crawled along the threadbare carpet of the dilapidated Brixton flat. The smoke was thick and acrid, carrying the telltale stench of whatever faulty electrical item the fire had originated from.

Gav and Tony shuffled past him, heading for the kitchen to put it out. Rupert shouldered open the door to the living room, feeling around for signs of the flat's occupants. His hand hit what felt like a couch. He patted down the cushions until he found an arm. Bingo. Rupert sat up on his knees and called out to the elderly man. There was no response. The man's body was limp—lifeless—and Rupert had been doing the job long enough to know he was likely already dead.

He lifted the man over his shoulder and radioed in. "Got one. Any word on the other occupants?"

"It's just him, O'Neil. We've got the wife out here. Bring him down."

Great. Rupert didn't fancy the task of laying the dead man at his wife's feet. Hopefully, there'd be an ambulance waiting so she wouldn't know until Rupert had slunk away. Heartless? Not really. Rupert had done his fair share of breaking bad news.

He carried the man out. A lone paramedic greeted him—no ambulance, just a bike with blues and twos. Rupert laid the man on the pavement. The paramedic pronounced him dead and covered him with a blanket. The wife's distraught wail should've gutted him. Should've torn him in two and etched itself in the part of his soul that never got over the death and destruction he witnessed time and time again.

It didn't.

He pulled his breathing apparatus off and went to the rear of the rig to clean down. Radio chatter told him the fire was out and the block of flats had been cleared of all residents. Their job was nearly done. An hour or so, and they'd be back at the station, showering and hanging around for another call.

"O'Neil?" Briggs, the watch manager, stood behind Rupert. "Everything okay?"

"Yup."

"Sure?"

"Yup." Rupert kept his gaze on the task at hand. Briggs was a good man—a friend—and he'd gone above and beyond for Rupert since Jodi's accident, but Rupert wasn't in the mood for a heart-to-heart. Not today.

Shame Briggs couldn't read minds. "Come and see me when we get back. 'Bout time we touched base."

Rupert sighed as Briggs walked away. Not a day seemed to go by without some well-meaning soul trying to persuade him to pour his heart out to them. When were they going to realise that no amount of tea and chatter would change a bloody thing?

The next hour passed in a haze of soot and grime as they made the flat safe for fire investigators. Rupert was the last man out. On his way, he passed a London Fire Brigade home-safety poster pinned up in the entrance hall. The cruel irony hit him hard. His crew spent much of their time out in the community, trying to prevent fires happening in the first place—smoke alarms, fire blankets, escape routes. Their message had clearly never reached this family.

Outside, he watched the grieving wife being coaxed into a police car, finally persuaded to leave the scene. Until a few months ago, Rupert would've perhaps gone with her, supported her until a family liaison officer arrived. Not now. Fuck that. It had been a while since he'd had the energy to counsel someone through what were often the hardest and most distressing moments of their life. A while since he'd had the stomach to meet the haunted gaze of a soul who'd lost everything they'd ever known in the blink of an eye.

Back at the station, he dodged Briggs and ducked into the showers. Whatever kind of job he'd been on, there was always something satisfying about watching hours of soot and grime disappear down the plughole, and he lingered under the hot spray as long as he dared. The coast was clear when he got out, or so he thought, until he got to his bunk and found Briggs waiting for him.

"Not hiding from me, are ya, O'Neil?"

Rupert sighed and tossed his damp towel on the bed. "No point with you fecking stalking me, is there?"

"S'pose not." If Briggs was offended, he didn't show it. He glanced around. "How's Jodi?"

Rupert looked around too, checking that they had relative privacy, though he didn't know why. His personal life wasn't much of a secret. "Pretty much the same."

"Still having seizures?"

"Not this week. They're hoping it was just a phase of his recovery." And dear God, so was Rupert. He'd spent the beginning of the last month dreading the moment the doctors decided Jodi was well enough to leave the hospital, but it hadn't happened. Instead, Jodi had been plagued by a run of terrifying seizures, and Rupert had regressed into fearing nothing but that damn-fucking shadow on Jodi's brain.

"And how are you bearing up? It's gotta be hard, Rupert. Two jobs and caring for Jodi. Don't know how you do it."

I don't, Rupert wanted to say. He'd handed his notice in at the club, and it had been a long time since he'd felt like he'd done anything properly, but he held his tongue. Briggs had waved the possibility of promotion to crew manager under Rupert's nose the day before Jodi's accident. He hadn't mentioned it since, and it was probably just as well. The bump in salary would've cleared the last of Rupert's postdivorce debts and allowed him to treat Jodi and Indie the way they deserved, but if—*when* Jodi came home, chances were Rupert would have to cut his hours to care for him.

And pay the mortgage with magic beans.

Briggs shifted his weight from one foot to the other. Rupert turned his back on him under the guise of pulling a wrinkled T-shirt—his clothes were missing Jodi's attention—over his head, counting down to the question he knew would come next.

"Don't suppose he's, er, talking yet, is he?"

"No, not yet." Rupert closed his eyes against the image of Jodi convulsing on the hospital floor, his dark gaze blank, and his mouth clamped shut, not uttering a sound. Was it wrong that Rupert longed for him to cry out? Even in pain? Anything to prove there was a scrap of Jodi left behind that hollow stare?

Briggs slapped Rupert on the back. "Chin up, mate. Never know, tonight might be the night you walk into that hospital and get yer boy back."

It wasn't. Rupert clocked out around midnight and jogged the short distance to hospital. The night sister met him at the nurses' station and ushered him to the quiet corner of the ward where Jodi had his bed. Rupert squeezed her hand in thanks. The ward managers had been incredibly tolerant of his fluctuating shift pattern, and let him in to see Jodi whenever he liked, providing he didn't disturb the other patients, which was unlikely considering his visits to Jodi were mostly spent in silence.

And tonight would be no different. Jodi was fast asleep, curled on his side, his good hand tucked under his chin.

"He didn't eat much dinner," the sister said. "I tried to tempt him with some of Caz's birthday cake earlier, but he wasn't interested."

Rupert's bones ached with sadness. Before the accident, Jodi's sweet tooth had been legendary. "Thank you."

The sister left him to it. Rupert adjusted the soft grey blanket he'd brought from home so it covered Jodi properly, then took a seat. "Hey, beautiful."

And beautiful Jodi still was, despite the purple smudges under his eyes and the pallor of his skin. His inky hair had grown a little, and Rupert had become addicted to the sensation of his thicker beard against his fingers. He scratched the wiry scruff now and squeezed Jodi's hand. "Sweet dreams, boyo. Be safe. I love you."

April 26, 2010

Jodi hopped off the bus in Harringay and took in the shabby buildings and monumental traffic congestion. Rupert was right. There really was nothing here but greengrocers with cabbages the size of small planets, Turkish/Cypriot cafés, and row upon row of scruffy bedsits.

"Welcome to bedshitland." Recalling Rupert's gentle sarcasm made Jodi smile, and the address he'd scribbled on a scrap of paper was burning a hole in his back pocket, but he had work to do and another address to find before he paid Rupert a long overdue visit.

He found the run-down meze bar a few streets from the bus stop. The owner, a wizened man who couldn't have been less than seventy, greeted him with a mug of coffee you could stand a spoon in. Jodi liked him—Spiros—straightaway. And the job was relatively simple too. Somehow, the old man had discovered the growing market for online takeaway ordering and wanted a functional website to help him offer the service. Jodi glanced around the tatty restaurant and considered his pricing. The old man likely couldn't afford his going rate—and Jodi had to wonder how he'd found him in the first place— but despite the peeling paint and cracked tiles, the place was spotlessly clean, and it smelled *amazing*.

On cue, Spiros placed a plate of grilled halloumi, tomatoes, and herby fried eggs in front of him, complete with fresh sesame bread and a glass of what looked like grappa. The food was rustic, honest peasant fare, and oddly beautiful. Jodi's stomach growled its approval. He took another glance around. The restaurant was clearly struggling, like any business that wasn't a fucking Wetherspoons. Did he really want to feel responsible for another shit-hot family business going bust? Hell no. Jodi downed the grappa and quoted Spiros a price that should've made him weep.

A little while later, he emerged into the grey world of Harringay under a haze of garlic and grappa. Spiros had invited him back for dinner, but Jodi had places to be—and people to see—and he was already half-pissed.

And late. Oops. He pulled out the scrap of paper he'd scrawled Rupert's address on. The bedsit was a five-minute walk from Spiros's place, so Jodi turned east and set off, passing the time by planning the restaurant's website. To fit in with its authenticity, the site couldn't be too flashy, but it had to work, and work well, which demanded a certain amount of slickness. Trick was to balance the functionality with ambiance and personality, something that would probably have to involve photographing Spiros. *Unless I could fudge a graphic of him.*

Hmm. Jodi couldn't draw for shit, but the idea had weight. He filed it away for later. Right now, he had eyes only for Rupert, who was standing on the pavement ahead, his phone tucked under his chin, and clutching the hand of a seraphic little girl Jodi knew from photographs to be his daughter, Indie.

Jodi trailed to a stop. Rupert hadn't said he'd have Indie with him today. Not that it mattered, to Jodi at least, but the lingering tickle of grappa in his belly gave him pause. Though his buzz had faded, it felt a little wrong to gatecrash a father-daughter day when he'd been drinking since breakfast time.

He considered slinking away, texting Rupert from the Tube to say his client meeting had run over and he had to get back to Tottenham, but as he warred between doing the right thing and indulging the craving need to see Rupert in any capacity he could, Rupert turned and saw him, and his window of escape was gone.

By Indie's curious smile, she saw him too. Jodi swallowed a shot of nerves and dug around in his pocket for chewing gum. He didn't have much experience with kids, especially girls, though he knew Indie was more into football than Barbies.

They met halfway, and it took Jodi a millisecond to see Rupert was as nervous as he was.

"I've been trying to call you," Rupert said. "Indie's childminder is ill, so I've got her for the day. I'm sorry. I tried to let you know."

"'S okay." Jodi bent to Indie's level and held out his hand. "I was coming past anyway. I'm Jodi. Nice to meet you. What's that on your T-shirt? A fairy?"

Indie took Jodi's hand and looked down at her T-shirt with the confusion of a child who'd put on whatever clothes they'd been told to that morning. "I think it's a mouse-dancer."

"A mouse-dancer, eh?" The cartoon character was more like a hippo to Jodi, but what did he know? "What are you two up to? Anything fun?"

"We're going to the park," Indie said. "You come too?"

Jodi glanced up at Rupert, who shrugged. "We'd love you to, but I won't be offended if you have better things to do."

"Erm, looks like I'm coming, then." Jodi squeezed Indie's tiny hand. "On one condition, though."

"I already brushed my teeth and I didn't make a mess."

"Oh." Jodi pretended to think hard and tried to ignore the faint shadow of guilt that darkened Rupert's features. "In that case, you'll have to push me on the swing instead. That cool?"

Indie giggled. "You too big for the swings."

"That right? Oh well, you can give me a crunchy cuddle when I fall on my bum, then."

"Cwunchy cuddle?"

"Yeah, one with tickles. We can practice on Daddy." Jodi lifted Indie up onto his shoulders and caught Rupert's surprised gaze. "Ready?"

"Erm, okay. Are you sure you want to do this? You don't—"

"Shut it," Jodi said. "I'm coming."

A while later, Jodi found himself at the top of a steep slide with Indie on his lap. "It's a long way down. Sure you don't want Daddy to catch you at the bottom?"

"No! Let's go! Let's go!" Indie banged her fists on Jodi's thighs.

Jodi laughed. Indie was a sweet girl, but her chubby cheeks and slender bones belied the rambunctious daredevil who'd been tearing around the park and run both him and Rupert ragged. He pushed off the slide and sent them zooming to the bottom where Rupert plucked Indie from Jodi's lap and swung her over his head. His grin was a mile wide, and Jodi was transfixed by the pair of them, identical in all but eye colour. Had he ever seen anything as innocently beautiful?

Not that he could think of, and the sight of Rupert and Indie dancing around the park in the sun reminded him that he'd crashed their playdate. "I'm gonna chip off," he said. "Call me later?"

Rupert set Indie on the roundabout. "Gotta get back, eh? Work to do?"

"Always. I'm home tonight, though, if you fancy a Skype chat?"

Rupert rolled his eyes. Jodi had been trying to persuade him to get Skype since they'd met, but he held firm. Apparently, technology was wasted on him. "I'll call you. Indie? Jodi's going now."

Indie hopped nimbly from the roundabout and climbed up Jodi's legs until she was safe in his arms. "Can we go ice skating next time?"

"Next time?" The thought of seeing her again was more heartwarming and appealing than he'd ever thought possible. "Sure, but you'll have to stop me falling on my arse—er—bum, okay?"

Rupert coughed, hiding his grin, and pried Indie back. "That makes two of us you'll have to supervise, kiddo. Say bye to Jodi."

They said their good-byes, and Jodi left them to it, fighting the urge to glance over his shoulder as he walked away. Kiddie time in the park wasn't how he'd expected to spend his afternoon, but he'd loved every moment, and though he really did have work to do, going home was the last thing on his mind. He caught a bus back to Tottenham. As Harringay disappeared behind him, he pulled out his phone and sent a text to the one person in the world he loved as much as he was coming to love Rupert.

Fancy some pie and mash?

Sophie met him in Tottenham at their favourite hole-in-the wall café, a dive that served all-day breakfasts and the best pie and mash in London. Jodi's Mediterranean brunch felt like a lifetime ago. He ordered as much as he dared before Sophie reined him in.

"Flipping heck, Jodi. I haven't got hollow legs, you know. Some of us can't eat our body weight in gravy and get away with it."

"Fuck off. I'm having two pies." Jodi placed his order, paid for both of them, then steered Sophie to a table by the steamed-up windows. "Besides, you're bloody gorgeous and you know it. More of you, the better."

Sophie pulled a face that did nothing to make her any less lovely. She'd put on a few pounds since she'd quit her job as an estate agent and retrained as a nursery nurse, and she looked amazing.

"So . . ." Sophie dumped sugar in her tea. "To what do I owe the pleasure? I've been trying to get you to buy me lunch for weeks."

"Hey, that's not my fault. You're never around when I'm free."

"That's because I work all day and sleep all night, like the rest of the world. Try it sometime."

"I'll have you know I went to bed at eleven o'clock last night." Jodi didn't add that by then he'd been up for thirty-six hours, rushing to meet a deadline he'd neglected in favour of rolling around on the floor with Rupert. He didn't have to. Sophie knew him well enough to fill in the blanks.

"So when do I get to meet this hunky fireman, then?" she said on cue. "How long have you been seeing him?"

Jodi counted back in his head. He'd met Rupert on Boxing Day, and it was April now. "Four months."

"Pictures." Sophie held out her hand for Jodi's phone.

He relinquished it, waiting until a waitress had set their plates on the table before he directed Sophie to the album where he'd stored the precious few snaps he'd managed to sneak of Rupert.

His heaping plate of two steak-and-ale pies with mash, peas, and gravy proved a welcome distraction as Sophie scrolled through them. He'd made good headway by the time she passed the phone back with a low whistle.

"He's *beautiful*. Fancy sharing?"

The question wasn't as innocent as it might have been between two other friends. Jodi and Sophie had ended their romantic relationship more than a year ago. They'd fallen into bed together a few times since, sometimes with company, but that didn't appeal to Jodi anymore. He loved Sophie with all his heart. Sharing *Rupert* though? Fuck no. Jodi couldn't imagine sharing him with anyone. Didn't want to. In fact, he couldn't imagine sharing a bed with anyone else ever again.

Like she'd heard his epiphany, Sophie smiled and patted Jodi's arm. "It's okay, babe. I can see how much you like him. This is the real deal, isn't it?"

"I think so." Heat flooded Jodi's face. He took a gulp of hot tea, which did nothing to quell the warmth filling his chest. "Just gotta hope he feels the same."

"How could he not?" Sophie's smile waned with a touch of the sadness she rarely let Jodi see. "Embrace it. I'm over the moon for you, Jojo."

Later that night found Jodi growling at his computer. Eventually, a glitch in the operating system froze the screen. He admitted defeat and shut it down, retreating to the couch with the old grey blanket that seemed to follow him around when the weather turned colder, a relic from his student days. It was tatty and holed, but combined with *Blackadder* on the telly, it felt like an old friend, and it wasn't long before he fell fast asleep.

A low chuckle woke him sometime later. "You look like a Hobbit, wrapped up in that."

Jodi grumbled and pressed his face into a cushion. He'd jumped a bloody mile the first time Rupert had used the spare key and crept into the flat under the cover of darkness, but he was used to it now. Loved it. There was nothing better than waking up to Rupert's comforting warmth beside him when he'd gone to sleep alone.

Rupert laughed again and pulled the blanket back from Jodi's face. "Wake up for me, boyo. I want to tell you something."

Jodi raised his head and cracked an eye open. "Mate, I already know you're gay."

"Very funny." Rupert scowled briefly, but he clearly wasn't annoyed in the slightest. In fact, he seemed happier than Jodi had ever seen him.

"That grin's gonna split your face. Spill."

"Indie loves you." Rupert grinned wider. "She's been talking about you all afternoon."

"Really?" Jodi couldn't name the emotion that stirred in him. He couldn't deny he'd been a little spellbound by Indie in return. She was nothing like the children he'd come across before. No snot and whinging. No constant trips to the toilet. "What did she say?"

"It's more what she asked."

Jodi sat up. "Asked?"

"Yeah." Rupert caught the blanket as it slipped from Jodi's shoulders. "She asked me if you were my boyfriend."

"Seriously? Where did she get that idea?"

Rupert shrugged. "I think she might've overheard something at home. Jen's big on slating me to anyone who'll listen."

"Still?"

"Aye, but I don't give a shit. Her big mouth's done me a favour. I've wanted to tell Indie for a long time. Just didn't know how."

A slow grin crept over Jodi's face. "So you told her I'm your boyfriend?"

"Er, yeah. That's okay, right? I mean, I know we've never—"

Jodi silenced Rupert with a quick kiss. They'd never had that particular conversation, but their casual friendship had slipped so seamlessly into a warm, companionable relationship, there hadn't been the need. They had much to learn about each other, but boyfriends? Fuck yeah, Jodi was having some of that. "I *am* your boyfriend."

"Thank God for that." Rupert's mile-wide smile returned. "Because I told Indie everything—the Disney version, at least."

"Wow. I don't know what to say. That's awesome." And it was. Jodi didn't have to know shit about raising kids to see how much being out to Indie meant to Rupert. "What about Jen, though? She won't do anything shitty and try to keep Indie away from you, will she?"

"She's going to do her nut, but there's nothing she can do about it. The courts have already told her she can't restrict my access to Indie because of my sexuality."

"You told the courts you're gay?"

Rupert nodded. "Didn't have much choice really. Jen outed me straight from the bat. Tried to paint me as a bloody deviant. Didn't do her much good, though. The judge took my side. First time anyone ever did that."

Jodi's heart ached. Rupert didn't give much away, but it didn't take a genius to figure out the scars he carried from his old life, both back home in Ireland, and here, with Indie and Jen. Some days, Jodi couldn't bear to think about it, but others, curiosity burned in his chest, and he wanted to know it all, no matter how painful it was to hear.

Today was a curious day. A thousand questions fought for dominance in Jodi's mind, but Rupert clearly had other ideas. He lunged at Jodi, catching him off guard, and covered him with kisses before Jodi could take a breath to speak.

Jodi fell back on the couch, but he'd barely touched the cushions before he found himself up in the air and bent double over Rupert's shoulder in a seamless fireman's lift. "Motherfucker!"

Rupert laughed, a sound Jodi was becoming gloriously used to. "Yup. Watcha gonna do about it?"

Nothing, obviously. Rupert was lean, but, damn, the bloke was strong. Jodi knew better than to waste his energy wrestling him. Besides, as Rupert carried him through the flat and dumped him on the bed, he had little desire to resist whatever Rupert had in mind. They'd fucked many times since that first time a month ago, and Rupert had grown in confidence with each heady night that passed. Jodi was a bossy lover by nature, but sometimes—just sometimes—it was fun to let Rupert have his way.

Rupert stripped Jodi of the jogging bottoms and T-shirt he'd fallen asleep in, then he drew his own zipper down slowly, revealing that he'd made the journey to Jodi's place sans underwear.

"Commando?" Jodi raised an eyebrow.

Rupert grinned. "Didn't know I was coming over till I was halfway here. Too late by then."

Jodi wondered what Rupert had been doing at home without his boxers on, but was quickly distracted by the cock pressing against his lips. He opened up and met Rupert's gaze as Rupert slid his dick into Jodi's mouth. Rupert licked his lips and shuddered with obvious pleasure, a far cry from the nervous wreck he'd been when they'd started messing around like this.

Not that either of them was messing around right now. Jodi craned his neck and drew Rupert closer, relaxing his throat and taking him as far down as he could manage.

Rupert groaned and gripped Jodi's hair. "I was thinking about this on the way over. Think about it all the time. You're fucking amazing, boyo."

Despite the context, the words seemed heartfelt, and they surged through Jodi. He sucked harder, clawing at any part of Rupert he could reach, until Rupert pulled his dick away and shed his remaining clothes.

Naked, he covered Jodi with his body and kissed him deeply. "I mean it. You and Indie, you're everything to me."

He took his kiss down Jodi's neck and chest without waiting for a reply. Jodi writhed as Rupert worked his way lower and lower, grasping the duvet, the sheets, searching blindly for something, anything, to hold on to. He found Rupert's hair and dug his fingers in, scraping Rupert's scalp with his nails. "The feeling's mutual, you know— Fuck!"

Rupert held the base of Jodi's cock and blew warm air over the head, a gentle warning, before he took him in his mouth.

Jodi arched his back and cried out as Rupert stroked and teased him with his tongue, moaning quietly, a low, vibrating hum that buzzed around Jodi's cock. *Jesus fucking Christ.* Jodi fought release, biting his lip and twisting Rupert's hair. Rupert was maddeningly good at driving him insane, coiling him tighter and tighter around an invisible string until he was so turned on he didn't know which way was up. Didn't know anything except that if he didn't come soon, he was sure to combust.

A thousand terrible firefighter puns flashed in Jodi's sex-fogged mind, but the coherency was fleeting. Rupert moved up the bed again. Jodi lunged for him and yanked him close, kissing him hard enough to clash their teeth. He wanted more. Needed more.

"Condom. Now."

Rupert took the command and leaned over to rummage in the bedside table. A condom and a well-used bottle of lube were dropped onto the bed. Jodi sat up. His hands shook, but somehow he managed to roll the condom onto Rupert and squelch enough lube out of the nearly empty bottle.

He slathered the lube on Rupert's cock, squeezing and releasing, until Rupert growled and batted his hands away.

"Get on your knees."

That was a new one, but Jodi obeyed without hesitation, rolling over and dropping his chest to the mattress. Rupert came up behind him, his cock pressing against him, pushing gently as Rupert aligned them.

"Ready?"

Jodi nodded. "Fuck yeah. Do it."

Rupert placed a hand at the base of Jodi's spine, warm and soothing, and a stark contrast to the coolness of the condom as he eased inside, slow and careful, pausing with every inch to mutter words of comfort Jodi rarely needed.

Jodi cursed softly, reeling at the exhilarating intensity of Rupert filling him, his senses on hyperalert. He'd always loved getting fucked, and with Rupert, he felt *everything*, from the feathery kisses on his back to the crazy-heat of Rupert's dick sliding ever deeper.

Rupert wrapped his arms around Jodi and eased his hips into motion, setting a steady rhythm that electrified the building inferno in Jodi's gut.

"Harder." Jodi gasped and gripped the bed frame. "Harder, Rupe. Please."

Rupert groaned. "Fucking love it when you say please." He thrust harder and brought his hand down on Jodi's thigh with a light smack, a blow that stung just enough to tip Jodi into an inescapable gauntlet of pleasure.

His legs shook, and he bit out another strangled curse. Rupert fucked him faster, and used his weight to force Jodi's hands from the bed frame, pushing him down into the mattress. "I'm gonna come."

"Race you." Jodi found the coordination to push his hips back, meeting Rupert hard in the middle. "I'm close."

A hot breath rushed past Jodi's ear. Rupert's arms tightened around him. Jodi cried out again and again, until sensory overload obliterated his awareness of anything but the deepest orgasm he'd ever had.

He came with a yell, tipped over the edge by Rupert's cock pulsing inside him. Rupert moaned and thrust twice more before he slumped over Jodi, panting, his body damp with sweat.

For a long moment, neither man moved, then Rupert kissed Jodi's neck and withdrew, retreating to the bathroom.

He came back with a warm flannel, and cleaned up with a grin. "All right?"

Jodi expelled a swift lungful of air. "All right? I'm in fucking bits. That was awesome."

"Yeah?" A bit of Rupert's old bashfulness coloured his features. "I didn't hurt you?"

"Honestly?" Jodi touched Rupert's cheek. "It did hurt, but I like that. It's not for everyone, but it blows my tiny mind."

Rupert snorted and rolled over onto his back, taking Jodi with him to rest his head on Rupert's chest. Jodi closed his eyes as Rupert combed his fingers gently through his sex-mussed hair. Having Rupert in his bed felt so normal. The nights they spent apart made no sense. Jodi let his mind drift, and imagined Rupert and Indie in Rupert's tiny bedsit, cooped up in one room and huddled together in Rupert's bed. Perhaps they liked it like that, but Jodi didn't. Indie was a growing kid. Soon enough, she'd need her own space—space Jodi had to spare.

"Where are you?" Rupert tapped Jodi's forehead. "You've dropped off the face of the earth."

Jodi raised his head and put his chin on Rupert's chest. "You know I have a spare room?"

"Erm, yeah? You said it's full of junk."

"It is, but it's junk I don't need. I want to chuck it all out."

"Okay." Rupert frowned, like he knew where Jodi was going, but couldn't quite believe it.

Jodi couldn't quite believe it either. After a mad few years flat-sharing after uni, and then living with Sophie, having his own place had been a relief, but the thought of seeing Rupert every day . . . every night, of building a life with him—damn. That shit felt like a dream he'd never known he wanted. "Live with me."

"What?"

"Live with me," Jodi said. "Move in. Paint the spare room pink for Indie and fucking *live* with me. Please?"

"Are you serious?" Rupert's gaze brightened, then faded again as caution crept in. "I mean, seriously serious? I've got fuck all, Jodi. I pay my bills, Jen's debts and CSA payments, and I don't have anything left. I couldn't—"

"We'll figure it out. My mortgage isn't huge 'cause I used the money my mum left me for the deposit."

"Your mum died? When?"

"Ten years ago."

"I'm sorry, boyo."

Jodi shrugged. "Thanks, but it's okay. We weren't that close. Everyone thought she was some kind of super mum because my dad fucked off before I was born, but the truth was she worked so much I hardly knew her. The nannies raised me . . . all six of them."

"That's pretty sad, but I get the not-being-close thing. My parents haven't spoken to me since Jen and I split, and we didn't talk that often before that. They never forgave me for leaving Ballyboden behind."

"Ballyboden?"

"My hometown, just south of Dublin. Population five thousand. There was no work unless I wanted to be a farmer, which I was shite at, and staying there my whole life would've felt like I was waiting to die, so I left, married Jen, and fucked that up too."

Rupert's tone was nonchalant, and Jodi let him have it. Families were a mystery to him, and up until he'd split with Sophie, he'd always assumed he'd have to make his own to understand how they worked.

"Fuck 'em. You've got a whole new life now. Live with *me*, Rupe. The mortgage is only a grand."

"*Only* a grand?" Rupert snorted. "Mate, I struggle to pay five fifty on a poxy room."

"So don't. Pay five hundred for a real home, for both of you, here, with me."

"You're bloody mad."

Rupert closed his eyes. Jodi could almost see the cogs turning in his brain in the long moments it took him to open them again. And even then, he said nothing. Just stared at Jodi like he wasn't quite real.

"Rupe." Jodi cupped Rupert's face in his palm and rubbed his cheek with his thumb. "I want this. I want *you*. Why is it so hard for you to believe that?"

"Because I don't get it. I'm a loser, mate. I've got nothing to offer you."

"Bullshit. I've got your heart, right?"

Rupert blinked. "It's yours. I fucking love you. So much."

"I love *you*." Jodi kissed Rupert once, hard, and lay back. "We love each other, so we won't ever need anything else. Fuck the money, babe. Just let yourself be."

Chapter SIX

December 26, 2014

"**D**addy?"

Rupert glanced up from the train track he was building on the living room floor: Indie's main present that he'd left under the tree for her on the first Christmas morning he'd spent alone in years. "What's up, love?"

Indie bit her lip, a habit she'd developed over the last few months when she wanted to ask Rupert something she wasn't sure he'd like. "Did Jodi buy my trains too?"

"Erm, kind of," Rupert said. "He helped me choose them."

The white lie burned his soul. He'd sworn to himself not long after Indie was born that he'd always tell her the truth, no matter how complex the situation, but it was a vow he'd found impossible to keep since the accident. How the fuck could he explain to an eight-year-old why the man she'd considered a virtual-stepfather had disappeared overnight? His explanation of a serious accident only went so far. He shuddered to think what Indie made of the fact that she hadn't been allowed to visit Jodi even once.

And Indie was no fool. She held a sparkly purple train up to the light. "Jodi doesn't like glitter. He says it sticks to his bum, remember?"

Rupert sighed. He missed Jodi's endearing lack of filter, despite his ongoing worry that Indie would go back to her mother and repeat things that would make Jen's ears bleed. "I remember, kiddo."

"Can we take a photo of my trains and put it in your photo album?"

"What?"

"The photo album, Daddy. The one me and Aunt Sophie made for you."

Rupert's gaze zeroed in on a clean spot in the dust covering the coffee table, trying not to picture the flowery photo album he'd shoved on a high shelf in Jodi's office the day before, unable to deal with it lying around the living room any longer. If he closed his eyes, he knew he'd see every page, composed with love by Indie and Sophie, documenting every family-friendly milestone of the life he and Jodi shared.

Had shared. It's gone now, remember? Rupert blinked hard. "I don't know where the camera is right now, sweetie. Maybe next time?"

"Okay." Indie went back to her train inventory, lining them up in colour order, the way Jodi kept his T-shirts, and Rupert's heart broke just a little bit more.

That evening, after a bittersweet day of presents, frosty games in the park, and SpongeBob's Christmas special, Rupert and Indie caught a bus across the city to deliver Indie home to her mother. Indie was quiet on the journey, tired out after talking Rupert's ear off for most of the day. Her incessant questions, which ranged from scarily astute to plain bizarre—*Do clams bark like dogs, Daddy?*—usually melted him into a biased father's puddle of goo, but as the bus rumbled along London's brightly lit streets, he was glad of the break. He'd been dreading Christmas for months, but now that it was over, the looming new year frightened him more, absorbing his thoughts as Indie dozed in his arms. Jodi's primary doctor had informed him on Christmas Eve that Jodi would be ready for discharge by January sixth, which left Rupert ten days to figure out what the hell they were going to do.

Or, rather, what the hell *he* was going to do. Jodi's doctors and social workers had agreed to release him into Rupert's care with ongoing outpatient support, and Sophie had volunteered to look after him when Rupert had to work, coordinating her days at the nursery with his shifts, but even with Briggs putting him on day shifts with only two overnights a month, life was going to be tough. And then there was the money. Jodi had earned a small fortune as a web designer, but he'd been self-employed and the savings they'd had were about to run out. Any compensation Jodi was due from the accident would take years to come through, and the paltry carer's allowance the state had offered Rupert barely covered the gas bill.

And that was just the half of it. What the fuck was he going to do about Indie? With Jodi still rendered mute and unresponsive by his injuries, there was no way Rupert could bring her to the Tottenham flat anymore. He couldn't bear it, and he knew the Jodi he remembered would never allow her to see him that way.

Rupert stepped off the bus in Wembley with a heavy heart. Saying good-bye to Indie was always hard, but with her off to her grandma's place in Wales for the New Year, it would be more than a week before he saw her again, and by then he had no idea where he'd be taking her.

The knowledge that he'd only grown used to seeing Indie so much because of the home Jodi had given them both cut deep, but he'd run out of time to worry about it. Jen opened her front door with her usual stony scowl and held out her hand for Indie's bag.

"Has she had dinner?"

"Hello to you too," Rupert said mildly. "Yeah, we had pizza."

"Pizza on Boxing Day? Nice. Indie, go upstairs and brush your teeth." With Indie inside, Jen started to close the door.

Rupert caught it before it shut in his face. "Can we sort out January's dates while I'm here? I've got my shifts."

"Really? Now?" Jen's sneer morphed into the irritated frown she saved for Rupert. "You'd better come in, then."

Rupert followed Jen and Indie into the plush town house they shared with Jen's latest squeeze—a mild-mannered banker with more money than sense, who was rarely around when Rupert brought Indie home.

Indie disappeared upstairs while Jen led Rupert to the kitchen and retrieved a diary from a drawer. "You can have her the second and fourth weekends. What weekdays do you want?"

Rupert breathed a silent sigh of relief. Not having Indie overnight until the second weekend of the new year gave him some breathing space. He handed Jen a list of possible afternoons he could take Indie out for tea.

Jen studied them, keeping him waiting long enough to remind him that she called the shots. "These look fine, but I'll have to check with Roger. I'll email you."

"Fine. I put January's maintenance in your account this morning."

Jen raised an eyebrow. Rupert had never missed a payment, but he'd been a few days late more times than he cared to admit, and never ever early. "What's the occasion?"

Rupert shrugged. "Just getting things in order. I've got a lot going on."

"Your boy toy out of hospital yet?"

"What do you care?" Rupert glanced around, looking for Indie, but she was still upstairs. "And don't call him that. It's not fair on Indie."

Jen rolled her eyes. "Whatever. I just want to know if I've got to put up with another six months of Indie asking me about him every ten seconds. If you've split up, you should tell her."

"We haven't split up. You know why I haven't let her see him." Rupert ground the words out through clenched teeth, knowing Jen would interpret his anger as the usual irritation that simmered between them. An interpretation that suited him, because, in reality, Jen didn't have a clue. She'd assumed that children hadn't been allowed on the neurological ward, and Rupert had never corrected her. She had no idea of the ongoing extent of Jodi's injuries, and Rupert wanted to keep it that way. It wasn't beyond Jen to fill Indie's head with all kinds of horrors and the less ammunition she had, the better. "Anyway, I'd better be off. Can I call Indie down to say good-bye?"

"Okay, but don't take too long. It's past her bedtime."

It wasn't, but Rupert didn't care to argue. It never got him anywhere. He called Indie down and gathered her to him in the bear hug she loved so much. "See you soon, kiddo, yeah? Have a nice time at Grandma's."

Indie squeezed him back with her tiny arms. "See you soon, Daddy, over the moon. Will you show Jodi my trains for me? And give him the pictures I drew him?"

Rupert closed his eyes and thought of the stacks of crayon drawings he'd hidden on top of the fridge at home. "Course I will. I love you, sweetie."

"Love you, Daddy."

Rupert showed himself out and caught another bus to take him to Camberwell. It was a long route, taking nearly an hour, and he was half-asleep by the time it stopped across the road from the hospital. Yawning, he hauled himself off the bus and drifted to the hospital's main entrance. He hadn't owned a car in years, but for some reason the parking payment machines caught his eye. The screens were lit up in bright blue on black, one of Jodi's favourite colour combinations, but it wasn't the graphics that stopped him short, it was the date: December 26, 2014, five years to the day since he and Jodi had met, a day—or night, really—that was etched on Rupert's heart in indelible ink. A night that had turned his sorry world upside down and made it beautiful.

A night that seemed so far out of reach now; the neon-blue digital numbers glowed belligerently and a wave of rage swept through him, heating his bones and burning his chest. The sudden need to smash something was overwhelming.

He turned away before he could punch the screen, and pushed through the hospital's revolving entrance. Autopilot led him upstairs to Jodi's ward. It was after nine, the time of night Jodi usually fell asleep, and for once Rupert found himself looking forward to the still quiet of his bedside, craving the familiar discomfort of the plastic chair. He was worn out, tired to the bone, and with a 6 a.m. start the following morning, a few hours' uncomfortable kip couldn't come soon enough.

A nurse buzzed him into the ward. He recognised her voice, but the station was empty when he tiptoed past. Jodi's bed was in the corner with the curtains pulled around it. Rupert slipped through them. Jodi was curled on his side, eyes closed, breathing deep and even. Rupert searched out the chair, his gaze cast downward. He drew it close to the bed and sat down, retrieving his phone from his pocket. The screen was blank. Fuck it. He'd forgotten to charge it. Not that it mattered. There was no one he wanted to speak to.

He settled into his chair and finally focussed on Jodi. Gleaming dark eyes stared back at him, alive, alert, and very much awake. Rupert blinked. "*Jodi?*"

Jodi sat up slowly, like a predatory cat, ready to pounce. "Who the fuck are you?"

"What?"

"I *said*, who the fuck are you?" Jodi pulled his lips into a scowl that stilled Rupert's heart, glancing erratically around him, staring at the drip in his arm and the ID bracelet on his wrist, before returning to Rupert, the hostility in his gaze increasing with every second. "Where's Sophie?"

Rupert grabbed Jodi's hand as Jodi struggled to sit up. Jodi jumped and smacked his hand away.

"Don't touch me!"

Rupert let go and tried to calm himself with gasps of air that stuck in his chest. He counted to ten and tried again. "Jodi, look at me. Do you really not know who I am?"

"What?" Jodi blinked, then glared at Rupert for a moment that seemed to go on forever. "Nope. Sorry. I don't know who the fuck you are. Now where the hell is Sophie?"

"Sophie?"

"Yeah, *Sophie*. Where's my girlfriend?"

Interlude

Jodi lay as still as possible, trying desperately to keep his vision under control, but his eyeballs felt like lasers, darting around the room, taking in the cacophony of medical paraphernalia—the machines, the tubes, the IVs jammed in his arms.

It's a nightmare. It has to be. Yeah, that was it. He was drifting in a dystopian fantasy. The woman in white at his bedside was some kind of zombie motherfucker and any minute now, he'd remember that he had a lightsabre or something awesome, rise out of the bed he seemed tied to, and cut her head off.

He looked for Sophie. She always appeared in his dreams, even the bad ones, chasing shadows away with her sherberty perfume and lilting laugh, but she wasn't in sight, and his gut told him she was nowhere nearby. "Where's Sophie?"

The woman patted Jodi's hand with a palm that felt unnaturally cool. "She's not here today, Jodi. What about Rupert? Don't you want to see him?"

"Who?"

"Rupert, your partner—your boyfriend. You live together."

Jodi stared and waited for the woman to crack a smile and explain the punch line of her twat-ish joke, but her face remained impassive. *Bitch.* Glowering, Jodi tried to sit up, but the one arm he could move wouldn't take his weight. He fell back onto the bed and tried again, struggling against a wave of dizzying pain until he managed to raise his head enough to read the laminate hanging around the woman's neck. *Dr. Rose.* "I don't understand."

"What don't you understand?"

What do you think? Jodi glanced down as sharp pain radiated from his palms to his shoulders. Blood oozed from his palms where he'd dug his nails in too hard. He eyed the wounds, welcoming the pain, hoping it would cut through the thick fog in his head and gift him some clarity. *Wake up, dickhead. You'll laugh about this in the morning.* But nothing changed. The woman's stare remained, and no one fucking laughed.

Jodi's patience evaporated. "Stop taking the piss. It's not funny. I don't know anyone called Rupert, and even if I did, I'm not bloody gay."

"No one's saying you're anything, Jodi, but Rupert *is* your partner. He's been here every day since the accident."

"Accident? What accident? Where's Sophie? Is she okay?" Silence. Panic slammed into Jodi's chest, forcing the air from his lungs as a machine somewhere nearby began a beeping tattoo in time with his speeding pulse. "Where's Sophie?"

The woman leaned forward. "Sophie's safe and well, Jodi. It was you who had an accident. I can tell you all about it, but I need you to calm down or we'll have to come back to this later."

"I . . . can't breathe."

"Would you like me to get Rupert for you?"

"No! I don't know any fucking Rupert—" Pain roared through Jodi's head. He fell back on the bed as the beeping went off the scale, and a deep, paralysing agony took hold, blinding him. He cried out and curled in on himself, but the sudden movement only brought more pain. "Oh God. Help me. Please."

Something tugged at one of the tubes in Jodi's arm. A cold sensation flooded his veins. For long moments nothing changed, then he felt it: a creeping buzz that lapped at the edge of the torture that tied him in a foetal ball on the bed.

The pain faded a little, taking with it some of the crazed panic seizing his chest, just enough for him to snatch a breath as his face seemed to melt into the scratchy sheet beneath him. "Please. I don't know who Rupert is. He's not my boyfriend. No one is. I want Sophie. Please. Please get Sophie for me. Please, I just need Sophie . . ."

". . . I don't understand." Jodi held his head in his hands as he stared at Sophie, trying to ignore Dr. Rose taking notes in the corner. "When did we split up?"

Sophie looked at Dr. Rose, who nodded surreptitiously, or probably thought she had. Jodi frowned. There'd been a lot of that since Sophie had finally arrived. Sometime earlier, he'd told himself he would feel better if only she'd just fucking get there. That she'd explain why the last thing he clearly recalled was heading across London to meet her for dinner. That she'd know why his arm wouldn't move and his head hurt like a bitch, that she'd know why he could hardly remember his name from one moment to the next. But so far she'd done nothing but gaze at him with a sadness he couldn't quite decipher, and pretty much tell him that he was dumped.

A waft of fruity perfume tickled his nose, and a painful shunt in his brain brought him back to the present. He winced. Sophie squeezed his hand. "What is it?"

Jodi opened his mouth. Shut it. The words weren't there. Sophie's gaze darted again to the silent doctor, and Jodi bristled, confusion and frustration conflicting so loudly in his aching head he felt dizzy. "Why aren't you my girlfriend anymore?"

"We split up years ago."

"How many?"

"Five. You're still my best friend in the world, though." The first flickers of a smile Jodi recognised brightened Sophie's features. "And I still love you to death."

Jodi loved her too, but five years was a bloody long time to lose, with or without her, and the harder he thought about it, the less sense it made. "I don't understand. Have I been in here since we split up?"

"No, sweet. You were in an accident five months ago, remember?"

Accident. Coma. Accident. Coma. That much was starting to sink in. "Five months . . . I've been out of it for five months?"

It was Sophie's turn to frown. "No, Jodi. The doctors told you this yesterday. You've been awake for weeks, walking and doing rehab. You just haven't talked. We thought you'd forgotten how, we never—" She pressed a shaky hand over her mouth. "I'm sorry. I can't do this."

Jodi tugged her hand, forcing her to meet his gaze again. "Do what, Soph? What is it?"

"Jodi—"

"That's enough for now," the doctor cut in. She tucked her pen into her breast pocket. "Get some rest, Jodi. We'll talk more tomorrow . . ."

Jodi studied the grainy images Sophie was scrolling through on her phone. He remembered this about her—that she took terrible photographs. Shame he couldn't recall the big bay windows and sleek oak furniture she claimed were his. "How long have we lived there?"

"We?"

"Sorry. I mean me. Where do you live again?"

"Primrose Hill. Your favourite place." Sophie sounded sarcastic, and for the first time, Jodi understood why.

"I hate that place. It's full of wannabe Britpop wankers."

"I know." Sophie smiled, but it faded a touch as she seemed to remember something.

Jodi reached hesitantly for her hand. *Do we still do that?* "What is it?"

"You were on your way to me when you had the accident."

Accident. Coma. Accident. Coma. Three days of supervised conversations came back to Jodi all at once. He pictured the stolen Astra the doctors said had hit him. No one seemed to know what colour it was, but in Jodi's mind it was the same horrible burgundy as the ageing Vauxhall Nova he'd bought himself a week after passing his driving test. "Where was I coming from, if you live in Twatrose Hill?"

"Tottenham, hon. You were twenty feet from your own front door . . ."

Jodi's head hurt so much he couldn't breathe. The room twisted to a blinding white light, and he slid from the bed, bracing himself to hit the hard floor. But strong hands pulled him up and instead of cold linoleum, he found himself lying on his bed, curled on his side, a pillow under his head and a soft blanket over him.

A warm hand closed around his. "Hang in there. The doctor's coming."

I don't want a doctor, I want you. But as the pain in Jodi's head amplified with every heartbeat, the comforting cloak of warmth faded, taking with it his ability to yearn for anything but oblivion. Something jostled his other hand. His skin began to burn, and a new voice startled him.

"The morphine's in."

"Jesus, don't give him that." The first voice lost its melodic softness. "It makes him sick."

Too late. Jodi opened his mouth to agree with whoever seemed to be reading his mind, but instead of words came puke, lots of puke, and most of it went over the side of the bed and covered a pair of scruffy trainers. Then he lost the magic hand. He tried to reach out, but nothing happened. A sob caught in his throat, and the hand returned, this time on his forehead, doing something distracting with his hair—stroking, brushing—until the voice came again, and he forgot to wonder.

"I've got you, boyo. Rest your head, I've got you."

Jodi obeyed without question, closing his eyes and letting darkness soothe what was left of the drilling tattoo in his brain, but as he drifted to sleep one question lingered: what the fuck was a "boyo" . . .?

"What do I need a social worker for? I'm not a kid."

The mousy-faced woman's gaze remained dull, as if she'd seen Jodi's increasing frustration a thousand times over. "Social services don't just care for children. We safeguard all vulnerable members of society."

Vulnerable members of society? Jodi's head spun. The woman had come to his bedside more than an hour ago, and he still had no idea what she actually wanted. He looked for Sophie, then remembered she wasn't there. The doctors had sent her away so they could torture Jodi in peace, and then this woman—a social worker—had arrived, and for some reason this conversation felt different to any other he'd had in his dubious recent memory.

The social worker said something. Her voice buzzed like a low-flying wasp at the base of Jodi's skull. Only one word stood out: Rupert, like it seemed to every time. Shame Jodi didn't know who *Rupert* actually was.

"*Jodi.*" The social worker frowned.

Jodi rubbed his eyes with the heels of his hands. "Sorry, what?"

"I said, Sophie and Rupert have told us they are going to help you take care of yourself when you leave the hospital. Is that an arrangement you feel comfortable with?"

Rupert. Rupert. Rupert. Jodi kept searching the patchy minefield his brain had become and eventually found the tall, blond dude who'd visited a couple of times. Sophie kept telling him they lived together, but Jodi could hardly remember home, let alone having a flatmate. Jodi trawled his brain again. A couch came to mind, scattered with black cushions and a tatty grey throw. The blanket seemed out of place, though Jodi couldn't see why. All he knew was the couch seemed to call to him, and abruptly his world narrowed to the way the seat cushions moulded perfectly to his back and the tatty blanket draped around his shoulders. *The blanket's around my shoulders, so why the hell are my legs warm?*

"Jodi?"

"*What?*"

"Do you want to go home?"

Do I? Jodi turned the question over in his mind, matching it with the tingly heat that was fast fading from his legs as he returned to the present. He needed that heat. He didn't know why, but something—everything—suddenly screamed at him that he wouldn't survive without it.

Jodi met the social worker's gaze as another wave of desperate frustration swept over him, clawing at his chest and veins. What did it matter that he couldn't remember his couch or his flatmate's name? What did any of it matter while he was rotting away in a place that made no fucking sense? "Please. I want to go home. I don't give a shit who counts my fucking pills. I just want to go home."

Part
TWO

Chapter SEVEN

J odi watched as Sophie bustled around the flat, unpacking clothes and filling the fridge with the groceries a Sainsbury's lorry had just delivered. For the hundredth time, he studied her movements and facial expressions, trying to marry them with the Sophie he thought he remembered. Same blue eyes, wild blonde curls, but her body was different—softer, rounder. And her face didn't quite fit.

Cold, creeping anxiety chewed on Jodi's heart. A week— No, ten days ago, he'd told himself everything would be better if he could just find Sophie, that the huge chunk of time and knowledge he was missing would come back, but it hadn't. She'd appeared at his bedside, flustered and crying, and—

And what? Jodi's mind went blank, all thought and emotion suddenly gone, like a lightbulb had blown. He blinked, trying to focus. Where the fuck was he again? The plain walls, high ceilings, and ornate, Victorian coving. The coffee table. The couch. Ah, yes. The flat . . . home, right? His gaze fell on a cluster of photographs, images of strangers. Sophie had told him this was his flat, that he owned it, with a mortgage and everything, but he wasn't sure he believed her. If the flat was his home, he'd recognise the people in the photographs, wouldn't he? But the blond bloke and the tiny little girl . . . Jodi stared and stared, but nope. He didn't have a clue, and he couldn't bring himself to care much, either. Panic-laced bewilderment and a never-ending headache had become his new best friends. There wasn't room for much else. "What day is it?"

Sophie glanced over her shoulder. "Thursday, sweetie. Why?"

"No reason." Jodi curled his legs under himself and rested his aching head on his good arm, the one without throbbing scars and metal bolts in the joints. "Where do you sleep?"

"At my house, Jojo. I don't live here. Rupert does."

Rupert. Jodi turned the name over in his head and matched it with the blond bloke in the photo who liked to hover and stare with tortured eyes that gave Jodi the creeps—his second carer and apparent flatmate. "Where is he?"

"At work. He'll be home tonight. Are you okay? You're so pale. Do you want to lie down? The doctors said you should rest a lot."

Jodi didn't want to rest. From what little he'd gleaned from the whispered conversations around him, he'd been resting—sleeping— comatose—whatever—for far too long already, but the bastard chiselling in his brain thought otherwise. His eyes grew heavy, even as Sophie helped him lie down properly and covered him up.

She held a tiny white pill to his lips. "Swallow this."

"What is it?"

"Codeine for your headache. There's stronger stuff if it gets really bad, so just let me know, okay?"

"Okay." Jodi swallowed the pill, wondering how deep the chisel needed to go before it justified better drugs, but he was asleep before he could give it much thought.

He awoke sometime later to low voices floating out of the kitchen. For a while, he lay still, letting odd snatches of the muted conversation meld with the remnants of codeine-fuelled dreams, but despite the lethargy lacing his veins, agitation drove him off the couch and into the kitchen, searching for a tonic to calm his nerves.

Sophie and the blond bloke stared at him as he shuffled between them and opened the cabinet he was suddenly sure contained what he was searching for. Bags of pasta and rice greeted him. *Damn it.* He slammed the cupboard door.

"What are you looking for?" Sophie asked.

"My fags," Jodi said distractedly. "Where are they?"

Sophie frowned. "You don't smoke."

"Yes, I do."

"No, you don't. You quit three years ago."

Silence. Jodi considered her words and tried to make sense of them. Couldn't. Fuck it. He retreated to the couch and put his head in his hands. His headache had faded to a dull roar, but dizziness still plagued him, like he'd moved too fast and his brain couldn't catch up. Like he'd never catch up. He thought back to the strained conversations he'd had with Sophie in hospital, the ones where, under the watchful gaze of an inscrutable doctor, she'd nervously explained that his mind seemed to be missing around five years of his life. The breakup, the flat, the mortgage. If he thought hard enough, he could comprehend all that, but giving up the fags? Why the fuck would he do that?

He was no closer to an answer when a warm hand on his shoulder startled him. Sophie set a plate of lumpy brown gloop on the coffee table. "Dinner."

"No, thanks."

"I wasn't asking. You need to eat, hon. Come on, you're wasting away."

Jodi eyed the plate. Its contents looked like shit and smelled like arse. "No."

Sophie sighed. "You didn't eat lunch either. What am I going to do with you? If you won't let us take care of you, the doctors might make you go back to hospital."

"Liar." Brain-damaged he might be, but he knew the doctors at the hospital considered him well enough to be at home. "What day is it?"

"Thursday, hon. Why?"

"When do I have to go back?"

"To the hospital? Erm, Monday, I think. Rupert's taking you to the physiotherapist."

"Rupert." The odd clicking in Jodi's brain returned. "Why can't you take me?"

"I have to work. In fact, I've got to get going soon. Rupert's going to look after you tonight."

"I don't need looking after," Jodi muttered, though he was beginning to accept that was far from true. Despite sleeping most of the day, he felt more tired than ever. He curled up on the couch and picked up the TV remote, studying the buttons. None jumped out at him. *Fucking idiot.* Frustrated, he closed his eyes.

He had no idea how much time had passed when Sophie roused him again a little while later.

"I'm going home," she said. "Do you want me to help you to bed before I go?"

"Wha—?" Jodi sat up. "What? What time is it?"

"Eleven."

Eleven. The room seemed to get darker. A familiar panic clawed at Jodi's gut. "Don't go."

"I have to, hon. I'm sorry. Rupert's here. Do you want me to get him?"

"I'm here, Soph."

The new voice made Jodi jump. He turned awkwardly to find Rupert leaning in the doorway with a hesitant smile, hovering in a way that set Jodi's teeth on edge. *Fuck's sake. He's gonna maul me like every other twat here.* "You're not going to touch me, are you?"

"No, mate. I won't. I promise. I'm sorry about what happened at the hospital."

Blankness hit Jodi. "What happened at the hospital?"

"Erm . . ."

Rupert glanced at Sophie, a clear plea for help if Jodi had ever seen one. A faint flicker of curiosity tickled his belly, but was gone before he could act on it. He turned away and flopped back on the couch. Sophie lingered, like she wanted to say something, but settled for a tight hug before she kissed his cheek and left.

The front door closed with a quiet *clunk* that sounded deafening to Jodi. He looked around the living room, at the plain walls, the photographs, the blank TV, anywhere but at Rupert. Somehow, he'd missed him venturing into the room and taking Sophie's place, perched on the coffee table.

"It's late," Rupert said. "You've got some medication to take. The antiseizure pills give you a bit of a stomachache if you don't eat. How about we get you to bed and I bring you some food before you take them?"

"No, thanks."

Rupert picked up the bowl of brown gloop Sophie had left and gave it a dubious stir. "Not up for Sophie's infamous chilli, eh? Don't blame you."

"Sophie can't cook?" It wasn't a question by the time Jodi finished the sentence. A click in his brain revealed years and years of dodgy roast dinners and soggy sandwiches, surreptitiously chucked in the bin the moment her back was turned. "She can't cook."

Rupert smiled. "No, bless her heart, she stayed up half the night making that swill. She does make a mean pot of builder's tea, though. She's left one in the kitchen. Fancy a cuppa and something less terrifying for your dinner?"

I own a goddamned teapot? What the fuck happened to me? Jodi couldn't think of a sensible answer to Rupert's questions or his own. He nodded and settled back on the sofa while Rupert disappeared into the kitchen, wrapping himself in the soft grey blanket Sophie had insisted on covering him with when they'd come home. The blanket smelled nice, like coffee and pine needles, and it was all he could do not to bury his face in it and go back to sleep. *Idiot. You've tried that already.*

"Nutella on toast." Rupert returned and held out a plate with a single slice of chocolate-covered toast.

Jodi had to admit it looked far more appetising than Sophie's efforts. "Do I like that?"

"I'd say so. You used to eat it enough, especially on a hangover. I slice a banana on top of mine. Drives you mad— Um, anyway. Take these and eat up." Rupert brandished a handful of pills far bigger and scarier than the tiny codeine Sophie had slipped past Jodi's lips.

"What the fuck are they?"

"The same ones you've been taking in the hospital. You don't remember?"

Jodi thought hard and made himself dizzy. *Hospital, pills, doctors . . . no, nurses.* Yup. He remembered the nurse—Caz—who'd appeared three times a day, clutching a tiny paper cup of mysterious medication. "I remember taking them, but I don't know what they are. No one told me."

"Do you want me to tell you?"

"I think so?"

Rupert set the plate of toast down and spread the pills over his palm. "Okay, but you should know most of these are preventative, so don't let them freak you out too much."

Easy for him to say. "Start with the big one and work your way down."

"The big one is your antiseizure medication. Do you remember having seizures while you were in hospital?"

"Maybe." Jodi recalled a vague memory of a similar conversation. "Actually, no. I remember Sophie telling me about them. When did I have them?"

"They started a few months ago, but you haven't had one for a while. That's why they let you come home. That and . . ."

"And what?"

Rupert shook his head. "Nothing. You just made some big improvements quite quickly. You couldn't hold a conversation like this a few weeks ago, and before that you didn't talk at all."

That rang a bell. Sophie had told him about the weeks and weeks he'd spent bumbling around the hospital, mute and useless. "How long was I like that for?"

"Three months."

"Did you visit me?"

"Every day."

"Why?"

The colour drained from Rupert's already pale complexion and left him ashen. Jodi frowned. What the fuck was his problem? It was a fair question, wasn't it? A question, it seemed, Rupert didn't want to answer, since he got up and turned his back on Jodi so fast Jodi's mind spun with him.

"I'll get you some water."

Weirdo. Jodi watched him go, recalling the few instances he did remember of Rupert visiting him in hospital. The way he'd hovered and stared, like he was waiting for Jodi to spontaneously combust, only to disappear abruptly behind the curtain. *Great. I picked a creepy flatmate.*

Rupert came back with a glass of water. "Ready for your pills?"

"Hmm?"

"Your medication." Rupert proffered a palmful of pills. "Do you want me to go through the rest with you?"

"If you like."

"It's not about what I want."

Jodi sighed. Rupert had that moody look on his face again, the look that made his skin seem dull and grey, and made Jodi slightly nauseous, though he couldn't say why. "Go on, then. Hit me."

"Okay, this one is your antiseizure, this one a strong painkiller to help you sleep through the night, this one an antibiotic for an infection you picked up from the catheter—"

"Infection?"

"A UTI," Rupert said. "A urine infection."

Jodi absorbed that. He wasn't altogether sure what a catheter was, but he recalled the burn plaguing his dick every time he took a piss and connected the dots. He pointed to the last pill. "What's that one?"

"An antidepressant."

"Why am I on antidepressants?"

Rupert considered the smallest of the four pills in his palm. "I asked that too. Apparently depression is quite common after a brain injury, and there's a slight scar over the area of your brain that controls emotions. This drug—citalopram—is supposed to regulate the balance of serotonin and help with your cognition."

"Cognition?"

"Thinking ability."

Jodi snorted. "So it'll fix my stupid, then?"

"You're not stupid, Jodi. You weren't before, and you're not now."

Yeah, yeah.

Darkness hit Jodi like a thick, black wall of choking terror. He bolted upright—his version, at least—flailing with his good arm for something—anything—tangible to tie him down to the bed and stop the inky cloud from sucking him in. His hand hit the bedside table, but instead of the cheap MDF of the hospital, he found solid wood—thick, textured oak that felt all wrong.

He lurched away from it, falling back onto pillows that were too soft and smelled like nothing he could ever remember smelling: a warm, spicy scent that made his heart beat too fast. His head swam, and every inch of his skin itched. Where the fuck was he? And where the hell was Sophie? He tried to call her name, but the power of speech had deserted him, and nothing but a garbled groan came out, a groan that was unnaturally loud in the heavy darkness of wherever the hell he was.

Hell. Perhaps that was it. As the devil drilling holes in his brain picked up its steady, sickening tattoo, it was all too easy to believe. Then his gaze fell on the bag he'd brought home from the hospital, and it came flooding back—the consultant discharging him, the cab ride home. Sophie abandoning him with the weird blond bloke whose name escaped Jodi.

Fuck this shit. Jodi fumbled around for a light switch. A lamp toppled to the floor and landed with a metallic clatter that set his teeth on edge. He swung his legs out of bed, stubbing his toe on the bedside table, and set off for the living room, the kitchen, anywhere but this black fucking death trap of a bedroom.

The hallway was dark too, but a beam of light under the living room door drew him in. He pushed it open. The blond bloke was throwing pillows on the couch. Jodi stopped short. In his headache-induced haze, he had forgotten about his babysitter. Rupert . . . yeah, that was his name.

"Can't sleep?" Rupert said.

"I woke up." It sounded stupid even to Jodi. "And my legs itch."

It was true. The pain in his head had woken him, but the creeping itch behind his knees was somehow worse.

Rupert nodded. "That's the painkillers. The doctors said a cool shower might help?"

Fuck that. Jodi shook his head. His bed had felt like a straitjacket, and standing in the living room in his PJs, he was bloody freezing. "What are you doing?"

"Making my bed."

"You sleep on the couch? Why? What's wrong with your bedroom?"

A long pause stretched out before Rupert replied, "I don't have one."

That didn't make any sense. Jodi had little memory of the flat, but he knew the room across the hall was a bedroom. "I don't understand."

"Have you been in the other room since you came home?"

"No."

"Come with me?"

For a moment, Rupert looked like he might hold out his hand, a notion that made Jodi feel slightly strange, but it passed quickly, and Rupert turned away.

Jodi followed him back to the hallway, to the closed door of the second bedroom. Rupert opened it and motioned inside. "Do you remember this?"

Jodi peered around Rupert. The room was like nothing he'd ever seen before. The white walls he'd expected to see were striped with candy pink, except the one by the window, which was painted blue and decorated with football paraphernalia, punctuated by a wooden slatted blind that alternated with the same shades of pink and blue. A tiny cabin bed completed the picture . . . blue duvet, pink pillow.

"Did a hermaphrodite kid throw up in here?"

"Not quite. It's my daughter's room. You decorated it yourself."

"Your daughter's room?" Rupert was taking the piss, he had to be. Stoned and half-dead Jodi may have been, but he would've noticed a child in the flat. Besides, he didn't even like kids. Why the fuck would he consent to living with one?

Then he remembered the photographs in the living room. "The blonde girl. That's your daughter?"

"Yup. That's Indie."

"She's pretty." It was all Jodi could think to say, and it was true. He couldn't recall ever meeting a child he liked, but the girl was beautiful.

And by Rupert's smile, it was clear he thought so too. "Thanks."

"You're welcome. So, where is she?"

"With her mum. She stays here every other weekend, though I wasn't sure if . . ."

"If what?" Jodi studied the pink stripes. The colour was vile, but he had to admit he'd done a cracking job at keeping them straight. Shame he could barely pull a pair of socks on anymore. "What weren't you sure of?"

Rupert stared into space before looking back at Jodi. "I wasn't sure if you'd want her here, or if it's a good idea for her. There's so much you don't remember, and you were close, really close. I don't want her getting upset when you don't know who she is."

"Upset?" Jodi jerked his head up a little faster than was sensible. "I wouldn't do that, would I? Am I that much of a bastard?"

"You're not a bastard at all. Indie loves you, but she won't understand why you don't remember her, and I can't let her get hurt like that. I'd move out if I could, but . . ."

Rupert's voice fell away, and though Jodi didn't understand the anguish in his gaze, an odd urge to dispel it swept over him, and it came to him far clearer than anything else had in a long while. "Does she know?"

"Hmm?" Rupert blinked, apparently startled, like he'd forgotten Jodi was there. "Know what?"

"That I don't remember her, or you?"

"No. Haven't quite figured out how to explain that one. I've told her some pretty heavy stuff before, but this . . . Shit. She won't understand this."

Jodi wondered why Rupert's pain mattered so much, but though the blank void in his brain made Rupert a stranger, the hurt in his hazel gaze felt somehow like Jodi's own. "I don't understand it either. Maybe it's better if you just let her forget."

Chapter EIGHT

Rupert's life had become a monotonous sequence of waiting rooms and squeaky chairs. It was a pink chair today—that vile, salmon pink that made him think of salmonella. The MRSA posters on the walls weren't much better, though they did remind him that no matter the tragedy of the last few months, Jodi had at least been spared a hospital-acquired blood infection. The persistent UTI had been bad enough.

The thought did little to cheer him up. Jodi had been home for a week or so, but the only change it had brought was they were now strangers to each other in the privacy of their own home rather than under the all-seeing gaze of the hospital team. Not that Jodi seemed to realise he was at home half the time. Barely an hour passed without him staring around the flat, confusion colouring his sunken features. And it was worse on the rare occasions he truly looked at Rupert. The doctors had said there was a good chance Jodi's amnesia would fade as he rehabilitated in once-familiar surroundings, but as the days passed and nothing changed, the other side of the coin—the dark, bleak side, where Jodi remained a subdued, bewildered shell of the punchy man he'd once been—became horribly more real.

"Are you waiting for me?"

Rupert tore his gaze from the shiny waiting room floor. Jodi stood in front of him, sulky and tired, like a teenager who'd just been scolded by their headmaster. "Of course I am. Said I would, didn't I?"

Jodi shrugged like he didn't care, and it was likely he didn't.

The psychiatric nurse who'd escorted Jodi to the waiting room peered around him, a kind, sympathetic gleam in her life-hardened eyes. "Come on now, Jodi. We talked about Rupert today, didn't we? He's taking care of you."

"If you say so." Jodi's eyes drifted to the window. There was nothing there, save a car park and a few tired trees. Rupert wondered what was holding his attention for so long. "Can we go home now?"

Rupert sighed as the nurse spared him another professionally pitying smile. An ever-fading glimmer of hope had carried him through the long months that had passed since Jodi's accident, but it was almost gone now. It had left, unbidden, the moment he'd realised Jodi had lost five years of his life.

"He's missing five years," Sophie whispered, her face streaked with tears. "He thinks we're still together."

Rupert sat down heavily, his breath leaving his lungs in a soft whoosh. His head had known this was coming—his short, fractured exchange with Jodi had told him so—but the stupid, naive idiot in him had held on to the hope that it was all a fucking bad dream.

But it wasn't a dream. Jodi was missing five years—five years that held the entire life he and Rupert had built together. Their past and present. Their future. Rupert stared hard at the hospital floor, sure he could see the remnants of their broken dreams, ready to be ground into the linoleum by the heels of whoever passed by next. He closed his eyes and whispered the question he already knew the answer to: "Did you tell him who I am?"

Sophie's voice cracked. "I'm sorry. I didn't know how. I didn't know what to say."

Rupert had wanted to be angry with her, but he couldn't. After all, *he* hadn't told Jodi, and no one else had either. How could they, when Jodi had reacted so badly to the doctor's first, failed attempts? Rupert remembered Jodi curled in a ball, sobbing in pain, and then later, when the drugs had kicked in and two days of silence had taken hold, and it had felt like they were back to square one.

Fuck that. Rupert couldn't be the reason Jodi's recovery faltered, and there seemed little chance Jodi would remember on his own. Save for a few minor details about random things—where the airing cupboard was, the name of next door's cat—he hadn't remembered anything, and he'd shown next to no interest in trying. No one knew the best way of persuading him either. Prompting him.

The psychiatrist—one of a long list of outpatient appointments Rupert had brought Jodi to that week—had been his last hope, but his private consultation with Rupert hadn't gone well.

"In cases like Jodi's, it's often best to allow the mind to heal in its own time. We can help him, of course, but pushing him to remember things he might not be equipped to cope with yet could be catastrophic."

Jodi's neurologist, Dr. Nevis, had agreed. "Try to be as honest as you can, but avoid planting ideas in his head. It's better to use intact memories to stimulate acceptance of new information."

Arguing that the "new information" was their whole bloody lives had been pointless, and he'd known the doctor was right. What the fuck had he expected? That they could sit Jodi down, hit him with every little detail of the lifetime he'd forgotten, and expect him to accept it all and just get on with it?

It wasn't going to happen, but that crippling realisation had left Rupert lost. Jodi had walked into the accident as a man who'd often described himself as a loose bisexual, but he'd woken up looking for his girlfriend with no memory of being anything other than straight, like he'd lost his entire sexual identity. And that had left Rupert as not much more than a barely tolerated babysitter.

"Rupert?"

Rupert came back to the present with a surprised jolt. Up till now, Jodi hadn't addressed him by name. Shame he didn't sound too happy about it. "Yeah?"

"Are we going, or what?"

There was no "or what." Rupert gave himself an internal shake. It was time to go home. He said good-bye to the hovering nurse, took Jodi's arm, and led him out of the hospital. Jodi didn't protest. He'd given up on that after Sophie had scolded him for being rude. Besides, Rupert wasn't taking his weight and guiding him for fun. To the outside world, Jodi probably appeared to walk pretty well, save the slight drag of his left foot, but when he'd had a long day, his balance often deserted him, leading him to stumble and trip, something that could do him far more damage than discovering he liked a bit of cock.

They made it outside. Rupert's stomach growled as the McDonald's opposite the hospital caught his eye. Breakfast felt a long time ago, but he knew there was little point asking Jodi if he wanted to stop. Jodi seemed to exist on bread, cornflakes, and an occasional packet of crisps. Gone were the late-night fry-ups and random Wednesday roasts. And it didn't help that Rupert and Sophie between them could barely fry an egg.

"You didn't have to cook for me," Rupert said. "Jesus, boyo. It's 2 a.m."

Jodi glanced over his shoulder, half an eye still on the mammoth pan of pasta he was adding bacon to. "Can't have you going to bed on an empty stomach. Besides, gives me stuff to do when I'm pining for your pretty face."

A bus ride later, they were at the Shoreditch pharmacy to pick up Jodi's prescription refills. With that done, Rupert ushered Jodi out and steered him toward the Tube station.

"Where are we going?"

"Home. That okay? Or did you want to go somewhere else?"

"It's fine."

Jodi's expression remained, as ever, blank and uninterested, but something made Rupert look again—a slight inflection in his dull tone, a nervous flicker in his dark gaze—*something.* "Are you sure? We can grab some food if you like?"

Whatever Rupert thought he'd seen evaporated as Jodi scowled. "You've asked me that three times today. I'm not fucking hungry."

"I asked you at breakfast, lunch, and dinnertime, and I'll probably ask you again before bed. You gotta eat, boyo." Rupert kept his tone mild with considerable effort, though he could tell Jodi was baiting him, probably hoping Rupert would snap at him, and then feel guilty enough about it to leave him alone.

But he was out of luck today. Rupert didn't fancy a silent journey home, even if it meant boring himself to tears with the sound of his own voice. He took Jodi's answering glare with a shrug and retrieved their Oyster cards from his back pocket. "How did you get on with the occupational therapist yesterday? You never told me."

Jodi didn't answer, distracted by swiping his Oyster card at the ticket barrier, a simple process made more complex by the damage to his cognitive thinking. Even evaluating the task seemed to take several seconds longer than the queue forming behind them was prepared to tolerate. Not that anyone said anything—it wasn't London's style—and thankfully, Jodi was occupied enough to remain oblivious to the pointed frowns grumpy commuters sent his way.

The escalators came next. Rupert took Jodi's arm and guided him on, something he'd done even before the accident, having seen too many gruesome incidents in Tube stations and shopping centres to trust anyone he loved to travel on them safely. In the past, the gesture had amused Jodi to no end. Not anymore. Now, he didn't seem to notice Rupert's deathlike grip on his good elbow and there was little life in him as they reached the crowded platform.

Staying true to another preaccident habit, Rupert stood between Jodi and the platform edge, shielding him from the backdraft of a couple of passing trains.

"So," he tried again. "How was your appointment yesterday?"

"Don't you already know? Thought the hospital had you and Sophie on speed dial."

Rupert suppressed a sigh. Despite Jodi's apparent disinterest, he often seemed irritated when he caught Rupert and Sophie talking about his recovery. "Why don't you tell me how it was for you?"

"It was bullshit. They made me play poker and write a shopping list at the same time. Like a trip to Sainsbury's will fix everything."

"You might be right there," Rupert said. "You never went shopping anyway. We got that shit delivered."

"Yeah?" Jodi's expression brightened for a fleeting moment. "Does that mean I don't have to go to that stupid bloody occupational therapy bollocks?"

"'Fraid not. We can't afford Ocado anymore."

"What the fuck does that mean?"

Rupert's reply was muffled by their train pulling into the station, and Jodi had blanked out by the time the noise faded. Relieved, Rupert gripped Jodi's arm again and guided him on, positioning him with his back against the wall, Rupert between him and the other commuters. The train rumbled. Jodi jumped, clearly startled. Rupert welcomed it, though he felt bad for doing so. Any animation was better than none. "So, did you do much else in the session?"

"Hmm?"

"The OT," Rupert repeated. "What else did you do?"

"Oh, er, nothing really." Jodi's gaze darted around as the train moved out of the station.

Rupert frowned. Jodi hadn't had any seizures at home yet, but he'd fast learned in the hospital that a jittery gaze was one of the warning signs. He checked Jodi for flushed cheeks and a slackening jaw. Jodi did look warm, but if anything his awareness, rather than slipping under the wave of an oncoming seizure, seemed more heightened than Rupert had seen since the accident. He took in Jodi's clenched fists and restless arms, the quickening rise and fall of his chest and the anxiety growing in his roaming gaze.

Against his better judgement, he touched Jodi's face, barely grazing the dark beard that had replaced the trendy stubble he'd sported before. "Still with me?"

It was a loaded question that Jodi would probably never understand, but as his terrified eyes met Rupert's, the weight of all they'd lost suddenly didn't matter. Most days, it was hard to remember that Jodi's glare didn't necessarily reflect what was going on inside his head—*or his heart, please, God, his heart*—but the fear in his gaze now was unmistakable. Rupert knew a brewing panic attack when he saw one.

The train picked up speed. Jodi inhaled sharply and flattened himself against the wall. Rupert moved his hand to Jodi's chest. Jodi's racing heart battered his palm as Jodi squeezed his eyes shut.

"Jodi, look at me."

Jodi shook his head.

Rupert took a chance and grabbed his hand. "Come on, boyo. It's okay. I can help you."

Jodi opened his eyes. For the first time in months, his gaze was as electric as Rupert remembered it when he lay awake at night, blocking out the present and drowning in the past—Jodi laughing hysterically at his own daft jokes, or bubbling with glee at a prank he'd played, or climbing all over Rupert and demanding to be fucked, loved, and owned from the inside out—but the fire in Jodi's dark eyes now wasn't love or laughter, or desire. It was pure terror, and Rupert had no idea why.

"Squeeze my hands," he said quietly. "Focus on me and let go of the breath you're holding."

Jodi made a strangled noise, a classic sign of someone fighting the urge to suck in a lungful of air they didn't need. A gasp they'd already taken and forgotten about as waves of crippling panic took hold.

Rupert found Jodi's hands again. "Let it go. Come on. Let it go and I'll show you how to breathe."

Whether Jodi truly believed him, Rupert would never know, but after what felt like a lifetime, he blew out a shaky breath.

"That's it," Rupert said. "Now breathe in, nice and slow, not too much."

It took a few attempts for Jodi to remaster the art of inhaling and exhaling at a pace that brought a little colour back to his cheeks. His shoulders relaxed, and his wide eyes drooped as exhaustion set in. Slowly but surely, his fingers tightened around Rupert's.

Rupert's heart leapt. He swallowed thickly and dampened it down. "There you go. Just keep breathing. Don't think about anything else."

Jodi opened his mouth. Shut it again. Took another breath. "Thank you. I—"

The train jolted, sending Jodi flying into Rupert's chest. Rupert stumbled backward as the lights went off, cloaking them in darkness.

"Jesus!" Rupert fought for balance, petrified he would fall and take Jodi with him. Common sense reminded him the lights went out on the Tube all the time, but as Jodi wrenched free from Rupert's grasp, backed against the wall and slid to the floor, covering his head, every ounce of his terror seeped into Rupert's battered soul.

Chapter NINE

Jodi woke up on the couch with a crick in his neck. As had become his normal, it took a few moments to place himself. The ever-present pain came first, radiating through his skull and creeping into every slowly healing injury, then the obligatory groan, the low, animalistic grunt he was never quite sure actually came from him.

He sat up in stages, taking in the dimly lit living room—the low-hung lamp in the corner, the TV flickering on mute. It was late, that much he could tell, but that was about it. What the hell was he doing in the living room and not segregated in the dark haunting bedroom he'd come to think of as a prison cell?

No clarity came to him as he pushed himself upright at last. *Shocker . . . not*, but the sight of Rupert fast asleep on the floor beside him surprised him, until he remembered he was lying in what Rupert called his bed.

Jodi frowned, and an odd sensation crept over him. Guilt? Shame? He couldn't name it. All he knew was Rupert sleeping on the hard wood floor felt wrong. In fact, everything felt wrong. His bones ached, and his mouth was dry, and the roiling in his belly made him want to puke. Where was Sophie? He needed her. She'd explain it to him.

A click in his brain reminded him that wasn't right either. *She's not your girlfriend, idiot. Remember?* For once he did remember. Sophie was at her own house and the only soul available to fill in the gaps was Rupert, but waking him and begging for reassurance was too much for Jodi to handle. The bloke already did far more than Jodi could ask for from a flatmate.

On cue, Rupert rolled over and opened his eyes. For a moment, he stared, then he sat up in a smooth, effortless movement that almost made Jodi weep with envy.

"What's up?" Rupert said. "You okay?"

"Um . . ."

Rupert waited, like he always did when Jodi lost his words.

Jodi found them. "Why am I out here?"

"You don't remember?"

"Obviously not."

He hadn't meant to snap quite so harshly, if at all, but after a flash of hurt that was gone so quickly Jodi was sure he'd imagined it, Rupert seemed unfazed. He pushed aside the balled up sweatshirt he'd been using as a pillow, and leaned forward, like he was checking Jodi for cracks.

Ha. Cracks. If only. Most days—nights—whatever—Jodi felt like a giant fissure had been mined in his soul.

"You had a bit of a turn on the Tube," Rupert said. "And you might have had a slight seizure when we got back. I'm not sure."

A seizure? Fucking brilliant. He'd been told about those, but had no memory of the ones he'd had in hospital. "What happened?"

"Er . . ." It was Rupert's turn to stutter. "You didn't seem to like the Tube. Have you been on it since you came home? I haven't taken you on it. Has Sophie?"

Jodi thought hard. "No. She keeps taking me on the bus with all the old fogeys."

Rupert smiled briefly. "Well, you didn't like it. You had a panic attack, and then the lights went out and I couldn't get you back. Pretty much carried you home, and you refused to go to bed. Then you collapsed in here. I put you on the sofa when you'd stopped shaking."

Embarrassment made Jodi's blood feel warm. Too warm. He kicked away the blanket Rupert must have draped over him. "Sorry."

"Don't be. It's what I'm here for. I'll always look after you, Jodi."

"Why?" The question escaped Jodi before he could stop it. "Don't you have anything better to do?"

"Not really."

Jodi let it go. He'd given up trying to figure people out. They all said he was the one with the problem, but didn't they understand none of this shit made any fucking sense? What kind of flatmate stuck around when the geezer they lived with lost his bloody marbles and practically needed his arse wiped? Sophie . . . Yeah, he got that. He'd accepted that the love he thought he remembered had morphed into one of those friendships that meant the world, but Rupert? Nope. The bloke remained a mystery.

"How are you feeling?"

"Sick," Jodi said absently. "Thanks for leaving the lights on, though. Probably woulda shat myself if I'd woken up in the dark again."

Comprehension flashed in Rupert's gaze. He studied Jodi a moment. "Perhaps that was it: the dark on the Underground, the noise, the heat. Sorry, mate. I should've thought about it more before I hustled you on it."

Why the hell is he apologising? It wasn't his fault that Jodi had become a bloody fruit loop.

"It's fine," Jodi said. "I'm sorry I fucked up your day and stole your bed."

"Boyo, that's the least of my worries."

"Okay, Jodi. Let's go back to the last thing you remember before the accident."

Jodi huffed out a sigh. This numb-nut psychiatrist was getting on his tits. "I already told you I don't remember the accident, or the day it happened, or the day before that. Last thing I remember I was going for dinner with my girlfriend—who's not my fucking girlfriend anymore."

"Does that upset you?"

"What? That I don't remember what I had for dinner that day? Or that I got dumped?"

The psychiatrist—Ken—tapped a pencil on his thigh. "What makes you think you got dumped? Do you remember Sophie ending your relationship?"

"No."

"Then let's stick to the facts, as you truly know them, for now. You've told me you remember going to meet Sophie for dinner.

She told the police you were coming to meet her on the day of the accident. Do you think it's possible that's the occasion you remember?"

Jodi sighed. He'd been over this with Ken, and Sophie, more times than he cared to count. The only person who didn't seem to want to talk about it was Rupert, which suited Jodi just fine. He hadn't felt like leaving the flat much since his epic meltdown on the Tube, and Rupert's quiet company was far easier to take than everyone else's constant questions.

"Jodi?"

"*What?*"

Ken sat back in his wheeled chair and folded his hands on his desk. "All right. That's enough for today. I can see you're tired. I'm going to give you a little work to take home with you, though, if that's okay?"

Jodi shrugged. He had a whole list of exercises—mental and physical—he halfheartedly practiced at home. One more wouldn't make much difference.

Ken pushed a sheet of paper across the table. Jodi humoured him and cast a disinterested glance over it. It appeared to be a record keeper—a journal, maybe.

"What's that for?"

Ken tapped his pen on the paper. "I'd like you to keep track of anything that makes you stop and think twice—things you might recognise, or think you've perhaps seen before but can't remember where."

"Like what?"

"Like anything," Ken said. "People, places, sights, and smells. Even just a feeling . . . a sensation, an instinct."

The only instinct Jodi had was a strong urge to roll his eyes, but insolence had no effect on old man Ken, save encouraging him to stare harder, studying Jodi with a watery gaze that set his teeth on edge. "How many things do I have to write down?"

"As many as you like. Your OT has helped you with your handwriting, hasn't she?"

Jodi nodded. It was true, though Sophie had gleefully informed him his handwriting hadn't been much cop to begin with. "*With your chicken scratch, Jojo, you should've been a doctor.*" Right. So he could sit across the table from miserable gits like him? Fuck that.

He left Ken to his humming and pencil tapping and found Sophie outside, smoking a long menthol cigarette.

"Shit." She stubbed it out, looking guilty. "I thought you'd be ages yet. Sorry."

Jodi eyed the cigarette butt. "You don't smoke."

"I started after we split up. I liked the smell."

"Oh." Jodi was a little nonplussed. Not for the first time, the distinct impression that he'd hurt Sophie in some way crept over him. "Can I have one?"

"No."

Okay. Jodi glanced up and down the busy street. His gaze fell on the Tube station. He shuddered and wondered if that was the kind of sensation Ken wanted him to note down. "Can we go home, then?"

"Of course." Sophie shoved her bag on her shoulder and took Jodi's arm, steering him to the bus stop. "How are you feeling? Do you want to do anything before we go back to the flat?"

Jodi shook his head. They'd only been out a few hours, but every part of him felt like lead, and he was cold too. He wanted his bed—no, the couch—and a three-hour nap. "I want to go home."

Sophie pulled him closer, and her body heat seeped into his bones. Jodi absorbed it and tried to recall a time when feeling her pressed up against him had excited him. Tried to recapture the many intimate moments they'd shared. But . . . nope. The memories were there, but Jodi felt nothing but platonic affection, tinged with a touch of sadness, and maybe regret? Hmm. Perhaps that was one for the diary, though Jodi couldn't imagine finding *anyone* attractive in this brave new world where his dick did nothing but burn like a bitch when he had a wazz.

Back at the flat, Jodi flopped onto the sofa, coat and shoes still on. Sophie tugged at his boots. "Help me a little?"

Jodi grumbled and sat up, fumbling with the laces. "Give it a rest. I wanna sleep."

"And you can, just as soon as you take your grubby boots off. Don't want dirt all over your couch, do you?"

Jodi didn't much care. The flat was a mess, and he liked it that way. Made it easier to find all the shit Sophie and Rupert insisted he needed. "Where's Rupert again?"

"Work," Sophie said. "Why? Do you want him for something?"

"No. Just wondering. He's been gone since yesterday."

Sophie shot him an odd glance. "Do you miss him when he's not around?"

"Why are you asking me that?"

"Just wondering." Sophie shrugged with the barest hint of an impish grin. "You seem to prefer his company to mine."

Do I? "Maybe because he leaves me the hell alone and lets me sleep."

Rupert asked his fair share of annoying questions, but he didn't nag Jodi about stupid dirty boots. In fact, he didn't nag at all, save his unnatural obsession with how much Jodi ate for dinner.

On cue, Sophie disappeared into the kitchen to fetch "a snack." Jodi curled up on the couch, hoping he'd be asleep by the time she came back, or at least look enough like it for her to let him be.

"Eat."

Or not. Jodi sat up *again* and stared down at the plate she'd placed in front of him; Nutella on toast. His brain clicked. *Nutella. Toast. Rupert.* No, that wasn't a blast from the past. That had happened last week, hadn't it?

"What's the matter? Rupert said it's all you'll eat when you're in a bad mood."

"I'm not in a bad mood," Jodi said absently, shifting over as Sophie sat next to him. "Have you made me this before?"

"Actually, no. The smell of that stuff makes me heave. Perhaps that's why we turned out better as friends."

"Eh?"

Sophie hesitated before her wry grin morphed into a reckless take on determination. "Nutella is your and Rupert's thing. He doesn't have much of a sweet tooth, but you always used to make him this when he came home from late nights at the club."

"The club?"

"He used to moonlight on the doors at The Cube."

"But he doesn't anymore." It wasn't a question this time. Jodi had heard Rupert and Sophie talking about this a few days ago.

"That's right." Sophie seemed pleased. She put her arm around Jodi and coaxed him to lie down with his head in her lap. He went willingly. Sophie was soft and warm, and he found himself cuddling closer, absorbing her warmth until drowsiness swept over him and he fell asleep.

He awoke with a jump sometime later. Rupert was home. Jodi couldn't see or hear him, but somehow he just knew, though it could've been simple logic. At some point Sophie had disappeared, taking her handbag from the coffee table, which led Jodi to conclude she'd gone home, leaving him in Rupert's care.

'Cause you're too much of a doughnut to be left on your own, remember?

As if he could forget. His lack of independence was the one constant.

On cue, Rupert came out of the kitchen, clutching a mug of tea like it was the only thing keeping him upright, and judging by the dark circles beneath his eyes, perhaps it was. "Morning."

"Is it?" Jodi glanced at the TV, which was playing BBC News 24. The clock read 5 a.m. Damn. He'd been asleep for over twelve hours. That had to be a new record for afternoon naps. "When did you get in?"

"A while ago. Sophie's got an early start, so I put her in your bed to get some sleep. That's okay, right? Didn't look like you'd be heading there anytime soon."

It was more than okay. Fuck that bedroom. Fuck the dark. Fuck everything. "It's fine. How was work? You've been gone for ages."

"Long." Rupert ventured a little closer. "How are you doing? Sophie said you were tired."

"I'm always fucking tired." Jodi hadn't meant to snap, but the harsh inflection in his tone made him cringe—Rupert too, if his backward step was anything to go by. Jodi thought about apologising, but the violent shiver that swept over him reminded him why he'd curled up on Sophie's lap in the first place. "It's cold in here."

"Is it? Do you want another blanket from the airing cupboard?"

Jodi thought about it and shook his head. He wanted—craved—warmth, but hiding under a pile of blankets seemed wrong.

Rupert took his headshake at face value and turned away to go back to whatever he'd been doing in the kitchen. A surge of panic drove Jodi to sit up and pretty much fall off the couch. "Wait."

"What?" Rupert looked over his shoulder. "What do you need?"

For a long moment Jodi could do nothing more than hold out his hands, unable to articulate, or even comprehend what he was asking for. All he knew was the comfort Sophie had offered him wasn't enough. That he needed that kindness from someone else. From Rupert. "I'm so cold. Will you sit with me for a while . . . please?"

Chapter TEN

R upert froze halfway to the kitchen. "You want me to sit with you?"

"Um . . . I need some company."

"Really?"

Jodi's outstretched hands wavered. He dropped them and wrapped his arms around himself. "You don't have to sound so fucking shocked."

Rupert *was* shocked. He'd grown used to coming home to a silent flat, whether Jodi was awake or not, and that silence continuing until Sophie broke the stalemate. *He said he was cold.* Rupert took a few steps toward the couch. Stopped. What the hell was he going to do when he got there? Cover Jodi's body with his own? Warm him from the inside out, then carry him to bed and love him all over again, like he used to?

Jodi sighed. "You're weird. You always look like you're about to say something, then you drop off the edge of the earth instead. What's up with that?"

If only you knew. Rupert shook himself and closed the distance to the couch. He sat tentatively, leaving a big gap between him and Jodi. "I'm just tired, boyo. Long night."

"Yeah? What did you get up to?"

"I was at work."

"Oh yeah, I knew that. Sophie told me. Why can't I remember this shit?"

"You will," Rupert said. "You've come so far already. This time last month you couldn't talk." *And I still had hope that you'd come back to me. How stupid was I?*

Like he'd heard Rupert's bleak thoughts, Jodi shivered and scrubbed his hands over his face. When he revealed his eyes again, his frustration was gone, replaced by the apathy that broke Rupert's heart anew whenever he saw it. "I don't know what I'm doing. I don't know who I am. All I know is, I'm so fucking cold I can't think about anything else."

And that was without the constant pain Rupert knew Jodi was in. Even now the telltale signs of a headache lined Jodi's face: the crease in his forehead, the slight droop of his left eye. "Then don't think about anything else. Get warm and worry about the rest later."

Rupert said the words absently, his mind, as ever, on Jodi's discomfort, mentally calculating which medication would be best to ease his pain. Jodi's shoulder jostled his, and he jumped a mile. Somehow he'd missed Jodi shifting closer.

"I'm stealing it," Jodi said by way of explanation. "The warmth. You're like a fucking radiator."

"Erm, okay." Rupert swallowed hard, fighting the suffocating sadness filling his chest. The old Jodi had been so tactile they'd worn each other like a second skin, and this inevitably brief reincarnation was almost unbearable. Rupert slipped his arm around Jodi's too-slim shoulders. The urge to pull Jodi close and crush him to his chest was strong—so fucking strong—but his head overruled his heart. Jodi didn't want that. Couldn't remember ever wanting that. He needed comfort, nothing more, and Rupert was all he had in this moment.

Jodi's soft moan broke through Rupert's brooding. He leaned into Rupert's loose embrace, half slumping into Rupert's lap. "Why am I so tired? I just woke up."

"You're still recovering. The doctors said it could take months for you to feel well again." *Or years*, if it happened at all. But Rupert didn't say it aloud. There was little point. In his stronger moments, Jodi seemed aware that his current state of physical health could be permanent, even with the gruelling therapy.

"I want to sleep."

"Then sleep." Rupert sat back to give Jodi room, though Jodi made no move to separate himself. "Get comfortable. You've got nowhere to be today."

Jodi met Rupert's gaze with glassy eyes. "No buses or musty clinics?"

"Nope. Not today."

Rupert waited for Jodi to snap his frustration at everyone else knowing his day-to-day life better than he did. For him to growl that they were smothering him. That he felt like a child. But today in the dim early morning, Jodi's anger didn't come. Instead, he let loose a rare half smile that claimed another crack in Rupert's heart, laid his head in Rupert's lap, and fell asleep.

Rupert was spellbound. He'd spent too much time watching Jodi sleep, but this felt different. The more he stared at Jodi, the more the pain in Jodi's face seemed to fade, and for a while, Rupert allowed himself to dream that nothing had changed, that the last six months really had been a nightmare . . . a nightmare that was over. He let his hands ghost to Jodi's hair; his jaw, half hidden by dark scruff; and his neck. Jodi's pulse was strong beneath his fingertips and with the weight of a long night shift pulling him under, it wasn't long before he found himself drifting into that sacred place where his dreams were real.

He woke to bright sunlight streaming through the living room window, a crick in his neck, and only a crumpled grey blanket to show Jodi had been there at all. Rupert raised the blanket to his face, inhaling its familiar scent. Indie missed the blanket almost as much as she missed Jodi.

A thud and a curse came from the bathroom. Rupert jumped up and darted into the hallway to find the shower running and the door closed. He tried the handle. It was locked. "Jodi? You okay in there?"

Silence. Rupert readied himself to barge the door down, but then Jodi's voice filtered through over the noise of the running water. "I'm fine. Just having a fucking wash. Leave me alone."

If only it were that easy. Jodi knew he wasn't supposed to shower without Rupert or Sophie guarding the door. Rupert hovered, torn between kicking his way in anyway and taking the consequences, and retreating to the kitchen—a room Jodi rarely ventured into—and dealing with the fact that he'd fallen asleep with Jodi in his lap.

He plumped for a compromise and backed away from the door, sliding down the opposite wall to sit on the floor, ears straining for Jodi's every move in the bathroom, which struck him ironic, given that Jodi had shown little interest in personal hygiene since the accident, showering only when Sophie bullied him into it, or because he wanted to get away from Rupert.

"You're not my fucking mother."

Rupert drew his legs up close and rested his elbows on his knees, surveying the cluttered hallway. Before the accident, Jodi had driven himself half-mad keeping the piles of coats and shoes to his obsessive order, but Rupert had let Jodi's standards slide. There were piles of shit everywhere, and he hadn't been able to bear to dig Jodi's once beloved Henry hoover out of the cupboard. Bloody thing never worked for him anyway. Jodi's favourite boots caught his eye, the tatty brown leather ones he'd often worn with the skinny jeans that made Rupert's head spin. Rupert hadn't had a sexual thought in months, but those boots had always done something to him. Jodi had been wearing them when they met, a damp winter night that seemed so distant now that Rupert was almost sure it had happened to someone else. Not that it was appropriate to reminisce about that shit anyway. Perving over Jodi when he couldn't even remember fancying blokes? When he was still so unwell he couldn't shower alone? *Nice one, dickhead.*

The shower shut off. Rupert held his breath as he listened to Jodi climb out of the bath, something that always set his nerves on edge. The thought of Jodi slipping and cracking his fragile skull on the sink kept Rupert awake at night. Usually, he stood in the doorway, averting his eyes to give Jodi privacy, while he tracked his movements, but now, with the door closed, he couldn't even hear if Jodi's feet had safely found purchase on the bath mat.

A wave of nausea washed over him. Was this how it was going to be now? Or was Jodi just in an odd mood? There was no way of knowing. Jodi had become as unpredictable as a London summer, and Rupert was no more at ease when he heard Jodi turn on the tap and rattle in the cabinet for his toothbrush.

It seemed like a lifetime had passed before the bathroom door finally cracked open. Rupert scrambled to his feet, his nerves still performing a painful dance in his gut. Jodi peered out. His eyes met Rupert's, and he frowned, but it wasn't his usual irritated scowl. Instead, he looked troubled.

"What are you doing?"

Rupert shifted awkwardly. "Waiting for you."

"Why?"

"To make sure you're okay."

"Why wouldn't I be?" Jodi edged out of the bathroom, dressed in the same clothes he'd slept in, and clutching his wet towel in front of him. "You don't have to loiter in the hall when I go for a piss."

"You weren't having a piss. You were in the shower." Rupert kept his words mild, but Jodi's tone grated him. How many times did he have to fucking explain himself? Like it wasn't enough that the life they'd built together was lying in piles of unwashed clothes all around them. Like it wasn't enough that Jodi didn't give a shit if Rupert snapped at him or not. That he didn't care if Rupert existed.

"I'm going to bed," Jodi muttered. "See you tomorrow."

"It's eleven o'clock in the morning."

"So? You're always telling me to rest."

Rupert raised his hands in surrender. "See you later, then."

Jodi shuffled off. Rupert watched him go, wondering what the fuck he'd missed this time. Jodi hadn't slept in his bed for days, choosing instead to sleep bundled up on the couch. What was so attractive about it now?

As ever, Rupert had no idea. He drifted to the living room. The plastic box containing Jodi's medication was on the coffee table. Rupert glanced at the clock. Jodi was due a dose of antiseizure drugs within the hour. He debated following Jodi into the bedroom, but his courage failed him. It could wait half an hour while he took a shower of his own and tried to get his head around the strangest morning he'd had since Jodi came home.

He stripped off his T-shirt and tossed it toward the basket overflowing with dirty clothes, then bent to peel off his socks. A noise from the doorway startled him. He looked up to find Jodi staring at him, his expression a dark molten mix of embarrassment and something Rupert couldn't quite decipher. "What's the matter?"

"Nothing! Fuck's sake. Stop bloody asking me that."

Jodi turned on his heel and stomped away, slamming the bedroom door. Rupert stared after him. *Did that really just happen?*

Chapter
ELEVEN

J odi lay stock-still in the bed, fists clenched at his sides, toes curled, gaze fixed on the ceiling. He counted the cracks in the Artex, the cobwebs around the light fitting, anything to distract him from the one part of his body that didn't hurt. But nothing worked. Despite his best efforts, all he could think of was Roomie-Rupert's bare torso and the resulting boner that just *wouldn't* piss *off*.

Groaning, he rolled over, skin crawling, sweat beading a path down his face, nausea churning deep in his belly. What the fuck was wrong with him? Most nights passed in a haze of dizzying headaches and infuriating coddling from Sophie and Rupert. In the morning it was usually hard to distinguish one from the other, but he remembered last night—morning, whatever it had been. Remembered the overwhelming compulsion to seek comfort in the warmth seeping from Rupert's body, the hypnotic effect of his arms . . . the probing heat of Rupert's erection digging into his cheek when he'd woken up in his lap sometime later.

And the answering hardness of his own dick.

Self-loathing shuddered through Jodi. Rupert had appeared to be asleep when Jodi had disentangled himself, even when he'd landed on the floor with a thud that had seemed to shake the earth, but what if he hadn't been? What if he'd been awake all along? Awake and aware that his dick had carved a hole in Jodi's cheek? And, worse, aware of *Jodi's* cock holding its own parade? *Oh God.* Jodi covered his face with his hands and curled into a ball, like he could crush his wayward dick into submission. It didn't work. In fact, the pressure of his stomach pressing his cock into his thighs made it worse.

In desperation, he swung his legs out of bed and yanked open the top drawer of the bedside table. He had no clear memories of living in the flat before the accident, only vague, blurred scenes that didn't make much sense, but he did remember where he'd kept his porn stash during his uni years—a pile of tatty magazines, loaded with images of long-legged women with brassy hair and huge knockers.

The drawer revealed no wrist manuals, just a box of condoms, a laptop, and . . . Jodi reached for the bottle of what looked like lube, then jumped back as it tipped over, revealing the shiny, bare-chested man on the label and the swirly sub line printed under the brand name. *Less sting for his ring.*

What the fuck?

Jodi kicked the drawer shut like it had burned him, his heart beating so loudly his ears throbbed. What on earth did he have anal lube for? As far as he remembered, he and Sophie hadn't explored *that* kind of sex in years, not since the first haze of initial attraction had faded and they'd discovered it wasn't something Sophie particularly enjoyed. Besides, this lube was brand-new, and clearly for men, so what the hell was it doing in Jodi's drawers?

The grinding in his brain returned full force. He clutched his temples and tried to get a grip on it before it spread through every nerve in his body. *"Don't fight it. Act on it."* The voice of his occupational therapist filtered through the pain. He straightened his posture and reached for the codeine and bottle of water Sophie and Rupert insisted he keep close by. His prescribed dose was three pills, but that often sent him to sleep, and for once, he didn't want that. Didn't want his dreams to be filled with greasy lube and shirtless men.

He took two and drained the bottle of water. His gaze fell on the ominous drawer again. The lube bottle seemed to call his name, and the momentary diversion of dealing with another fucking headache had done little to pacify his dick. He needed a distraction.

With his eyes averted, he opened the drawer and grabbed the laptop, slamming the drawer shut before the creepy bottle jumped out at him. He crawled under the covers and booted up the MacBook. A box asking for a password flashed up. He searched his brain but inevitably found nothing. Instinct told him the password would have something to do with Sophie, but that logic had proved deeply flawed of late. He tapped the keyboard as his mind jumped from one notion to another too fast for him to keep up. What if it wasn't even his computer? He was missing five years, after all, and he knew the shiny iMac in the room Sophie and Rupert called the office was his. Why would he need two computers?

No sensible answers came to him, then he remembered the business card pinned to the fridge. Fire Kat Design. Something clicked. He closed his eyes and tried to chase it down, but it evaporated as quickly as it had come.

Fuck it.

He opened his eyes and typed in *Fire Kat Design* with his birth year tacked on the end. The laptop flashed to life. Jodi blinked, but his surprise was fast tempered by the image that greeted him on the screen: a photograph of Rupert in even less clothes than Jodi had seen him in that morning.

So much for the distraction.

Heat flooded Jodi's veins, burning him from the inside out. *What the actual fuck?* Was this Rupert's laptop? It had to be, right? Clearly, his flatmate was some kind of narcissist. There was no other reason his admittedly sketchy logic could find for Rupert's half-naked form filling the screen.

So shut the damn laptop and put it back. But Jodi did neither. He growled in frustration, but couldn't find the will to break his stare. He leaned forward and studied the image, comparing it with the virtual stranger he shared a home with. They didn't look like the same man. Putting aside the vast swathes of flawless skin that continued to send Jodi into a tailspin, he'd never seen Rupert smile like that. Jesus, he rarely saw Rupert smile at all.

That skin, though. Jodi took a deep, shuddering breath. It was perfect: pale and smooth, and wrapped around a body that put the dude on the lube bottle to shame. And Rupert's eyes . . . fuck, his eyes. Jodi was lost in them and didn't notice his hand slip under the duvet until his fingers brushed his cock.

He froze, but it was momentary because the stolen, bewildering pleasure of the featherlight touch on his dick was too intense to ignore. He wrapped his fingers around his cock. The relief was instant but fleeting, as a desperate need for more took hold. He moved his hand up and down, squeezing and pulling. Twisting. His eyelids drooped, but he fought them, unwilling to break the thrall that Rupert's warm gaze had cast on him. *This is wrong.* But it didn't feel wrong. It felt right, like it was the only thing that had made sense in as long as he could remember, and fuck, it was good—better than good. It was fucking amazing.

Jodi pushed the laptop back, cradling it between his thighs, and shoved the duvet away. The cool air on his dick made him shiver, but the heady heat in his veins remained, boiling over until an animalistic groan escaped him, echoing around the room, bouncing off the walls and reverberating through his bones. He jammed his fist in his mouth, biting down on his knuckles. Jesus Christ, this was insane—perhaps *he* was insane—but he couldn't recall wanking ever feeling like this, arresting, enthralling, and so utterly consuming that he couldn't see how it would ever end.

But it did end. He came with a rush and a strangled yelp, shooting all over his T-shirt with more jizz than he'd ever seen.

For a long moment, he didn't dare move, but as his gasping breaths returned to normal and his sweat cooled, reality and perspective hit him like a train. Disgust crept over him, and left him empty, like his back had no bones and his stomach had sunk through the mattress. Nausea roared, an urge that, this time, he couldn't ignore. He dove for the bin as fast as his limited body would allow, and heaved his guts up until there was nothing left but bile and shame. *Great.* Like it wasn't enough that he had the brain function of an eight-year-old. Now it appeared the accident had short-circuited his sexuality too. Was that even possible? To go into a coma with a—albeit, as it turned out, imaginary—girlfriend, and come out wanting to touch your flatmate's dick?

Jodi shuddered, and his stomach heaved again, but nothing came up. Panting, he pulled his sticky T-shirt off and wiped his mouth, then stashed it under the bed to retrieve and dump when no one was looking—not that he expected that to happen anytime soon.

On cue, the bedroom door opened. Jodi lunged for the laptop, slamming it shut, and hurling it clumsily into the drawer.

Sophie frowned. "What are you doing? Are you all right?"

"Um . . . I threw up?"

"Shit." Sophie bustled in, swiping the bin before Jodi could protest. "Do you have a headache?"

"No more than usual. I took some codeine. It came straight back up, though."

"Ah, bet you didn't eat breakfast either? Do you never learn?"

Apparently not. Illicit wanking aside, even Jodi could remember the countless times the cacophony of pills he needed to take had pickled his empty stomach.

Sophie disappeared, presumably to the bathroom, leaving Jodi to cast a furtive glance around, checking there were no stray signs of his masturbatory meltdown.

"Now what are you doing?"

Jodi glanced up from peering under the bed. "Nothing."

"Are you looking for something?"

"Um . . ." Jodi's brain malfunctioned, and he blurted out the first thing that came to mind. "My laptop."

Dickhead.

Sophie came round the bed and peered into the evil drawer, not seeming to notice the condoms and lube that were all Jodi could see. "Here it is. What do you need it for?"

"I don't know."

It was an honest answer. Jodi took the computer from Sophie and crawled back under the covers, leaving room for her to slide in beside him with little conscious thought.

She slipped under the covers. "We do still do this, in case you're wondering."

"Hmm?"

"Lazing around in bed together, eating shit, and gossiping like a pair of old women. It's usually my bed, though. Plays havoc with my sex life."

Jodi processed the sudden influx of new information, absorbed it, and found it fit. Being in bed with Sophie felt normal, though five years ago it *had* been normal. "Why does it fuck with your sex life?"

"Would you want your, uh, partner, spending the day in bed with their ex?"

Jodi couldn't think of an answer. Sophie drummed her nails on the laptop. "Are you going to boot this thing up, or what?"

Jodi opened the laptop and tapped in the password, ignoring Sophie's curious stare. Rupert's shirtless torso filled the screen once more. Jodi looked away under the pretence of scratching his neck, but his eyes betrayed him, drinking in Rupert's skin just a split second later. "Is this Rupert's laptop too?"

"No. I don't think Rupert knows how to turn one on."

Jodi had some sympathy for him there. "So it's just mine? No one else uses it?"

"Unless you count me pinching it to shop on ASOS, no. Why, honey? What's up?"

Jodi turned the screen to face Sophie, giving her the full Rupert experience. "That's what's up. Why the hell do I have this shit as my wallpaper?"

Sophie bit her lip, a sure sign that she was nervous, an emotion that bewildered Jodi's already fragmented mind. "You live with Rupert. Why wouldn't you have his picture on your computer? This is from when you took Indie to Cornwall last summer."

Last summer meant nothing to Jodi. Why would it? And Sophie's answer made no more sense than the open lube bottle in his bedside drawer. "But—"

"Anyway," Sophie cut in. "What did you want to do on here? Check your emails or something?"

"My emails?"

"Yeah. I called the clients in your account book when you had your accident, but I might have missed some. Let's see." Sophie peered at the screen and drew her finger over the mouse pad. "The mail app isn't on here. Maybe you have it on the iMac? Or your browser? Can you remember? What's your email password?"

The barrage of questions made Jodi's head spin. He tried to catch them all as they jumbled in his brain, but it was no good. His cognition short-circuited and the axe of blackness fell. "Sorry, what?"

Sophie moved the mouse over an icon that was vaguely familiar. "Maybe it's this . . . Oh, no, this isn't it."

"What is it, then?"

"Haven't a clue, so it's probably some fancy program you use for work. Click on it and see."

Jodi tapped the mouse pad. Nothing happened.

"You have to press a bit harder, hon."

Jodi pressed down and the icon sprang to life, eclipsing Rupert's face and chest with a bigger logo that eventually merged into a convoluted interface. Jodi leaned closer and studied the tool bar. His fingers itched, and his previously heavy eyes suddenly felt jammed open. He found the file list and clicked on the first one he saw. A monochrome website template opened, modified for what appeared to be a hipster cafe that served a gazillion types of herbal tea. The site was crisp and clean . . . almost. The sidebar header was positioned too far left and the font on the interactive buttons didn't match up.

He made the adjustments, working on instinct. It took him a while to notice Sophie had gone quiet—scarily quiet—and was watching his every move, tracking each click and drag. "What?"

"This software is new, Jodi. You only got it a month before the accident, and you said it was completely different to the program you were using before, that you had to teach yourself how to build sites all over again."

Jodi frowned. "Thought you said you didn't have a clue what it was?"

"I wanted to see if you did. That's why I didn't tell you that you don't have the internet connected on this computer to stop you pissing around when you're doing your layouts."

"You wanted to see— What the fuck? Why would you do that? I'm not a bloody lab rat, Soph. What else are you testing me on?"

"I'm not testing you on anything." Sophie shrank back from Jodi's anger. "The doctors told us not to plant memories in your head. They said no one interprets the past in the same way, and we had to let you remember things on your own."

"What things?"

"I don't know. Just things. Don't shout at me, Jodi. I'm doing my best."

"What aren't you telling me?"

"*Nothing.*"

Jodi stared her down. He barely knew which way was up anymore, and the distinct sensation Sophie was keeping shit from him wouldn't quit. Did she know about the lube in the drawer? Or why his laptop was plastered with photos of Rupert half-naked? Or was it something else? Something bigger and even more fucked up? Jodi's anger faded, and in its place came fear. He didn't want to know. He didn't want to remember. He—

"*Jodi.*" Sophie took his hands and squeezed them hard until he met her gaze. "Don't be angry, please. I want to give you all the answers, but I'm so scared I'll get it wrong and hurt you. That we'll lose you all over again. I can't do it. You have to remember. Please. You have to remember."

"Remember what?"

"Who you are, Jodi. You have to remember who you are."

Chapter TWELVE

One Sunday morning, ten weeks after Jodi came home from hospital, Rupert emerged from a quiet night shift into the first spring sun of the year, the kind of sunshine that teased London at the close of winter, promising an end to the dreary grey frost, only to disappear again like it had never been there at all.

Knowing this far too well, Rupert stood in the eerie calm of early morning Brixton and tilted his face to the sky, absorbing the gentle heat, letting it seep into his bones. As ever, his thoughts turned to Jodi, who was no doubt tucked up in bed with Sophie watching over him, and the warmth stalled, blocked by the cool grip of sadness around his heart. There'd been a few fleeting days when he'd almost believed they were getting somewhere, but over the past week or so, Jodi had become more silent than ever, retreating to the bedroom the moment Rupert came home, only coming out to pick at the food Rupert fudged for him, or to take a shower, an occupation he seemed to have a renewed interest in.

Rupert sighed and opened his eyes. Jodi's physical recovery was progressing as well as anyone could hope for, but caring for someone who wouldn't even look at you was more soul-destroying than he could ever have imagined. Still, the situation didn't seem like it was going to change anytime soon and the sun's appearance had given him a faint charge of energy he couldn't ignore. He caught the Tube to Finsbury Park and jogged the rest of the way home. With his bag slung on his back, the four-mile run was hard work—he hadn't been to the gym in months—but the strain on his lungs and the lactic acid in his legs felt good, cleansing, and he was almost sorry when the flat appeared on the horizon. He slowed to a walk, catching his breath. The light in the bedroom was on, but that didn't necessarily mean anyone was awake. Jodi didn't care for the dark, and there was no reason for Sophie to be up this early on a Sunday.

He let himself in and dumped his bag in the corner with the rest of the clutter. His makeshift bed on the couch called his name, but he needed to eat first or he'd never find rest. Empty cupboards and an empty fridge spoiled the party. A closer inspection revealed there was nothing edible in the flat save half a packet of pasta Rupert couldn't be arsed to cook and a fun-size KitKat.

Rupert took the KitKat and a mug with the last teabag into the living room, mentally writing a shopping list to take to the supermarket later that day, and cursing himself for letting the cupboards get so bare. Grocery shopping was one of many things he'd yet to get used to, even after all these months.

"Morning."

"Jesus!" Rupert jumped, sloshing hot tea over his hand. "What the fuck are you doing sitting in the dark?"

"Trying to figure out the HTML code for a website I can't remember building." Jodi eyed Rupert from the rarely used armchair, his gaze inscrutable. "Didn't think you'd be back till later."

Rupert set his mug down, shaking his hand. "Why? I came off shift at six."

"I know, but you're always late at weekends."

"So?" Rupert glared at Jodi, irrationally irritated. Jodi had often waited up for him in the past, unable to sleep until he knew Rupert was safe, but those days were long gone, and Rupert didn't feel like explaining himself to someone who didn't give a shit.

Jodi took the hint and turned back to his laptop, his face a study in concentration. Despite his chagrin, Rupert was intrigued. He dropped his chocolate on the coffee table and rounded the armchair to squint over Jodi's shoulder. What he saw meant little to him, but Jodi's work never had. Jodi's passion for web design had always impressed and baffled him in equal measure.

"Weird, isn't it?"

"Hmm?" Rupert tore his gaze from the screen to find Jodi staring at him again.

"That I can remember how to code, but not how the central heating works."

"No one knows how the central heating works in this place, mate. Bloody boiler's got a mind of its own."

"If you say so. Still doesn't make any sense, though."

Nothing does.

Rupert left Jodi to it, flopped on the couch, and went to sleep.

He woke a few hours later to the metallic clang of the weights Jodi had been given to strengthen his arms and legs. Yawning, Rupert sat up and checked the time: 10 a.m. *Damn it.* He'd had dreams of sleeping until at least midday, but it wasn't to be. Unlike Jodi—both before and after the accident—once Rupert was awake, he was awake, and there was little point pretending he wasn't, especially when there was no big, warm bed and welcoming arms to make lying around in his pants any fun.

Get used to it, dickhead. Rupert scrunched his eyes shut and pinched the bridge of his nose, ignoring Jodi and his weights, and willing away the cloud of pessimism he wasn't quite ready to deal with yet, but his mind refused to play ball, instead sweeping through every nightmare he'd had since Jodi's accident, including the ones where nothing ever changed. The ones that became more and more real with every day that passed. The ones where Jodi continued to frown at his computer screen, and Rupert spent the rest of his life rotting on a lonely couch. *'Cause even if he never looks my way again, I'll never love anyone else.*

Rupert rubbed his eyes and focussed on Jodi, who seemed to be having trouble packing the weights away in their box. Guilt fast replaced depression as he recalled biting Jodi's head off just a few hours before. "Do you need some help?"

"No."

Of course he didn't. Rupert suppressed the compulsion to check Jodi had taken his medication and breathed a silent sigh. Jodi's mood, like his own, was unlikely to change as the day went on. Sophie wouldn't be back until tomorrow night, leaving Rupert at the mercy of Jodi's apathy for the next thirty-six hours. *Great.*

"You can hold my feet . . . if you want?"

"What?"

Jodi looked amused, an emotion Rupert had almost forgotten existed. "I've done most of it already, but I gotta do sit-ups now, and I can't keep my feet down."

He might as well have asked Rupert to fly him to Mars. Since when had Jodi followed the daily exercise routines his recovery team had devised for him of his own accord? Without growling at Rupert and Sophie first? Or simply being too tired and ill to cope with it?

Rupert slid off the couch and shuffled to where Jodi had lain down on the rug. "You sure about this? It's been a while since we last tried."

A month, to be exact, and they hadn't exactly tried. Rupert had got as far as holding up the abdominal exercise sheet before Jodi had called him a cunt and left the room. The time before that, he'd fainted, leading Rupert to deduce that particular worksheet was cursed.

Perhaps Jodi didn't remember, or care. He answered Rupert's question by pointing to his feet. "Hold them down."

Rupert held them down. Jodi took a breath, then slowly, painfully, hauled himself up.

It was hard to watch. Jodi had never been bothered by exercise or personal fitness, but with his lank and leanly muscled frame, bright smile, and general good health, it had never mattered.

"This hurts," Jodi said.

"Where?"

Jodi shrugged like Rupert had asked the most bone-stupid question in the world.

Rupert tried again. "Everywhere, right? Okay, let me grab a pillow."

Rupert snagged a sofa cushion and placed it behind Jodi, trying to ignore the clean, familiar scent of Jodi's sweat. *He's not that Jodi, remember?* "Gives you a little less work to do like this. Will hurt less if you drop too."

"Got all the answers, haven't you?"

"I wish, boyo. I wish. Straighten your spine a little."

Jodi obeyed and fixed Rupert with an odd stare. "Are you okay?"

"Me? I'm fine. Why do you ask?"

"You don't seem yourself."

"How would you know what that is?" The words were out before Rupert could stop them, spilling from him with a flat despondency. An emotion he couldn't name flashed in Jodi's dark gaze. Hurt? Sadness? Guilt? Or was it the dull rage that had become their constant companion?

Either way, it was gone before Rupert could decipher it. Jodi lowered himself to the pillow and took a deep breath, effectively ending a conversation Rupert didn't really want to pursue anyway. What was the point? Jodi didn't remember him. Didn't want to remember him. And this was their reality.

"Ready?" Rupert asked.

Jodi nodded and pulled himself up. He did it with more purpose this time, faster and bolder, yet seemed surprised when he found himself upright. "That wasn't so bad."

"Try it again," Rupert said. "The sheet says to do ten, but it's just a guideline."

"Guideline, my arse," Jodi muttered, but he followed Rupert's instructions and completed the exercise again and again until he reached number ten.

"One more," Rupert said. "You're winning, come on."

Jodi's glare was murderous, but as he hauled himself up a final time, Rupert was amazed to see laughter in his eyes. "Bloody hell. I don't think I've ever finished one of these sheets."

"You must be having a good day."

Jodi shook his head. "I feel different, have done all week. It's like I've dropped something somewhere and I don't have to pick it up again."

His analogy was so honest and simple that Rupert had to smile. "That's really great. Hold on to it until the next breakthrough comes."

"Do you think there'll be another one?"

Rupert got up and held his arm out for Jodi to use as leverage. "What do you mean?"

"Just feels like everything's been shit for ages. I'd pretty much resigned myself to it staying that way." Jodi stood, his eyes glazing over briefly.

Rupert waited for his equilibrium to catch up, then released his arm. "Nothing ever stays the same. Even if your recovery doesn't work out the way you want, you'll get better at living with your injuries."

"S'pose it helps that I can't remember what I was like before."

"Only you know that, boyo."

Rupert watched Jodi until he was safely on the sofa, then picked up the exercise paraphernalia Jodi had left on the floor.

"Why do you call me 'boyo'?"

"Hmm?"

"Boyo. You say it all the time, and I don't know what it means."

"Erm, I guess it's the same as 'mate' or 'lad' if you're Irish. My dad used to say it to me and my cousins."

"Used to?"

Rupert turned away and snagged some stray socks that had been under the coffee table for more than a week. "We haven't talked in a while."

"Why not?"

"Long story."

"You don't want to tell me?"

Rupert said nothing. It was probably high time he told Jodi he was gay and dealt with the consequences, but he wasn't in the mood today, especially without Sophie for backup.

"I used to know, didn't I?" Jodi said when Rupert didn't answer. "And now you know everything about me, and I know nothing about you."

The sadness in Jodi's tone made Rupert look up. "What do you want to know?"

Jodi shrugged. "Dunno. I like talking to you, though. Did we used to talk a lot before?"

Rupert smiled in spite of the weight dragging his heart through the mud. "Yeah, we talked. You were the best friend I ever had."

If that meant anything to Jodi, it didn't show. His only response was another absent shrug before he rose from the couch and left the room.

"Where are you going?"

Rupert glanced over his shoulder as he stamped into his scruffy trainers. "Sainsbury's. Why? Do you need me for something?"

"No."

Jodi leaned on the living room doorframe, hands in his pockets, looking for all the world like he didn't give a shit, but his dark, brooding gaze compelled Rupert to close the distance between them. "What's wrong?"

"Nothing."

"Sure? I can stay if you want? Wait until Sophie gets here tomorrow? We'll have to order Domino's for breakfast, but—"

"I want to come with you."

It was the last thing Rupert had expected Jodi to say. Aside from his many medical appointments, Jodi rarely left the flat at all. "You want to come to the supermarket?"

"I want to go with you."

"With me?"

Jodi started to roll his eyes, but seemed to change his mind. "I think I feel better when I'm with you. I know that doesn't make sense, but everything is more . . . logical, maybe."

Rupert had been lost for words many times since the moment he'd met Jodi, but this felt like the first time all over again. Like it had been that long since Jodi had truly wanted to be in his presence. "I guess you'd better write us a list, then."

Half an hour later found them in the frozen section of the closest supermarket, trying to decipher Jodi's scrawled list.

"It could be sausages," Jodi remarked sagely. "Or maybe salami?"

"It definitely isn't salami." Rupert squinted at the list. "And you don't like frozen sausages. You never let me buy them before. Said they were full of trotters and ball sacs."

"They probably are. What was my handwriting like before the accident? Was it legible?"

"Just. To be honest, it wasn't much better than this."

"That's what Sophie said."

Jodi seemed relieved, though it left them no clearer as to what they were looking for. Rupert was beginning to regret challenging him to open the fridge-freezer and write down what he thought was missing.

"Maybe it's a *B* not an *S*?" Jodi's frown deepened.

"Fuck it." Rupert crumpled the list into a ball and tossed it into the empty trolley. "Just get whatever you fancy."

Jodi coughed and turned away, grabbing a package from the nearest fridge.

"Potato waffles?" Rupert raised an eyebrow.

Defiance flashed in Jodi's eyes. "Yeah."

Fair enough. The waffles went in the trolley, along with fish fingers and Findus Crispy Pancakes. Rupert grabbed a bag of peas in a feeble attempt to be healthy, then steered them out of the frozen crap aisle. He couldn't cook for shit, but he couldn't bring himself to let Jodi subsist on junk either.

They made their way to the meat aisle. Rupert forced himself to bypass the bacon and picked up a whole chicken. "We could do a roast?"

"Really?" Jodi frowned. "Do you know how to do that? 'Cause I haven't got a fucking scooby."

Rupert studied the label on the chicken. "You used to. Said you learned how to cook when your ma moved down under, because her cooking was the only thing you missed about her."

"I don't remember missing her at all."

"You don't." Rupert chose his words with caution. "Or you didn't before the accident. You told me she worked so much when you were young that you grew used to her not being around, so when she moved to Australia, and then, um, died, it didn't mean a lot to you."

Jodi looked thoughtful. "It's true. My childminder raised me until I went to school, and then I kinda raised myself."

It was nothing Rupert hadn't heard before. An old man jostled him from behind. He started to get out of the way, but Jodi's hand on his arm stilled him. "So I wasn't upset when she died?"

"I only know what you told me. You'd have to ask Sophie to be certain. It happened before we met."

"Of course it did." Jodi frowned, though he seemed more bemused than upset.

"You okay?" Rupert nudged him gently.

"What? Oh, yeah. I just feel like I've forgotten loads outside of the last few years sometimes, you know? There's stuff I should know that just isn't there until someone puts it back for me."

"No one can put anything back for you. You just have to trust it's still in there somewhere." *If only it were that simple.* If Jodi had any memory of the men he'd been with before Rupert, men that had been and gone even before Sophie, perhaps the prospect of prompting Jodi to remember Rupert and all they'd meant to each other wouldn't be so impossible.

It was Jodi's turn to nudge Rupert. "What are you going to do with that chicken?"

"I have no idea," Rupert said absently, his mind still on the illogical gaps in Jodi's brain. "Shall we get it anyway and wing it?"

Jodi pulled a face. "Sophie cooked chicken the other day. It was bloody minging."

Back to sausages then. Rupert put the chicken on the shelf, retreated, and grabbed a pack. "How about toad-in-the-hole?"

"If you say so."

It was as close to a "yes" as Rupert was likely to get from Jodi. He threw the sausages in the trolley. "Sold. Come on. We need some other bits if we're going to smash this shit."

Rupert had never been an optimist, but "smashing" a toad-in-the-hole turned out to be even more complicated than he'd feared. He eyed the kitchen counter, cluttered with every pan they owned and dusty with flour, and wondered if *he* was the one who'd had a bang on the head. What on earth had he been thinking?

"Can't you just google it?"

Rupert tossed a halfhearted glare over his shoulder. The fact that Jodi had chosen to stay in the kitchen with him, settled at the breakfast bar with his laptop rather than skulking away to the couch, meant the world to him. "I tried, but the Wi-Fi isn't working."

"So? You have a data allowance on your phone, don't you?"

"Nope. I have a pay-as-you-go sim card. I only have an iPhone because you forced your old one on me."

"Why?"

"Because I was as skint as a boozer's widow when I met you. Could barely afford to pay attention."

Jodi snorted. Rupert tore his focus from the lumpy batter he'd concocted in a jug that was far too small for it. "What's funny about that?"

"I'm not laughing."

The gleam in Jodi's eyes gave him away. Rupert rolled his eyes. "*Anyway*, I've never bothered to upgrade it because there's Wi-Fi here and the fire station picks up the signal from the Costa across the road. You made me take your old phone because you were fed up of my old one dying when I was on shift."

"On shift?"

"Yeah." Rupert busied himself pouring fat into what he hoped was a nonstick baking dish. "It freaked you out when I was late home and you couldn't get hold of me."

Jodi's gaze turned reflective again. "So that's the answer, eh?"

"The answer to what?"

"Never mind."

Jodi slipped abruptly from his stool and left the room. Rupert assumed that meant their day together—which had been slightly bizarre by its normality—was over. So he was mildly surprised when Jodi reappeared five minutes later, clutching his phone.

"I called Sophie's mum. We can google it if we get stuck," he said. "But I think I can remember what she told me. Can we try?"

Rupert was at the point with his lumpy batter where he'd accept help from just about anyone. He slid the jug across the counter and stepped back. "Have at it, boyo."

Chapter
THIRTEEN

The next day was the second consecutive morning Jodi had come awake feeling halfway human. It was also the second morning he'd woken up with his hand stuck to his dick and his mind freeze-framed on Rupert's hard chest, leanly muscled biceps, and strong, perfectly veined forearms.

And the umpteenth time he'd wanked over them.

Damn it. Jodi sat up and wrenched his hand from his groin. Vague flashbacks of Rupert helping him to bed after he'd fallen asleep in the armchair filtered into his consciousness, bringing with them an all-too-clear memory of the long hours he'd lain awake after, wrestling with the heat that Rupert's platonic, caring touch had stirred in him. Heat that hadn't abated as he'd slept.

Jodi placed his palm on his chest, feeling his heartbeat quicken as he drifted back to the only thing that made his long, lonely nights in the bedroom bearable, but he caught himself as his fingers brushed his cock, and shoved his hand in his pocket. *Stop it. You're not gay.* He didn't feel gay. He *wasn't* gay. Couldn't be. He liked girls, right?

He closed his eyes and chased down the memories he had of sleeping with Sophie . . . her soft skin and rounded body. Her breasts. He thought of other women he'd slept with too: women of all shapes and sizes, beautiful inside and out. Arousal and desire rippled through him, and he took a deep breath, letting his hand drift back to his cock. His mind swam and his body responded, heating his blood and driving sweat from his skin. He lay flat, recalling every touch and sensation, letting them expand and evolve until he had new fantasies, illusions that intensified with each pull and twist until he came with a low cry.

Gasping, he opened his eyes as he spilled onto his stomach, toes curled, heart pounding. Did one straight wank cancel out a week of gay ones? Was that how it worked? Jodi had no idea. Besides, obsessive wanking be damned, none of it explained the primal compulsion he felt to be as close to Rupert as possible. He'd spent weeks avoiding him, hiding in bed or skulking in the bathroom, hoping the yearning would reveal itself as another figment of his battered imagination, and trying to convince himself that his obsession with Rupert would fade, but Rupert had proved him horribly wrong yesterday morning when he'd come home from work early, sheened with sweat, his cheeks flushed from whatever he'd been doing to leave him out of breath. Jesus Christ. The next thing Jodi knew he'd been watching Rupert sleep like some kind of creep, counting his breaths and wondering what it would feel like to trace his strong arms with his fingertips, squeeze his hand, and bury his face in his neck. After that, sausage shopping in Sainsbury's had seemed like the easy option.

Rupert was nowhere to be seen when Jodi ventured out of his room later that morning. He searched the flat and came up blank. For the first time in as long as he could remember, he was truly alone.

Jodi stood in the kitchen and absorbed the quiet. He'd pretended to be asleep when Rupert had checked on him just after eight, but the lingering scent of fried onions made him regret it. Closing his eyes, he pictured Rupert fumbling his way through creating Jodi's patchy recollection of Sophie's mum's toad-in-the-hole. Shivering, he found himself missing that curious gaze and gentle smile. He'd been craving solitude for months, but now that he had it, it felt all wrong.

The front door opened. Jodi jumped, but the light footsteps told him it was Sophie, not Rupert. His stomach sank, and he shuddered again. When had Rupert's absence begun feeling like a hole in his damn heart?

Sophie appeared at his shoulder. "What's the matter?"

"Nothing. What's the matter with *you*?"

"Hope you haven't been growling at Rupert like that." Sophie rolled her eyes, clearly unfazed by Jodi's scowl.

"What if I have? What the fuck does it matter? He's no different to you, is he?"

"Not really. There's no reason for you to talk to me like I'm something you stepped in either."

Her sharp tone caught Jodi off guard, catching his runaway temper in a snare of contrition. "Sorry."

"You're forgiven. What's up? Did you have a bad night?"

"No, not at all. I had a fun night."

"Fun?" Sophie raised an eyebrow. "That's not a word I've heard you use in a while."

"Yeah, well." Jodi pushed past her, lacking the words to explain the Rupert-shaped bubble he'd spent the previous evening in. He left her to whatever it was she did in the kitchen and retreated to the living room to take his pills and go through his daily exercise routines.

He was puffing his way through leg curls when Sophie appeared above him, clutching a plate overflowing with toad-in-the-hole leftovers.

"Who made this?"

"Me and Rupert did."

"You did?"

"Yup. I asked your mum how to make it, and I even ate some too."

"That's amazing."

"Is it?" Jodi finally unstrapped the weights from his legs and gave Sophie his full attention. "What the fuck are you crying for?"

"Why do you think? Jesus, Jodi. You're such an arsehole sometimes!"

Sophie turned and fled back to the kitchen, slamming the door. Jodi stared after her, perplexed. What the hell had he missed this time?

It became no clearer as the sudden silence enveloped him like a thick, choking smog. He wished Rupert was there to explain it to him, then killed the thought before it could take root. This was about Sophie, not Rupert, and he didn't have the energy to figure out why they felt like one and the same.

He got up and took a deep breath, then approached the kitchen door, tapping lightly on the frame before venturing inside. "Soph? Are you okay?"

Sophie didn't look up from the pile of carrots she was obliterating into tiny pieces. "I'm fine."

"Why are you crying, then?"

"I'm *not*."

"Yes, you are." Jodi came up behind her and stilled the knife in her hand. He drew her into a tight hug, then cupped her face in his palms. "What's wrong? Tell me?"

Sophie pushed Jodi's hands away and wiped her eyes. "I can't tell you, because it doesn't make any sense."

"So? Nothing makes sense to me these days. Doesn't mean I can't listen."

"You always used to, you know. Even after we'd split up, and before, when we'd stopped having sex and started seeing other people, I could always talk to you about anything. You're my best friend."

"I am?"

Sophie sniffed. "Of course you are. But it's not the same— You're not the same. Or maybe you are. Sometimes you sound just like you used to, and it hurts, Jodi, because we miss you, *I* miss you. I'm with you all the time, but I miss you so much."

Jodi didn't know what to say. It was the second occasion in as many days he'd been called someone's best friend, but he didn't believe it. Couldn't. How could he be anyone's best friend when he didn't have a clue who he was? "Why are you crying today? I don't understand."

"Oh, I don't know." Sophie shrugged and grabbed a sheet of kitchen paper from a nearby roll. "It's hard to keep up sometimes. We had a lovely day last time I was here, and it felt like I had you back—as my friend—and you said you had fun with Rupert too. Then the next thing I know you're biting my head off again, and it's upsetting, you know? It's like the old you gets dangled in front of me, then ripped away. I can't imagine how Rupert—" Sophie bit her lip.

Jodi raised an eyebrow. "How Rupert what?"

"How Rupert copes without you. Jodi, you're everything to him. You and Indie. You know that, don't you?"

Did he? For a moment it felt like every other question Jodi couldn't answer, then Rupert flashed into his mind, with his steady hands and unwavering gaze, and Jodi knew Sophie was right.

He loves me.

"You haven't wanted to talk about Rupert since our sessions began. What's changed?"

Jodi sat back in his chair and considered Ken's question. He'd come to the session under the usual cloud of apathy and boredom, but he'd barely sat his arse in the squeaky leather chair before he'd found himself confessing his ever-growing infatuation with Rupert.

Ken's reaction hadn't been as clarifying as Jodi had hoped. *"What's changed?"* Fuck's sake. Hadn't Jodi just bloody told him?

"Everything's changed," Jodi said. "I woke up one day thinking about him, and I haven't stopped since."

"I doubt it was as cut-and-dry as that. Perhaps something triggered these thoughts. Have you read back through your journal?"

Jodi resisted the urge to roll his eyes—it made him dizzy—and shrugged. "Er, I never really got round to starting it."

It wasn't strictly true. He had written a few entries, but none of them were about Rupert, and it had been weeks since he'd even thought of it.

Ken didn't seem surprised or annoyed. In fact, for a brief moment, he looked almost amused. Then his expression sobered. "So, you have feelings for Rupert that you don't remember having before the accident."

"I don't remember Rupert at all from before the accident."

"Don't you? You mentioned the Olympics in our last session. Said you went to the women's weightlifting at Excel Arena."

"So?"

"The Olympics were in 2012, two years after you met Rupert."

Jodi blinked. "I don't remember that."

"You don't remember the event? Or you don't remember telling me?"

Jodi wanted to say both, that he couldn't remember either, that Ken was mistaken, but the harder he thought about it, the clearer the recollection of his last session with Ken became. They'd been talking about sports in general and Jodi had admitted he cared little for football and rugby.

"What about a big occasion? Like the World Cup, or the Olympics?"

"Just give them a ball each. I'd rather see someone do something incredible . . . like lift twelve times their body weight in bags of nails."

The image of himself and Rupert watching Chinese women doing just that had manifested moments later, so clear and strong Jodi couldn't deny it was real, could he?

A hand on Jodi's shoulder made him jump.

"Jodi?" Ken's voice sounded unnaturally close. Jodi's vision cleared to reveal Ken had left his desk and was now kneeling on the floor in front of him. "Would you like some water?"

Jodi shook his head. "No . . . I'm fine."

"Sure? You've gone a little pale on me. Have you eaten today?"

"Yes. Rupert massacred an omelette for me before he went to work."

"Good." Ken stood and returned to his side of the desk. "What shift is Rupert working today?"

"Six till six."

"You were up early, then?"

Jodi nodded absently. He'd got up that morning to have a piss, and met Rupert in the hallway on the way back. Following him into the kitchen had felt so natural he'd hardly noticed himself doing it.

"You know, I ask you quite often about Rupert's movements, his shift patterns, how he spends his time when he's at home. You never used to know . . . like you didn't care enough to keep track. Have you noticed your awareness improving in general? Or is it just Rupert you're paying more attention to?"

Ken spoke with his gaze down, studying the meticulous notes he scribbled on a pad with a Snoopy cartoon in the corner of each page, but he looked up as he posed his last question, leaving Jodi nowhere to hide.

"I don't know," Jodi said honestly. "I know I'm getting better, but I'm not the same as I used to be."

"How do you know that?"

"Sophie . . . and Rupert. They seem so sad when they look at me. I feel like I'm failing them."

"Sophie is very dear to you, even now when you haven't been a couple for a long time, and you know she loves you, but what about Rupert? Are your feelings for him the same? Or something else?"

"Something else. And he loves me too. He's never said it, or done anything to make me think he has the same weird thoughts as me, but I know he loves me . . . in a different way than Sophie."

It felt good to say it out loud, but Ken didn't give Jodi long to enjoy it. "What makes you think your thoughts are weird? We've never talked about sexuality. Do you remember feeling this way about other men before the accident?"

Jodi opened his mouth. Shut it again. Then a perspective he'd been lacking since he'd opened his eyes in that damn fucking hospital crashed into him like a train. "Oh God."

His voice had faded to a whisper, but Ken heard him. "What? What is it?"

"I—I have felt like this before . . . I think. Sort of. I went out with a bloke at uni for a while. I didn't sleep with him . . . I didn't. I don't think I even wanted to. But I fancied him. I did. I know I did." As the memory firmed up, Jodi spoke to himself as much as Ken. "Why didn't I remember this before? I thought it was only the last five years I'd lost. What does this mean? I don't understand."

"The main bulk of your amnesia has centred around the past five years, but it would've been impossible for the doctors to know for sure that you'd retained every memory you had before then."

The notion that the gaps in his mind could be more vast than he'd imagined made Jodi feel sick. "How will I know?"

"I don't know if you ever will. Perhaps it would be wiser to consider your sexuality as it stands now, rather than brooding on what it might have been. Do your feelings for Rupert upset you?"

"Yes."

"Why?"

"Because I don't understand them."

Ken made a note, then turned the page over, like the subject was closed. "Have you talked to Rupert about this?"

Or maybe not. "Fuck no. I can't do that."

"Why not?" Ken fixed Jodi with a stare that made him want to sink through the floor. "You and Rupert were close before the accident, and you have become close again now. Why not confide in him?"

"You want me to tell my flatmate I'm having pervy thoughts about him? What the fuck's wrong with you?"

"He was your friend before," Ken said as though Jodi hadn't spoken. "One who cared enough to put his life on hold to look after you. He has seen you at your very worst moments and stayed by your side when you've pushed him away. I think it's unlikely there is much you could do to make him turn his back on you now."

Easy for him to say. He wasn't the one fantasising about a bloke who was clearly the best friend a man could ever have. *Great way to repay Rupert, eh? Daydreaming about his cock . . .*

Jodi left Ken a little while later with his mind more fragmented than usual. He walked half a mile to the bus stop, checking his pocket for the Oyster card Rupert and Sophie made sure he had with him every time he left the flat, even when they were with him. Except they weren't always with him now. A few days ago, the whole world—Jodi's world, at least—had sat him down and informed him that he'd regained enough of his faculties to be left to his own devices a few afternoons a week. Afternoons that he mainly spent walking five times further than he needed to, as despite his newfound freedom, no one seemed keen on him crossing the street by himself.

The bus rumbled into the stop. Jodi double-checked the number and route, then felt like a twat. He knew it was the right bus because it was the same bus he'd taken two days ago when he'd come to his occupational therapy appointment. The same bus he'd taken with Rupert two days before that when he'd seen the brain doctors in the opposite building.

He boarded the bus and swiped his Oyster card, then found a seat near the driver so he could ask for help if he lost track of the stops. It would've been easier to take the Tube—he could follow a bloody straight line—but he hadn't been in the Underground since he'd lost his shit on it a few months back and wound up clinging to Rupert's leg like a hysterical cat.

That's got to change. The notion and accompanying determination took Jodi by surprise. Until now, it hadn't seemed to matter. Why would it? It wasn't like he needed to go anywhere he couldn't get to on the bus. But there was something about sitting at the front of the bus, surrounded by elderly women counting their change, that suddenly rankled him. What the fuck was so hard about taking the damn Tube?

Now felt like as good a time as any to find out.

Without pausing to think, Jodi pressed the Stop button and rose from his seat, making his way to the door as the driver pulled the bus into the next stop. There was a Tube station twenty metres away.

He manoeuvred through the crowds and shoved his way down the steps. Below ground, self-doubt kicked in. He stared at the brightly coloured map on the walls and tried to trace his journey home. Instinct drew him to the Victoria line. He closed his eyes and called on the logistical memories his brain had managed to retain. He couldn't remember ever needing to come this far south before the accident, but the conviction that he had done, many times, was suddenly overwhelming.

He opened his eyes and studied the map again, following the bright blue line down from Tottenham until it came to where he was now . . . Brixton. What the hell was in Brixton? And then it came to him, and the answer was the same as it had been for many other questions he'd asked himself recently: Rupert. Rupert worked in Brixton, at the fire station, and he had done so since long before they'd apparently met. Jodi took a deep breath and another piece of the invisible puzzle slotted into place. He couldn't think of a reason why he'd come to Brixton with Rupert—to a fire station of all places—but he had. *Knew* he had. Felt it in the bones he'd longed to leave in Ken's stuffy office.

In a daze, Jodi tore himself away from the map and followed the signs further underground. Then the heat of the looming platform hit him, and his thoughts of Rupert evaporated. Since the accident, he'd grown used to the oddly slanted perspective that often plagued him—a shifting sensation that made him feel like he was walking sideways—but today, as the ground rushed up to meet him at an alarming rate, the lack of equilibrium had never been more terrifying.

The slam of concrete never came. As he braced himself for impact, strong hands caught him and held him upright.

"All right there, mate?"

Jodi blinked as the bottleneck platform entrance he'd stumbled in returned to normal. His rescuer came into focus . . . a thick-set, ruddy-faced man who looked familiar. "Thanks."

"No worries. Thought you was gonna hit the deck."

"Me too."

"You okay?"

Was he? Jodi took stock in the slow, measured way his OT had taught him. *Can you walk? Can you talk? Do you need help?* Yes, yes, and . . . probably not. Jodi nodded slowly. "I'm fine. Just lost my balance."

"Not surprising. Not long been outta King's, have ya?"

"Um—"

"Don't worry, Jodi, mate. Don't worry. I'll let you get on. Good to see you out and about, though. Your old fella's not been himself since you got clobbered. Tell 'im I'll buy him a pint next time he comes down the Chequers. You too. Look after yourself."

With that, the gallant stranger was gone, swept away in the crowd of commuters who'd disembarked from the train that had pulled into the platform while Jodi had lost and regained his bearings. Jodi stared after him, watching the back of his head as it disappeared. His cockney slang was far from native, but Jodi knew enough to know "your old fella" could mean anything from someone's dad to their—

Fuck.

Jodi staggered to a nearby bench and sat down. His pulse—which had slowed while he'd attempted conversation with the ruddy-faced man—roared in his ears. *"Your old fella." Jesus bloody Christ.* Rupert wasn't Jodi's father, which left only one feasible reality, a reality that up until now had seemed nothing more than a perverted, twisted dream. A fantasy forced on him by having his skull smashed into Tottenham High Road. Rupert loved him, of that he was certain, and the affection, attraction, and addiction Jodi felt in return was real.

So fucking real.

Another train rumbled out of the dark tunnel and stopped at the platform. Jodi stood and mechanically boarded, drifting to a vacant seat. The journey passed in a blur of whiplash-inducing emotions he struggled to name, but he couldn't deny the relief flooding through him. Nothing had made sense to him in months. Nothing had been tangible, like it was really his to feel.

The tannoy called out for Tottenham. Jodi stood, moved to the door, and jostled his way above ground. The flat was a stone's throw from the Tube station, and he found himself home before he could blink.

Inside, a flashing red light on the landline phone caught his eye. Jodi checked the log and saw he'd missed three calls and a voice mail from the same number. He pressed the Play button. Rupert's soft Irish brogue filled the hallway. "Jodi? Pick up your damn phone, will ya? I called you a million times. Fuck's sake—"

The message ended abruptly. Jodi frowned. Rupert sounded stressed. *"Pick up your damn phone."* Jodi patted his pockets. Shit. He'd left his phone in the bathroom when he'd taken a shower that morning and forgotten all about it.

He found his phone by the sink, the screen jammed with missed calls and messages from Rupert and Sophie. Jodi fired off a text to Rupert, then deleted his messages without reading them. He did the same with Sophie, trying to ignore the guilt tickling his veins. House rules were that he stayed in touch with Rupert and Sophie when they left him alone, letting them know he'd made it through another few hours without stepping in front of a speeding car. Most days he remembered, but not today. Today, it had been hours since he'd last checked in and the fear that he'd worried them made him feel like a dick.

Sophie's reply came through in minutes, but he found himself loitering, waiting for Rupert's. And waiting, and waiting. He drummed his fingers on the countertop. His mind was abuzz with a million things he needed to say to Rupert, but, albeit briefly, for some reason a couple of electronic words felt like they'd be enough. If only he could think of anything coherent.

He stared at the phone, fixated. It was a while before he realised it had grown dark. Damn it. Some days he couldn't care less if it was night or day, but the sensation of time disappearing while he languished in his chaotic thoughts was, at best, annoying.

At worse it was terrifying, but Jodi had too much on his mind to worry about the holes in his brain today. All he wanted—craved—right now, was any sign he was on Rupert's mind as much as Rupert was on his.

Finally, Rupert's name lit up his phone screen. Jodi swiped the message open, preparing himself for the subtle disappointment in him Rupert could never quite hide, even in the short messages they exchanged when he wasn't around.

The whole-screen paragraph took Jodi aback. He scanned the message, and his heart sank. Far from the gentle admonishment he'd expected, Rupert had sent a list of things Jodi needed to do before he went to bed. Things Rupert usually helped him with. Things Jodi would have to do alone because Rupert wasn't coming home.

Chapter FOURTEEN

The greasy, choking heat of burning oil came at Rupert from all sides. He crouched down and felt his way through the blazing chip shop, searching for any sign of the elderly owner who was still unaccounted for. His hand hit something that could've been a shoe. It wasn't. Further inspection of the object revealed a chip scoop.

Rupert cast it aside and pressed on. He'd just searched the flat above the shop, but the smoke was thickening by the second and time was running out. Another few minutes and anyone still alive on the ground floor would be dead. And Rupert didn't need a body on his hands. Not today. His crew had already attended a fatal industrial accident, and he wasn't in the mood to lay another dead soul in the back of an ambulance.

So he pressed on, trying not to count how many chip-fat-based fires he'd attended over the last few months. Did people never learn?

He reached the service counter, creeping closer and closer to the heart of the fire. A window at the back of the shop blew. He ducked lower, dodging the surge in heat as the backdraft gusted through the burning shop. Adrenaline quickened his pulse. Six years on the job had dulled his fear of flames, but the thrill of dancing around them never got old. Running out of oxygen worried him more. His tank sounded its warning alarm. He didn't have much left. Just another few steps—

The radio crackled. "Stand down, team one. Stand down. All persons accounted for. Withdraw. Repeat. Withdraw."

Or not.

He picked his way out of the chip shop as the hose crews continued to tackle the blaze. It wasn't the biggest the crew had seen that week, but they didn't have long to get it under control before it spread to nearby homes. Rupert glanced back over his shoulder. Smoke still billowed from the roof and windows, but the flames were no longer visible. Green Watch had it covered.

At the rig, he stripped out of his breathing apparatus and scrubbed a clammy hand down his face. Briggs appeared from nowhere and passed him a bottle of water. Rupert took it gratefully. Whatever the weather, crawling through burning buildings was sweaty work. "So the old boy turned up then?"

Briggs grunted. "Old git, you mean. His daughter found him up the road in Corals. Reckons he probably left the fryers on in his hurry to catch the dogs."

"Dickhead." And Rupert meant it. He'd seen too many tragedies to forgive such blatant idiocy and knowing he'd risked his life searching for some twat who'd been in the bookies all along just about summed up his day.

Briggs moved off to check on the other crews. Rupert climbed into the rig and retrieved his phone from the dashboard while he waited for them to regroup. It had been a few hours since he'd had to tell Jodi a major incident with the station's other rig meant he couldn't come off shift until dawn. Jodi had replied with a flat *OK*, and with calls rolling one after the other ever since, Rupert hadn't had time to check that he really was okay, that he felt well enough to be by himself all night when he'd already spent the day alone, a day Rupert had spent reminding himself how to put his worries for Jodi to one side while he got on with his job.

He swiped his phone. There was nothing from Jodi, but the screen was jammed with four missed calls from Jen. He called her straight back; she'd only keep calling otherwise until she'd got what she wanted.

She answered on the first ring. "What took you so long?"

"I'm on shift. What do you want?"

"My dad's had a stroke. They don't think he'll be able to come home, so I need to drive up to Coventry in the morning to get things sorted."

"Okay." Rupert couldn't find the words for sympathy he didn't mean. His ex-father-in-law had made his life hell, even before the truth had come out. "Are you taking Indie with you?"

"I can't really do that, can I? You know what that house is like. There's nowhere for her to sleep, and she hates it. You need to have her for a few days."

"I can't." Rupert cringed, hating himself for being caught between the two souls he loved so much. Since Jodi had come home, he'd been having Indie at Sophie's place—the world's girliest apartment in Primrose Hill—but Sophie had gone away and wouldn't be back until the end of the week, leaving Rupert with no access to her apartment and no one to care for Jodi in his absence. He'd already left him for far too long. "I'm sorry, I just can't. I have to—"

"I'm not asking you, Rupert. I'm telling you. You need to get over here and take care of your daughter. I don't care if you have better things to do. I need you here tomorrow morning."

She hung up before Rupert could respond. He called again, but she didn't answer, and by then the rest of the crew were boarding the rig, ready to go back to the station. There was barely time for a piss before they were called out once more, and the calls kept coming. It was three in the morning before he checked his phone.

He activated the screen. Three messages, all from Jodi, and spaced three hours apart, the last one more than two hours ago.

Come home
Please
I need you

"Let me out here."

The taxi jolted to a stop. Rupert threw the fifty quid he'd withdrawn for food shopping at the driver and jumped out. He dashed up the steps and jammed his key in the exterior door. The door stuck. He kicked it open, slamming it into the wall behind, and took the stairs two at a time.

He shoved his way through the flat's front door. "Jodi? Jodi? Where are you?"

There was no reply. Rupert charged through the flat. Living room, kitchen, bedroom, bathroom. But they were all empty. Jodi was nowhere to be seen.

Rupert pulled out his phone and hit Jodi's speed dial for the hundredth time since he'd read his messages, but it went to voice mail.

Panic swept over Rupert. He dashed back to the hall, heading for the front door. What the hell had happened? Had he fallen and hurt himself? Called 999 himself? Or one of the neighbours? With Sophie away, his ad hoc double shift had been badly timed. Fucking idiot. Why the hell hadn't he told Briggs to do one, and come home?

He fell over Jodi's feet, landing on his knees to face an expression he'd never seen on Jodi's face before. "Jodi?"

Jodi didn't blink. His bloodshot gaze remained bewildered, exhausted, and . . . something else. "You came home."

"Of course I did. I would've come sooner, but I didn't get your messages until I came off a job."

"That's why I didn't call you. Because you were at work and you can't answer the phone at work."

Jodi recited the words, repeating the instructions Rupert had given him when he'd left the day before.

"That's right," Rupert said. "They let me carry my phone on silent and leave it on the rig, but I can only use it in an emergency. That's why I left you the station number as well, so you could call for help if you needed it. What's happened? Are you okay? Did you hurt yourself?"

"No. It's not me. It's her."

"Her? Who? Sophie?"

"No. Her."

Rupert followed Jodi's gaze through the open doorway he was slumped in. Followed it into the pink and blue bedroom, all the way to the tiny humped body of Indie, curled up in the bed she hadn't slept in since Jodi came home from hospital five long months ago.

A surreal calm came over Rupert. He stood and went to Indie's bedside. She was fast asleep, clutching the battered wolf toy Jodi had bought her from London Zoo soon after Rupert had introduced them. She always slept with it when she came to the flat. In her absence, Rupert had stashed it on top of the fridge, unable to face his failure to give her a stable base while Jodi had been so unwell. Somehow it had found its way home.

Rupert touched Indie's cheek, for a moment lost in its ethereal smoothness. He hadn't seen her all week. Had she grown again?

"Rupert?"

Rupert closed his eyes to Jodi's hoarse whisper. Something had happened in this room while he'd been at work, something huge, and he felt it in every fibre of his being, but he needed this quiet moment, the calm before the storm. And in this turbulent new world, only Indie could give him that. He needed her as much as he needed Jodi. More. But Indie was sleeping, at peace in her world of princesses playing football, or whatever it was she dreamed about. In all her eight years, he'd never known her to have a nightmare. No. The nightmares were his, and he'd take every one if he could spare her a moment of pain. He'd take a bullet for her, and Jodi. He'd die for them both.

Jodi. Rupert breathed a silent sigh and turned away from Indie, treading noiselessly out of the room to Jodi's side. He crouched down and tentatively brushed Jodi's hair from his forehead. "What happened?"

"I—I don't know."

"Yes, you do. Tell me from the beginning. Why is Indie here?"

"Her mum brought her."

Rupert had figured that much but swallowed his impatience. Jodi looked shell-shocked, and no good would come from pushing him to explain himself faster. "When?"

"Seven, maybe? Her mum said it was nearly her bedtime."

"What else did she say?"

"That she'd be back in a few days."

"That's it?"

"I think so."

Jodi's gaze faltered. For a moment, Rupert thought Jodi might faint, or worse. He slipped Jodi's good arm over his shoulders. "Come on. Let's get you up. What are you doing out here anyway?"

"I couldn't sleep, Rupe. I was so scared I'd break her."

Rupe. Rupert wanted to cry. It had been so long since Jodi had last called him that. "I can't believe Jen left her here without telling me. I'm so sorry."

"Jen? Is that her mum?"

"Yes. She called me earlier, asking me to have Indie here for a few days, but I told her no. This is her way of getting even."

Jodi took slow, shuffling steps across the hall into the main bedroom, leaning on Rupert for support, a telling sign of how tired he was, until he reached the bed and sank down on it. "I didn't know her. I opened the door, and she just started yelling. She wouldn't let me speak, and she was gone before I could tell her I didn't have a fucking clue who she was."

Rupert was livid. It was so Jen to show up and dump Indie like a stray cat without a thought for anyone but herself. Lord knew, she'd done it before, to him, to Jodi, but that was before Jodi had survived an accident that could've killed him, only to live a life trapped behind a shadow on an MRI scan. Before Jodi had become a man barely able to take care of himself, let alone a child. Rupert had long ago lost the will to bear Jen much ill feeling, but fuck, in that moment he *hated* her.

Movement on the bed brought him back to the present. Jodi had scooted across the bed and wrapped his arms around his knees, making himself as small as possible, his gaze apprehensive, perhaps, even afraid.

Rupert touched his arm. "What's wrong?"

"I'm sorry I didn't know her."

"What?"

"I'm *sorry*, okay?" Jodi's voice rose. "I'm sorry I didn't remember her, or Indie, or you. I'm sorry I can't remember anything that matters. I just— I'm trying. I'm trying all the time, then people tell me stuff that doesn't make any sense, and I don't know what to do. Then Indie came, and I didn't know what to do. I made her toast and milk and put her to bed. She made me sit with her, and she was talking to me like I was her best friend, and I didn't know what to do. I never know what to do. I'm sorry, Rupert. I'm so fucking sorry."

Jodi broke off with a racking sob that obliterated what was left of Rupert's shattered heart. He took Jodi in his arms before he truly knew what he was doing, crushing Jodi against him, holding him as tight as he dared, like he could draw the hurt out of him with a simple embrace. "It's all right, boyo. It's all right. You're okay."

"I'm not, though, am I?" Jodi raised his head. His face was wet, and his eyes more lost than Rupert had ever seen them. "Your daughter knows me better than I know myself, and I can barely remember her name. What's okay about that?"

Rupert sat back on the bed so Jodi could relax against him—or escape if he needed to. "It'll get better. It *is* getting better."

Jodi said nothing, but he made no move to disentangle himself. If anything, he pressed closer, like he was trying to hide away in Rupert's chest. Rupert hugged him tighter. Seeing Jodi so distraught was gut-wrenching, but he couldn't deny it felt amazing to hold him. To feel him, touch him, breathe him in, and revel briefly in the fact that Jodi had chosen to be so close. He shut his eyes. Perhaps if neither of them spoke, the world would stop turning and they could stay this way forever.

"Indie showed me the dress she wants to wear to our wedding."

"What?" Rupert's eyes flew open.

Jodi stared back at him. For the first time since the accident, he didn't look bewildered.

"She told me I was your boyfriend, that I had been since she was tiny, and she wants us to get married."

Words failed Rupert. He'd always known Indie would give him away, if Jodi even believed her, which was doubtful. He hadn't believed anyone else. "I—"

"Why didn't you tell me?"

"Jodi—"

"Why didn't you tell me?" Jodi's voice was low, but the anger in his tone left nowhere to hide. "All this time I thought I was going fucking mad and you *knew*. Everyone knew, didn't they?"

"Knew what?"

"Don't give me that shit." Jodi scrambled from the bed, lurching to his feet. Rupert stood too and moved to steady him, but Jodi blocked his reaching hands. "Why didn't you tell me? Some bloke stopped me in the street and called you my boyfriend, then I come home and a child I can't even fucking remember does the same. Can't you see how messed up that is? Why didn't *you* tell me?"

Rupert took a deep breath as he absorbed Jodi's fury. He'd waited so long to finally tell Jodi the truth, part of him had made a tired, warped kind of peace with the fact he probably never would. That all he and Jodi had shared would remain confined to a past Jodi would never remember. "Indie told you whatever she told you because she was the only one I didn't ask not to."

"That doesn't make any sense."

"What does? Oh *God*." The enormity of what was about to happen nearly sent Rupert to his knees. "Jodi, please, you have to understand. You'd been awake for ages, but you hadn't spoken . . . I didn't know what to do."

Jodi stared, his gaze a potent mixture of rage and confusion. "I know all this. I know I was a walking zombie for months. It doesn't explain why you never told me something so fucking important."

Rupert should've found hope in the fact that Jodi felt what Indie had told him was important, but his mind was in bits. What if Jodi believed it and rejected Rupert anyway? Rejected him once and for all? Living in limbo had left Rupert a broken man, but with no end in sight it had been too easy to imagine another world, a world where Jodi had woken up remembering how much they loved each other.

How much I still love him. "I tried to tell you when you first woke up, but you didn't understand. Then the doctors tried to tell you too, and you got really ill—you deteriorated, you didn't speak for days. It was like you couldn't bear it, like it horrified you so much you'd rather be dead—" Rupert faltered. "You came back, but you didn't remember being awake, and you didn't remember me at all."

"I still don't remember you."

Rupert tore his gaze from the floor. "I know, and I've come to accept you probably never will."

"I should, though, shouldn't I?" Jodi took an unsteady step forward. "I should remember you because I was in love with you."

Was. Rupert swallowed the bile in his throat. "Is that what Indie told you? That you were in love with me?"

"No. She told me I was your boyfriend. I'd already worked the rest out for myself."

"Eh?" Rupert felt dizzy. "I don't understand."

Jodi snorted. "Not nice, is it? To feel so much about something that doesn't make any sense?"

Rupert sank backward onto the bed. "You had your voice back. You could speak up for yourself, tell the doctors what hurt so they could help you get better. Tell Sophie you needed her. It seemed like you'd been trapped behind that fucking scar on your brain for so long, I couldn't be the reason you lost yourself again."

"That wasn't your decision to make. You should've told me who you were to me. All that time I thought you were some creepy flatmate who stared at me a lot. Scared the shit out of me when I found myself gawping at you too."

Rupert blinked. "What?"

For a moment it seemed Jodi might leave the room, but he didn't. He sat down beside Rupert, close enough that their legs almost brushed. "I wish I could remember how it felt to be in love with you, but I can't, because I don't know you."

"I get it," Rupert said. "The doctors kept warning us not to put ideas in your head, that we couldn't lead you to the memories that meant the most to us—to me. I'm so sorry, Jodi. I just didn't know what to do."

Jodi sighed. "I'm tired, but to be honest with you, I'm fucking relieved. I thought I had a glitch in my noggin that was making me gay or some shit, like the accident had twisted my dick and pointed it in the wrong direction. To know it's real—that it's tangible. Fuck. It makes more sense than anything I've ever known."

"I don't know what to say." Rupert felt like he'd been dropped into a vortex that took his wildest dreams and stretched them around a muted reality that didn't quite fit. "If it's any comfort, as far as I knew up until the accident, you still liked girls too."

"So I'm not gay? Jesus Christ. I've only just caught up."

Rupert laughed a laugh that wasn't as hollow as he expected. "You're not anything, boyo. You're *you*, like everyone else."

Chapter
FIFTEEN

Jodi rolled over in bed and collided with a warm, comforting mass. He reached out, finding soft cotton and then skin, smooth skin that felt like nothing he'd ever touched before. He opened his eyes, and the last time he'd been awake, whenever that had been, came flooding back to him. The day that had seemed to go on and on, and the night that felt never-ending until Rupert had finally come home.

The rest of the previous day was a little blurred. The session with Ken, the dazed Tube ride. The never-ending wait for Rupert to return. And then the knock at the door that had accelerated the slow journey his damaged brain was taking to the conclusion that, by now, felt almost inevitable.

Couldn't say he cared for Rupert's ex much, but the girl? Indie? Despite the bombshells she'd unwittingly chucked Jodi's way, he'd found himself spellbound by her. Indie was bright, fierce, and beautiful. Jodi couldn't remember loving her any more than he remembered loving Rupert, but he'd adored her from the moment she'd pulled on his beard and told him he looked like a troll.

"Don't let Daddy grow a beard. It turns orange when it gets too long and scratches my face."

"How would I stop him?"

"He listens to you. That's what boyfriends do."

Jodi stared at Rupert. In his hazel eyes, there was a lot of Indie, but beyond the beautiful little girl, he saw Rupert, really saw him, perhaps for the first time since he'd set eyes on him after the accident. Rupert seemed nervous, and tired, like he hadn't slept a wink in days. Jodi tried to speak, to tell him something, anything, to let him know he was okay—that they were both okay, together—but nothing intelligible came out.

"Shh." Rupert touched Jodi's face briefly, like a whisper. "You're exhausted. Go back to sleep. We'll talk later."

Jodi was powerless to protest. His mind was alive with a million questions, but his body was weak, and he could barely summon the energy to close his eyes.

But he did close them, and the next time he woke, he was alone, and the spot where Rupert had been lying was cold.

He shivered and sat up slowly, testing his equilibrium for the dizziness that sometimes plagued him first thing in the morning. Not that he knew whether it was morning. With the blinds closed and the bedside lamp on, he had no idea what time it was. Or where Rupert was.

Anxiety lanced Jodi's heart. In recent weeks, he'd grown used to the comfort of Rupert's presence, and his absence now was terrifying. What if it had all been a dream? What if he'd imagined the resolution to the turmoil he still felt deep in his belly? What if it never went away? *What if, what if, what if.*

Fuck this shit.

Jodi stood just as the bedroom door opened. Indie danced in and scampered onto the bed.

"Mum and Daddy are arguing outside because Daddy made her come back for me. Can we watch your old Bucky O'Hare videos?"

Okay. So the part about Rupert's bitch of an ex and his mesmerising daughter showing up on the doorstep definitely wasn't a dream. Jodi blew out a breath and sat down again. "I don't know where they are."

Indie hopped off the bed and opened a drawer. "You keep them in here, silly, with your *South Park* DVDs, but you don't let me watch them. Daddy says they're rude."

"Yeah? He's probably right."

"Probably. You always say he is." Indie retrieved a battered VHS case and jammed it in the dusty machine Jodi had assumed was broken. "Where's the video remote?"

"Um . . ." Jodi glanced around. He hadn't used the TV at the end of the bed since he came home from hospital. "Are you sure you've got time? Isn't your mum here to pick you up?"

"That's what they're arguing about. She wants me to stay until Saturday. Dad says he has to work, but that doesn't matter, does it? You can babysit me."

"Haven't you got school?"

"It's half-term."

Jodi had no answer to that. He stayed put on the bed, not trusting himself to get up and walk around just yet. Indie crawled in front of him, brandishing a battered remote control and a sparkly pink hairbrush.

"Found it," she said. "Can you put my hair in bunches? I want to look like Bucky."

Lacking any better ideas, Jodi took the brush while Indie pressed Play and the dormant TV flashed to life, filling the screen with images of a fluorescent-green space rabbit cartoon he remembered from the late eighties. He couldn't remember anything important, but *this*? Yep, this, he remembered. *Bucky O'Hare and the Toad Wars.* For fuck's sake.

Indie stood patiently while Jodi gingerly ran the brush through her long hair. "You want bunches?"

"Yup. High ones, so they're like Bucky's ears."

"You don't want to look like Jenny?"

"Ew. No. I don't like cats."

"Seriously? I thought everyone liked cats?"

"Not cartoon ones. I like real ones, like Knob Cat."

"Knob Cat?"

"I brought one home once," Rupert said from the doorway. "Rescued it from a tree. You called it Knob Cat."

Jodi winced. Knob Cat? Seriously? The old Jodi sounded like a bit of a dick. "Bet you didn't like that."

"You're quite right. We changed it to Bob Cat until her mummy came to get her. Speaking of which, Indie, go and say good-bye to your mum. She's waiting."

Indie bounced on her heels. "I'm staying?"

"Until Thursday."

"Yes!" Indie spun around and planted a lightning-fast kiss on Jodi's cheek. "We can go ice skating."

She darted out of the room. Jodi watched her go, bemused. "Knob Cat?"

Rupert treated him to a tired grin. "It took you a while to get used to having a kid around who repeated everything you said to everyone she met. You didn't mean any harm, and it was pretty funny until she said it at nursery and Jen went ballistic."

"Jen's your ex?"

"Ex-wife, yeah. We don't get on much, but we tolerate each other for Indie's sake."

"She seemed like a bitch."

"She is." Rupert's eyes flashed with an emotion that made Jodi lean forward, his hands half-outstretched, but Indie returned before he could pull Rupert to him and examine his face until he understood the pain Rupert tried so hard to hide.

Indie returned to her position between Jodi's legs. "I'm back."

"So I see," Jodi said. "Bunches. Right. Have you got bands?"

Indie held up her hand, which was filled with brightly coloured hairbands. "Lots."

"Okaaaay." Jodi studied her hair. He'd had an ill-advised man bun for a few months at uni, *way* before they'd become ubiquitous with twats, but it had been a while since he'd last attempted to manipulate long hair. He looked at Rupert. "Have I done this before?"

"Aye, you're much better at it than I am. I'm not allowed to touch her hair if you're here."

Fair enough. Jodi set about wrestling Indie's hair into two high ponytails.

"Fold them," Indie instructed. "So they're like ears."

Jodi obeyed and the result wasn't half bad. Rupert seemed impressed. "Amazing what you can do when you don't think too hard, eh?"

"Hmm?"

"You couldn't move your hands like that a month ago. You're fucking amazing, boyo."

"Daddy!"

"Sorry, kiddo." Rupert winced. "I've made you some lunch. Why don't you go eat it in the living room while I have a chat with Jodi?"

"I want to watch Bucky."

"Later. Jodi's tired."

Jodi hadn't long woken up, but he couldn't deny his brief encounter with Indie had left him craving a nap. He gently tugged one of Indie's looped bunches. "Go on, love. We can watch it in a bit."

Indie left reluctantly, glancing over her shoulder as she went, like she was afraid Jodi would disappear the moment she turned away. Rupert watched her go with an odd expression on his face, then turned back to Jodi. "She's going to be here for a few days, that okay with you?"

"Of course," Jodi said. "You don't have to ask me that. This is your home too. I can't believe you've been having her at Sophie's place all this time."

"It was the best thing for everyone," Rupert said. "You wouldn't have wanted her to see you while you were so ill, and later . . . I don't know. Perhaps I should've told her the truth, but it was just something else I couldn't face. After a while, staying at Sophie's became normal for her."

"Like sleeping on the couch? Does that feel normal for you now?"

Rupert shrugged. "Not much feels like anything, boyo. It just is."

A cloud of overwhelming sadness descended on Jodi, like the sudden darkness that came before a rainstorm. And with it came the certainty that he wasn't the only one whose life had been stolen by the accident. Jodi didn't remember the life he'd lost, but Rupert did. He remembered everything, and the loss in his haunted gaze hurt Jodi more than any physical pain ever had.

"I'm so fucking sorry."

Rupert shook his head. "Don't do it to yourself. Trust me, it won't help. We can't look back and fix what isn't there anymore. I'm going to take Indie to the park. Will you be okay by yourself for a bit?"

"Um, yeah. Are you—?"

"Jodi." Rupert held up his hands. "Please. Just don't, okay?"

He left the room. A few moments later, the front door slammed. The sound reverberated in Jodi's head, like his skull was empty now that Rupert had gone. Like Rupert had taken everything that mattered with him. Then the silence took hold and it was deafening. Jodi pressed his fists into his eyes, willing his brain to just fucking *remember*, but nothing happened. The silence remained.

Jodi let his hands drop with a heavy sigh. The room came slowly back into focus, along with the clothes he'd been wearing since yesterday morning. Rupert had stopped reminding him to shower, trusting Jodi to follow the lists he'd written with his occupational therapist, but it didn't take much for Jodi to forget until something—like a grimy T-shirt—prompted him.

He made his way to the bathroom and took a shower, standing under the spray until the water ran cold. It wasn't his wisest move. Since the accident, the cold had bothered him. Some days, he just couldn't get warm.

He walked out of the bathroom, distracted as ever by the riddles in his brain. Then he caught sight of the clutter piled up in the hallway and something clicked. In the bedroom, he threw on a T-shirt and a pair of trackies, then went back to the hallway. He picked up a pile of coats and hung them on the nearby hooks. They didn't look right, so he took them down and hung them again, this time in size order. With that done, he moved quickly around the hallway, scooping up dirty clothes and stray shoes. He chucked the shoes in the cupboard and shut the door. Opened it again and put them neatly on the rack.

Then he stood back, and the calm order of his surroundings filtered into him. He'd grown used to the clicks his brain sometimes sounded when a piece of information he'd given up for lost suddenly reappeared. They usually came one at a time, and sporadically, but now, as he stared around the tidy hallway, his senses came alive. Purpose, perspective, compulsion. Everything seemed brighter, clearer, and though the gaps in his mind were still too vast for him to comprehend, a new sense of purpose overcame him.

Jodi paced the flat, picking up dirty dishes and clothes, newspapers, post, and shoes—*more shoes?*—until he saw carpets or floorboards in every room. He loaded the dishwasher and studied the buttons. Gave up and googled the fucker. With the dishwasher running, he tackled the washing machine, which proved far simpler as he could remember using one before.

That left the bathroom and a wrangle with the vacuum cleaner. Jodi fetched the hoover from the bedroom cupboard. He plugged it in and switched it on. So far so good, then he pulled it along the wooden floor and the wheels stuck, and the resulting crunch in his brain was so loud he jumped.

He stepped back from the hoover and pressed his hands over his ears. Images filled his brain—a mad rush to do something . . . something he couldn't quite see, and then the hoover—this hoover—running over his foot. Talking into the phone—*"Henry tried to kill me this morning. Ran over my foot, bloody dick-splash..."*—but who to? *"Be safe, Rupe. I love you."* Jesus. It wasn't a conversation, it was a message, and he'd left it for Rupert.

Oh God. Revelations had been battering him all day, but somehow, this one hit the hardest, like a train—no, fuck, like a speeding car. Jodi sank to the floor as another chunk of reality slotted into place with a thud that shook his insides. He'd left the message right before the accident, he was sure of it, and the sickening crunch in his brain hadn't been an epiphany at all, it was a memory, a real one, and Jesus Christ, it *hurt*.

Jodi sat on the floor for a long time. His mind-bending headache faded, and no more memories came to him, but the sensation that something had yet again changed remained. He gazed around the half-tidy flat. Over recent months, he'd come to accept it was his home, that it had been way before the accident, but until this moment, it had never felt familiar, safe, or warm, especially when he was home alone . . . alone without Rupert.

He was warm now, even without the hoodie he usually wore indoors. His newfound energy had returned. He stood and considered the hoover. The brush attachment was fucked and the hose bound together with duct tape. Damn thing looked like a prop from a sci-fi film. *Henry.* The name was emblazoned on the side of the battered machine. Jodi wondered why they hadn't bought a new one. Perhaps he'd ask when Rupert came back.

If Rupert comes back. Jodi pictured the bewildered frustration in Rupert's gaze before he'd fled the flat. Despite Jodi's almost constant state of introspection, and the lingering disquiet from discovering Rupert had kept something so huge from him, Jodi felt Rupert's distress like it was his own. Rupert had lost as much as Jodi—perhaps more.

I wouldn't blame him if he ran for the fucking hills.

Though common sense told him Rupert could've abandoned him long ago if he'd really wanted to, the thought of Rupert doing just that was too much to bear. Jodi plugged the hoover in and switched it on. A whistling shriek filled the room, along with the scent of a damp dog, and Jodi wrinkled his nose. It smelt like the bag hadn't been changed for months . . . It probably hadn't.

He searched the cupboard for spare bags. Found them and replaced the old one. The hoover still stank, but it was likely as good as it was going to get. He set to work hoovering every available surface in the flat.

He'd just finished the skirting boards in the bedroom when the front door opened and Indie's bell-like voice filtered through the flat. But she didn't come looking for Jodi, and disappointment swept over him, an emotion that puzzled him as he unplugged the hoover, retracted the chord, and stowed it away in the cupboard. By all accounts, he hadn't seen Indie since a week before the accident, and, of course, he didn't remember that meeting—or her—so why did he crave her company so much now, twenty-four hours after her mother had forced a pretty fucking awkward reunion?

"What happened in here?"

Jodi jumped, though he didn't know why. Rupert *always* checked on him when he came home, no matter how twat-ish Jodi had been to him before he left. Except, Jodi hadn't been a dick this time, had he? Jodi had no—

"Seriously. What the hell happened?"

"I cleaned up a bit."

"A bit? Looks like an army of maids had a party in here."

Jodi shut the cupboard door with more care than necessary, unable to tell if Rupert's tone carried any humour. Had he done the wrong thing by cleaning up? Did Rupert like it messy? Or was it simply that, covered in sweat and dust, his eye half-closed from the persistent ache in his brain, Jodi was an even less attractive prospect than he'd been before Rupert went out? *Gone are the old days, eh?* "Sorry."

"Don't be sorry, boyo. I'm just surprised. It's been a while since you pulled your Dot Cotton routine."

"Dot bloody Cotton?"

Rupert was grinning when Jodi found the balls to turn round, though it seemed strained. "You used to be obsessed, in a healthy way, not like OCD, or anything. You liked things clean and tidy. Everything had its place."

"What happened?"

Rupert stared at Jodi like he'd grown horns. "What do you think? The accident happened and no one was ever here. Then you—we came home and nothing fucking changed."

Jodi didn't miss Rupert's slip, and anger surged in his veins. *It's not my fault I got my head caved in.* But the emotion was short-lived. Rupert had rarely snapped at him since he came home from hospital, leading Jodi to believe he hadn't much before either, which meant that Rupert was the kind of bloke who only spoke harshly when he was upset.

"I'm sorry," Jodi said. "I know it's hard to believe, but I didn't notice the mess until today, or I would've done it sooner."

"It's okay, mate."

"No, no, it's not. I don't work, or have a kid; I've got nothing to do but sit around this shithole, so it shouldn't *be* a shithole."

"Well, it's not now, is it?"

Jodi grumbled. "That's not the point. I can't believe it's been like this for so long. I swear, I looked around today, and it was like a lightbulb came on. I couldn't stop until everything was done."

He left out the hours he'd spent staring at the dusty floor, trying to match the churning emotions in his gut with the fragmented memories his delinquent brain had kept throwing up when he least expected them. Something told him that would fast quench the bare hint of a genuine smile that was dancing on Rupert's face.

"You know, that's Jodi of old," Rupert said. "Drove me up the wall, rearranging your DVDs at three in the morning 'cause you couldn't sleep knowing they weren't in alphabetical order, and that was without the obsessive cleaning."

"Obsessive?"

"Okay, I'm exaggerating. I guess I could've kept on top of it a little better all this time, but I think, maybe, I might have been waiting for you to do it, or *want* to do it, like I thought you doing the bloody dusting would fix everything else. Stupid, eh?"

"Nothing about this is stupid. I feel like I've wiped cobwebs from my eyes. It's been a hell of a day."

Rupert hummed his agreement. "Sure has. Listen, I need to get Indie to bed soon, but she's dying to come and watch those videos with you. Would you mind keeping her busy for a bit? I'm not going anywhere, but I've got some calls to make."

"Of course. Send her in. Do you want—"

"Boyo, please. I don't need or want anything more than I've got already."

For the second time that day, Rupert left Jodi hanging, turning on his heel and fleeing the room before Jodi could blink.

Indie appeared a few moments later, dressed in pink pyjamas and clutching the wolf Jodi had retrieved from the kitchen for her the night before. "Can we watch Bucky now?"

Lacking any brighter ideas, Jodi picked up the TV remote and flicked on the VHS Indie had put on earlier in the day. The lime-green space rabbit filled the screen. Indie smiled, and Jodi found himself under her spell. She sprang onto his bed and burrowed under the covers, holding the duvet up for him to do the same. Powerless to refuse, Jodi obeyed and crawled into bed.

Indie cuddled into his side and put her head on his chest. "It's nicer in here than earlier. Did you put the fairy dust down?"

"The what?"

"That white stuff you put on the rugs to make the fairies' feet smell nice. Daddy says it makes Henry stink less too."

For a moment, Jodi was lost again. *Who the fuck is Henry?* But then the hoover appeared in his brain, neatly put away in the cupboard . . . directly below the bottle of Shake n' Vac. "I didn't use it today. Forgot it was there. You can do it for me next time, if you like?"

Yeah, 'cause that's every little girl's dream, isn't it? To help her dad's retarded boyfriend destink the pit he calls home?

The venom lacing the errant thought caught Jodi off guard. Did Rupert see him that way? Did Indie? Two days ago it hadn't mattered; now it mattered more than anything.

Indie hadn't answered Jodi's question, or, if she had, Jodi had missed it in the ramblings of the devil on his shoulder. He looked down, but she was asleep, the wolf squashed under her arm and her thumb jammed in her mouth. Jodi smiled and pushed her fine hair off her forehead. Her innocence was a balm to the riot playing everywhere else he turned, and it wasn't long before his own eyes felt heavy.

"Still awake in here?"

Jodi opened his eyes to find the TV had switched itself off and the room was in darkness, something that didn't bother him with Indie safe in his arms. Or perhaps it was the fond smile Rupert was treating him to from the open door. "I think so."

Rupert snorted and ventured closer. He reached under the covers and deftly plucked Indie from Jodi's grasp. He tucked her against his chest and padded out of the room, presumably to put her to bed, though Jodi had no idea what the time was.

A few minutes later, Rupert returned to his leaning post in the doorway. "You okay?"

"Me?" Jodi sat up. "I'm good. What about you? How did your phone calls go?"

Rupert grimaced. "I could do without taking any more days off work, but it is what it is. Indie—and you—you both come first. Who needs money, right?"

Money wasn't something that had occurred to Jodi in a very long time, and the bolt of common sense that struck him felt, as ever, like a sledgehammer. Tottenham wasn't an exclusive area of the capital, but Jodi remembered enough general knowledge to know that London property prices were insane, especially compared to a firefighter's salary—a firefighter with a child to support. "How the hell are we managing?"

"Managing? You mean financially?"

"Yeah. How much is the mortgage on this place?"

Rupert frowned. "A thousand, plus bills, food, and everything else, but I don't want you to worry about that. You took out a critical-illness policy when you got the mortgage. It doesn't cover it all, but we're doing okay."

"I should go back to work."

"No, you should concentrate on your recovery. That's what insurance is for. And anyway, do you honestly feel up to spending eighteen hours a day staring at a computer screen, like you used to?"

"Eighteen hours a day?" Just the thought of it was enough to turn up the volume on Jodi's perpetual headache. "Did I really work that much?"

"Sometimes. We both used to work a lot."

Rupert didn't have to explain why he'd cut his hours down—even Jodi could figure that. "That insurance policy won't pay out forever. What are we going to do if I can't go back to work?"

"Nothing," Rupert said. "All *you* need to do is get better, and not worry about things I've got under control."

"But—"

"But nothing. You looked after me for years. It's time you let me return the favour."

Rupert left the room again. Jodi thought about following him and forcing him to talk about the whole new can of worries they'd somehow opened. Jodi couldn't comprehend going back to a life he couldn't remember, but, more than anything, all he wanted was to throw his arms around Rupert and kiss him—kiss him until both of them believed everything was, eventually, going to be okay. *'Cause it will be okay, won't it?*

Jodi had no idea. His heart screamed at him to force his tired body from the bed and chase Rupert down so they could close the door on the doubt that had hurt them both so much, but he didn't move. Rupert loved him, of that Jodi was certain, but loving him and wanting—desiring—him weren't the same thing, and as Jodi drifted to sleep, the courage to find out how Rupert truly felt deserted him.

Chapter SIXTEEN

"**I** just don't get it." Rupert walked out of the fire station and turned his face into the drizzle, letting it refresh his scratchy, sleep-deprived eyes. "He says he still doesn't remember anything, but he keeps doing all this shit that he used to do, like he does remember. It doesn't make any fucking sense."

"Hang on." Sophie closed a door at the end of the crackly phone line. "Since when has anything about this made sense? He recalibrated my MacBook for me when he came over yesterday, but he doesn't remember learning to use the one he bought himself two years ago."

"You should see the living room too," Rupert said. "Remember he was on about moving the couch to the back wall last summer?"

"Don't tell me he's gone and done it?"

"Yup. I came home to find he'd moved the whole room around—the furniture, the TV, everything. Thought I'd walked into the wrong flat."

Sophie laughed, but Rupert couldn't find any humour in the situation. The flat looked different every time he came home, and after months and months of upheaval and heartache, Jodi's renewed housekeeping obsession was taking some getting used to.

"Anyway," Rupert said. "I'll let you get on. Sorry for bending your ear. I didn't know who else to call. I miss you."

Sophie's answering sigh was hard to take. "I know, hon. I miss you too. It feels weird sleeping in my own bed so often, but it's better for everyone. Jodi needs to think about you now, not that he needs much encouraging."

She probably meant to cheer Rupert up. Everyone else seemed to think the progress Jodi had made over the past month was nothing short of miraculous—and something to celebrate, but Rupert hadn't seen much to rejoice about. So what if Jodi now knew Rupert was— had been, whatever—his lover before the accident? Indie's sleeping arrangements aside, not much had really changed. Jodi was asleep every time Rupert came home, or exercising, or cleaning. What the hell was Rupert supposed to do? Wrestle the hoover from him and demand to know exactly where this vague imitation of their lost relationship was going?

Yeah, because things weren't fucked up enough already.

He wished Sophie a good night and let her get back to her own life with a heavy heart. He'd meant it when he said he missed her. Jodi could fend for himself when Rupert was at work, and with Indie slotting neatly back into life at the flat like she'd never been gone, there was no need for Sophie to stay over as much. In fact, it had been a week or so since Rupert had last seen her at all, and her absence was like another punch to the gut. Missing someone, even when they were right there, seemed to be what his life had become.

He caught the Tube heading north and found a seat, slouching with his hood up and his earphones jammed in. London wasn't a city where strangers interacted much, but he kept his gaze down anyway. He wasn't in the mood for half smiles and pointless small talk.

Forty minutes later, he walked into the flat to find Jodi working through the strengthening exercises for his injured arm. *Great.* Rupert ducked into the kitchen without a word and opened the fridge. A few months ago, watching Jodi struggle to so much as touch his toes had been enough to move Rupert to tears, but things had changed in recent weeks. Now, Rupert could hardly look at Jodi's flushed cheeks and sweat-sheened skin without his eyes watering for an entirely different reason—one that made Rupert hang his head in shame. What kind of bloke perved over someone while they recovered from a feckin' brain injury?

A bloke like Rupert, apparently.

"Rupe?"

Jesus Christ, I wish he'd stop calling me that. Rupert pulled his head from the fridge. "Yeah?"

Jodi grinned. "You okay? You scuttled in here with a face like a drop-kicked pie."

And there was another thing Rupert couldn't get used to: the reemergence of Jodi's *ridiculous* sense of humour. Rupert had spent four years laughing until his stomach ached, and so many months yearning for Jodi to raise a smile, but now, faced with Jodi's relaxed grin, Rupert felt like puking. *I should probably tell him that I'm a complete fucking pervert.* "Did you take your tablets?"

"Yeah." Jodi's smile faded. "I ate lunch, went to the ortho quack, and did my exercises, then I managed to buy a loaf of bread from the Tube station without trying to pay with bananas."

"The Tube station? What were you doing there?"

Jodi looked at Rupert like he was an idiot. "Coming home from the hospital. My TARDIS is broken."

"You took the underground?" Rupert couldn't hide his surprise. He hadn't taken Jodi on the Tube since his meltdown a few months ago, and Sophie hadn't for even longer. Jodi didn't like the Tube, not since the accident. "Was it okay?"

"It was fine. I've been doing it for a while now. Face the fear, and all that."

Rupert ignored the unease that came with knowing Jodi had been on the Tube by himself. "What was it you were afraid of?"

"The dark." Jodi shrugged, like it was nothing. "I didn't realise that's what it was at first, but it felt the same as when you used to turn the light off and close the door when you put me to bed. Like I was trapped in a hole, like I was—"

"Locked in," Rupert finished. "That was one of my biggest fears, you know, when you were in that bloody coma. That your senses were still working, you just couldn't tell us. It was worse than imagining you dying..."

He didn't go on. Didn't have to. Jodi stepped closer to Rupert and closed his hand around Rupert's arm, his gaze suddenly darker, his grip tight and brutal. "I *wasn't* locked in. I don't remember anything about it. First thing I knew, I was waking up to your face."

Rupert laughed bitterly. "And it was the last thing you wanted to see, right?"

"No," Jodi snapped. "I just didn't know why I was seeing it, or where I was, or why every part of me hurt so much I wished I was fucking dead."

Jodi stormed out of the room. A minute later, the bedroom door slammed shut. Rupert sucked in a shaky breath, rocked, as usual, by the sheer speed he and Jodi could tumble into a row neither of them understood. He closed his eyes and counted to ten, trying to pull himself back to the few moments when he'd truly felt encouraged by Jodi's progress.

His mind took him to the morning after Indie's impromptu arrival. After a conversation Rupert was still trying to wrap his mind around, Jodi had fallen asleep beside him, and stayed asleep for most of the day, save a few nonsensical mumbles. For the few hours Rupert had been able to watch over him, he hadn't dared close his eyes, terrified he'd wake up—on the couch—to find Indie's bed empty and Jodi's gaze as blankly apathetic as it had ever been. Nothing had prepared him for the week that followed, those few blissful days when he'd almost been able to convince himself everything was going to be okay. Jodi seemed fascinated by Indie, and for a while, they'd shut the rest of the world out.

But it hadn't lasted. Indie had gone back to Jen's, and the very next day, Jodi had come home from a neurologist's appointment in the blackest mood Rupert had ever seen. He hadn't spoken for two days and now, two weeks later, Rupert still didn't know why. And Jodi's sudden return to good humour on the third day had made even less sense. *How the hell am I supposed to keep up?*

Rupert put the kettle on, then flicked it off. Opened the fridge, shut it again. Then, with world-weary sigh, left the kitchen to face the music.

He found Jodi sitting on the bedroom floor, squinting at something on his laptop screen.

"Sorry for being a dick," Rupert said. "I'm knackered, not that I'm making excuses."

Jodi didn't look up. "Don't worry about it. Sophie told me I've been a dick to you ever since the accident."

"That's a little harsh."

"Is it? She seemed to think she was being kind."

Rupert ventured further into the room. "When did you speak to her?"

"This afternoon. She rings me every day after work."

"Ah, like she used to, eh?"

"Yeah?" Jodi finally tore his gaze from the laptop. "I like that. I was worried I'd never get to talk to her when she stopped staying over. I couldn't work out how the three of us—and Indie—all fit together."

"Like a melted welly boot."

"What?"

"Your words, not mine." Jodi stared, clearly mystified. Rupert let it go and sat on the bed, trying not to read over Jodi's shoulder. "Are you hungry?"

"No."

"Sure? I'm going down the chippie."

"I'm fine—" Jodi started to shake his head, then appeared to think better of it. "Actually, can I come with you?"

As if Rupert could refuse. As if he wanted to, because despite his fears that Jodi's newfound well-being was too good to be true, he couldn't resist an opportunity to do something so normal with him, sloping off down the chip shop like they used to.

While Rupert had been contemplating what his life had become, with his head in the fridge, outside, it had grown dark. Jodi gazed up at the stars like he'd never seen them, apparently oblivious to the Friday-evening bustle of Tottenham's streets. "I like nighttime better, don't I?"

"Aye, you're a night owl."

"A night owl who's scared of the dark? What a cunt."

"We've been over that." Rupert took Jodi's arm to cross the road at the traffic light fifty yards away from where he'd been run down. "Besides, you've been taking the Tube, haven't you? Doesn't seem like you're scared of anything."

Jodi grunted. "Still sleep with the fucking lamp on, though."

"So?"

Jodi's only answer was a glare.

Rupert guided him across the road, then released his arm. "What were you doing on your laptop? Working?"

"Hmm?" Jodi blinked like he'd forgotten Rupert was there. "Oh, no. I was doing some memory exercises online. Trying to retrain my brain." He pulled a face that, despite the dark scruff on his chin, made him look like a twelve-year-old.

Rupert chuckled. "How's that going?"

"Shite, but I'm not surprised. Dr. Nevis told me I'm pretty much done with my neurological recovery. He doesn't think I'm going to get any cleverer."

Rupert frowned. "When did he say that?"

"A while ago."

Rupert did the maths. "A while as in . . . about two weeks ago?"

"If you say so."

"Makes sense," Rupert said. "You didn't say a word all weekend after your last appointment."

Jodi winced. "Sorry. It kind of threw me."

"I get that, but why didn't you tell me later on?"

"You weren't here. You went to work on Monday and you didn't come home till Wednesday morning. I was over it by then."

It was Rupert's turn to be contrite. A factory fire in Stockwell had pulled Green Watch out of their jurisdiction and stretched Rupert's shift so far into the following day there had been little point going home before the next one. "How do you feel about it now?"

Jodi shrugged. "Dunno. Some days it doesn't seem to matter, and others it's the worst shit in the world."

"What is?"

"That I have to start from the beginning with the things I want the most, and I don't even know if you want them too."

They'd reached the chip shop, and Jodi ducked inside, leaving Rupert with his mouth open. *Is he serious?* How on earth could Jodi not know Rupert wanted him back—wanted him now—more than anything in the world?

He followed Jodi inside and found him at the back of the queue, staring at the hot-hold counter, clearly bemused. "I don't know what I usually have."

"What do you *want*?"

"Are we still talking about chips?"

"You tell me."

But Jodi couldn't, and Rupert knew it. He tapped his finger on the warm glass of the hot-hold counter. "You usually have two steak pies, large chips, mushy peas, and a battered sausage."

"Two pies? Really?"

Jodi looked so horrified that Rupert couldn't help chuckling. "Shall we just get one to start with? Ease you in?"

They settled on a pie, a bag of chips, and a couple of jumbo sausages, and took it all home to share. On the way, Rupert waited for Jodi to pick up the conversation where he'd left off, but he didn't, and back in the flat, without Tottenham's busy streets as a buffer between them, an awkward silence took hold, suffocating the tentative good humour they'd shared in the chip shop.

Rupert picked at his food, his agitation growing as he watched Jodi do the same, like they'd got off the roundabout for the hundredth time and gone back to the start. Frustration overwhelmed him. "I'm sick of this. It's doing my feckin' head in."

He got up and tossed his plate on the coffee table, storming into the kitchen without waiting for Jodi's response—if there was to be one. Chances were, there wouldn't be. They'd become experts at half conversations that went nowhere. Masters of scratching a wound until it was open and bleeding, and then leaving it to fester.

He didn't expect Jodi to follow him.

Jodi chucked his own plate in the sink. Chips scattered across the draining board. "It's doing *your* head in? At least you know what you're fucking missing, if you're missing it at all? Maybe you're not. Maybe you dodged a bullet, eh?"

"What?"

"Oh, come on. Just because we were together before, doesn't mean we should've been. Doesn't mean we were happy, does it?"

"Happy? Of course we were— What the fuck? What makes you think we weren't happy?"

"You don't seem happy now."

"What have I got to be happy about? So, you know we were together ... doesn't change much. You still don't want me."

"Don't I?"

"Do you?" Rupert hadn't meant to challenge Jodi so bluntly, but the words were out before he could stop them, laid bare between them.

"I *do* want you," Jodi said. "I just don't know if that means I wanna bang you and leave, or hold you all night long after. And I don't know how to learn. I thought it would come back to me, eventually, but Dr. Nevis says it probably won't, that if I want to be with you, we have to start over again. And I don't know how to do that. Or if you even want to. Why the fuck would you? Why would you—"

Jodi's voice cracked. He clamped a shaky hand over his mouth briefly, then let it drop, fixing Rupert with a gaze that hurt Rupert's heart. "I'm broken, Rupert, and I can't be fixed. Why the hell would you want me now?"

"Jodi." Rupert closed the distance between them and gripped Jodi's shoulders. Only Jodi's injuries stopped Rupert from shaking him. "Jodi, you're not bloody broken, you hear me? And I do want you, as much as I ever did, I just . . . I don't know what that says about me. I'm your carer, Jodi. I shouldn't be thinking about stuff like that. It's not right."

"Oh God." Jodi twisted himself from Rupert's grasp and abruptly sat on the floor, like his legs wouldn't hold him any longer.

Alarmed, Rupert dropped beside him and took his face in his hands. "What is it? Are you okay? Are you dizzy?"

"I'm fine." Jodi pushed Rupert's hands away. "It just feels like we're going round in circles. Am I being totally fucking dense, or are we both saying the same thing? You think it's wrong to want a broken man, and I think I'm too broken for you to want me in the first place?"

Rupert replayed Jodi's words. Matched them with his own, then sat back on his heels as a crashing wave of perspective rocked his equilibrium. "Jesus."

Jodi laughed humourlessly. "I know, right? I think one of us needs to spell it out, and it has to be you, because I need to believe it. Will you do that for me? Please? I need to know it's real."

"It's real, boyo. I promise." But was it? Jodi's emotions had been volatile and unreliable since the accident, often swinging from one inappropriate reaction to another too fast for Rupert to keep up. What if this was just a cruel trick played by the shadow clouding his brain? What if they woke up tomorrow and Jodi hated him all over again?

He never hated me. He just didn't know me. And as far as being wrong goes . . . we're both bloody wrong, or not. Perhaps we never were.

For once, Rupert's relentless inner monologue was worth listening to. He crawled closer to Jodi and put his hands on his bent knees, waiting for Jodi to meet his gaze. It didn't happen.

"Listen to me," Rupert said. "Something terrible happened to you, to us, and it took everything we had. This," he gestured around the dimly lit kitchen, "all of this, is just the remnants, but it's enough for us to build something new. I want to, Jodi, because I want *you*, because I love you. I know you can't say the same right now, but maybe, if we go back to the start, you might learn to love me again."

Jodi finally looked up. His eyes were red-rimmed and watery. "Do you really love me?"

"Yes. Have done since the moment I met you."

"Do you want me?"

"More than ever. It just scares me a bit."

"I know how that feels," Jodi said. "But I wish I'd known the rest of it from the beginning."

Rupert swiped at his face. "I'm so sorry. I told you every day until you started talking, then I got scared, because you were scared too, and I didn't want me loving you to be the reason you couldn't get better."

Jodi moved, his body blurring in Rupert's gaze until they were nose to nose. "I think I got better *because* you still loved me, even though I was gone. I must have known on some level, because it feels so right now."

"Yeah?"

"Yeah. Now all we need to do is figure out how to make it awesome."

"Awesome?"

"Indie told me we were awesome. She said I made you happy. I want to do that again."

"Sounds like we want a lot of things." Rupert blew out a breath.

Jodi frowned. "Is that bad?"

"No, just means we've got a lot of work to do."

"Then we're going to need some more chips. I kinda chucked mine away."

Rupert laughed, feeling somehow lighter than he had in a long time. "Get your coat then, boyo. Chippie shuts in ten."

Chapter
SEVENTEEN

That night, with Rupert by his side, Jodi slept better than he could ever remember doing before: long, deep, and pain-free. He felt like he'd just blinked when he opened his eyes in the morning. Shame he hadn't meant to fall asleep in the first place.

He rolled over, searching for Rupert's warmth, but found only cool sheets. He bolted upright. Panic roared through him. Had he dreamed it all? Had the long hours talking into the night, stretched out on the bed with a bag of chips between them, been nothing more than a figment of his defunct imagination?

"Easy, boyo." Rupert popped up from nowhere at the side of the bed, his hand comforting and warm on Jodi's knee. "Gonna give yourself whiplash, sitting up like that. What's the matter?"

Jodi shrugged, unwilling to admit he'd been on the verge of a meltdown. "What are you doing on the floor?"

"Cleaning up. We passed out in a bit of a mess last night."

"Did I fall asleep first?"

"Yup." Rupert grinned. "With a mouthful of chips and a can of Tizer in your hand. Reminded me of those nights you used to get tanked on JD and wait up for me, only to KO before you took your bloody clothes—"

Rupert stopped, flushing guiltily.

"Go on," Jodi said. "Tell me."

"Not sure it's something you want to know."

"Why do you think that?"

Rupert didn't answer. Jodi replayed his last sentence. *". . . only to KO before you took your bloody clothes—"* "Did I summon you home on a promise and let you down?"

"You've never let me down, Jodi."

It was sweet of Rupert to say, but Jodi doubted it was true. Whoever he used to be, he couldn't have been perfect. Lord knew, he wasn't now. "Did we have sex a lot?"

The blush returned full force to Rupert's fair cheeks. He got awkwardly to his feet and made a meal out of stuffing crumpled chip papers in the nearby bin. "Why do you want to talk about that?"

"Talked about everything else last night, didn't we?"

"Aye, but we never figured out what we were going to do about it." Rupert left the room.

Jodi thought about following, but something told him to stay put and do all the things Rupert usually had to remind him to do.

He'd just swallowed the last of his morning medication when Rupert reappeared, sheepishly brandishing a mug of tea and a plate of Nutella toast.

"Sorry I keep walking out on you," he said. "This is way harder than I ever imagined it would be."

"What is?"

"You getting better. I thought we'd done the hard bit, but it feels like we're just getting started."

Jodi twisted the cap back on his antiseizure drug bottle. "Is that why you won't talk about sex?"

"Jesus, Jodi." Rupert scrubbed a hand down his face. "Why do you suddenly want to talk about that?"

"Because it was the first thing that came back."

"What?"

Shit. It may have been the first part of his attraction to Rupert that had returned, but it was the last thing Jodi had ever intended to say. Still, there wasn't much he could do to take it back. He got up and turned away while he stripped off the T-shirt he'd slept in and rummaged in a drawer for a clean one. "I started dreaming about you a few months ago before I . . . before I knew about, um, us."

"Dreaming?"

"Yeah." Jodi had never been so glad he couldn't see Rupert's face. "Except it happened when I was awake too."

"What kind of dreams?"

"Erm . . ."

"Oh."

The single syllable wrapped Jodi in a cloak of heat. He turned around. Rupert was staring at him, eyes wide. Jodi chanced a grin, and tried not to fixate on Rupert's teeth digging into his bottom lip. "Whatever you're thinking, you're probably right."

"You don't want to know what I'm thinking."

"Don't I?"

"I have no idea, but I know I sure as hell don't want to tell you."

Jodi pulled a T-shirt on. Part of him wanted to take pity on Rupert and leave it alone, but the more selfish part of him won out. "I kept thinking about being with you. It scared the shit out of me for a while before I realised it was real. It drove me fucking crazy. I thought I was a freak."

Rupert flinched. "Why would you think that?"

"Why do you think? I didn't know I was supposed to feel that way, or that you felt that way about me."

"I'm so sorry."

"Don't be," Jodi said. "Just don't keep anything else from me. I know you're worried about putting ideas in my head, but you don't need to be—they're already there. Now I just need to know the truth."

"The truth about what?"

Jodi sighed. "Have you always found it so hard to talk about sex?"

Rupert came further into the room and sat on the edge of the bed. "Actually, yes, but I'd never really tried until I met you. Before then, I did everything I could not to even think about it."

"But you were married before you met me. Why didn't you think about sex then?"

"I was married to a woman. The kind of sex *you're* talking about scared the bejesus out of me."

"Oh." Jodi processed Rupert's words and tried to match them with the "Rupert Files" in his brain. "So, you were married, then you split up and came out? And then you met me?"

"Pretty much. Look, I'm not saying we can't talk about it. I know we should . . . that we probably need to. Give me some time, yeah? I'm still getting my head around the fact that you want to be in the same room as me again."

Jodi felt bad then. It was hard enough to keep up with himself. How the hell did he expect Rupert to? "I'm sorry."

"I told you: don't be. I'm over the feckin' moon. I just need a moment to pull myself together."

Except that moment was going to be far longer, as Rupert had to leave for work and he wouldn't be back until the evening. Jodi tried to hide his disappointment. Failed. Rupert put two fingers under Jodi's chin and gently forced him to meet his gaze.

"We can talk about this later, if you still want to. I promise I won't freak out. I'm in this for as long as you want me. Just gotta man up."

It was on the tip of Jodi's tongue to tell Rupert he was all the man he'd ever need, but was that true? How many men had come before him? Would Rupert know the answer? Did Jodi dare ask?

"Jodi?"

"Hmm?"

Rupert shook his head slightly. "This is surreal, but I've got to go. Are you going to be okay today? You've got an appointment with Ken, haven't you?"

Jodi scowled. *Fucking Ken* . . . "I'll be fine. Do we need any shopping?"

"Maybe some bread and some milk? Haven't had a cuppa yet today. Gonna be raging by the time I get to work. Can you remember the PIN for your debit card?"

"Nope. Gonna get it tattooed on my arse."

"Good luck looking it up when you're at the front of the queue in Sainsbury's. It's one-seven-nine-three. Start from number one and draw a U shape." Rupert stood and drifted toward the door. "Sure you're going to be okay?"

"I'll be *fine*," Jodi snapped. "Jesus. It's not like you've never left me."

"Don't be an arse."

"Excuse me?"

Rupert fixed Jodi with a steady gaze. "I said, 'Don't be an arse.' It's not unreasonable for me to worry about you a little bit. The last time I left you without a second thought, you got mowed down by a stolen car."

Guilt returned full force. Jodi closed his eyes and imagined how he'd feel if their roles were reversed—if Rupert was snatched away when Jodi was just beginning to comprehend loving him.

There was no worse feeling. There couldn't be. Jodi opened his eyes and found Rupert on his knees in front of him. "Don't leave me," Jodi said. "When you come home tonight, I need you to sleep in the bed with me. I don't care about the sex—I don't even know what the fuck I'm talking about . . . I can't remember it, but I need you with me. I can't be away from you anymore."

Rupert cupped Jodi's face and stroked his cheek with the pad of his thumb. "If that's what you want, boyo. I'm there, every night I'm home. I love you."

"I love you too."

"So things are good at home, then?"

"Hmm?" Jodi tore his gaze from the window and struggled to focus on Ken. "Oh, um, yeah. It's all kind of falling into place. At least, I think it is. It's not like I know what it should be like."

Ken raised an eyebrow. "Sounds to me like you know exactly what you want, and why can't that be how your life should be?"

"You tell me."

"I don't need to, Jodi. You might not remember every moment of your past, but you know how you feel right now. You love Rupert. You want to be with him. If that's what Rupert wants too, there's no reason you can't have it. Is it what Rupert wants?"

"He says it is." Jodi chewed on his lip. "He wouldn't lie, would he?"

"What do you think?"

"I think— I know he loves me. I knew it before he told me."

Ken smiled. "Then focus on that and don't let yourself be distracted by any negative thoughts. Talk them out, with Rupert or with me, and then move forward. There might be bumps in the road, but you and Rupert have overcome so much already, you should both be proud of how far you've come."

Jodi couldn't speak for Rupert, but as a faint sense of pride bloomed in his belly, he realised Ken was right. So much had changed in the last few weeks alone, but it was all for the good. He was no longer lost and lonely; he was loved, like he'd always been, only now he knew it, believed it, and had made it his own.

He left Ken and began heading home, stopping at the supermarket for milk. On the few occasions he'd ventured out to do the shopping alone since the accident, he'd deliberately chosen the quiet corner shop near the flat, ducking in and out with the exact change, counting it carefully before he went in. Today, with his last conversation with Rupert keeping him company, he braved the Sainsbury's he and Rupert had bought the toad-in-the-hole ingredients from all those weeks ago.

The shop was busy. Nerves tickled Jodi as he searched for the milk aisle. It was a big store, but as he navigated through it, the ceiling seemed to get lower with every step. Anxiety roared in his ears, growing louder and louder, until the urge to bolt and run became too strong to ignore.

Just gotta man up. Jodi sucked in a breath and pulled his phone from his pocket. He craved Rupert's gentle, comforting voice, but Rupert was on shift and couldn't answer. So he rang Sophie, preempting her usual afternoon call.

"I'm in Sainsbury's," he said by way of greeting. "I don't like it."

Sophie's laugh was like a bell. "Oh honey. Are you by yourself?"

"Yup. Tied my laces myself and everything."

"Don't be a dick."

Jodi stopped walking, ignoring the trolley that banged into his ankles from behind. "Am I really that bad? Rupert called me an arse this morning."

"Did he mean it?"

"I think so, and he wasn't wrong. I forget sometimes how much this has hurt him. It's like that gap in my head swallows me up."

"But that doesn't happen as much as it used to, does it? And the gap's getting smaller."

Another trolley collided with Jodi's ankles. He moved out of the way and found a quiet-ish spot by the lacto-free milk. "Not anymore it's not. Dr. Nevis says I'm probably done with my neurological recovery."

"I know that," Sophie said. "But he also said that nothing was definite. Anything could happen, Jodi. Besides, even if you never remember another thing, you've got the rest of your life to plug that gap with new memories. You won't need to be certain of your old past, because you'll have a new one."

It sounded pretty fanciful to Jodi, and he would've called bullshit to anyone else, but Sophie's dreams had always felt real. "He said he loves me."

"He does love you."

"I know. I love him too."

"I know."

"Do *you* love me?"

Sophie sighed. "Of course I do—not the same way Rupert does, though. I thought I did for a while after the accident, but I don't."

"What does that mean?"

"It means you're the love of my life—for now, at least, and even though I adore Rupert, there was a tiny twat-ish part of me that enjoyed the fact that you forgot about him and loved me all over again. But I was wrong to like that. I feel so much better knowing you and Rupert are working things out. It's like the stars are aligning."

Sophie finished her monologue with another sigh, and Jodi wanted to cry. He often forgot that damn-fucking car had hit Sophie too. "I'm sorry."

"Don't be sorry, Jodi. Don't you bloody dare. We've had this conversation a hundred times. I want you to be happy. Rupert makes you happy. Just let him."

"I'm trying," Jodi said. "I think I'm freaking him out, though. Reckon he's got too used to me being a wanker."

"Be patient. He's waited this long for you. It's your turn to have a little faith."

Sophie said good-bye and hung up, leaving Jodi to realise that he was still in the milk aisle. He grabbed a pint of semi-skimmed and some butter. Logic took him to the bread section, where he picked up a sliced loaf. That done, he headed for the checkouts and found queues at every till.

Sod this. Jodi considered ditching the groceries and running for home, but then he pictured the empty bread bin and Rupert trying to have a cup of tea with no milk, and joined the shortest queue. A battle with the thinnest plastic bag in the world ensued, but with a little prompting from the "Rupert Files," he remembered the PIN for his debit card and made it out of the store with most of his dignity intact.

As ever, he was surprised at how uplifting it was to complete a bonehead task without a babysitter. Energy buzzed in his veins, and he didn't feel like going home to an empty flat. He didn't much fancy another supermarket excursion either, though, and shopping aside, he couldn't think of anything to do, or anyone he wanted to see. *Wait.* That wasn't true. He wanted to see Rupert. Jodi checked the time. It was nearly five; Rupert would be done in just over an hour. Which meant Jodi had plenty of time to retrace his steps and meet him from work.

It didn't take much deliberating. Jodi caught the Tube like he'd been doing it all his life, and made his way back toward Camberwell, where the hospital was. He was usually exhausted and dizzy after he'd taken the Tube to the hospital, disoriented from being rocked about for twelve long stops, but today, the surge of energy he'd had on the street outside the supermarket stayed with him, and he emerged in Brixton, a stop before the hospital, feeling like he could take on the world. Whether he'd win or not was another matter, but for now, searching out the fire station would have to do.

Luckily the maps app on his phone took care of that, and before long, Jodi found himself across the street from the listed building that housed Brixton's fire brigade. He checked the time again. Five to six. Perfect. Or was it? What if Rupert left through the back? Or finished late? What if Jodi had got it wrong and he wasn't there?

Nerves bubbled in Jodi's gut. Rupert had asked him for some time, but that was just about sex, right? He hadn't said he didn't want to see Jodi at all . . . No, of course he hadn't. He'd told Jodi he loved him and he would see him at home. Except Jodi wasn't at home. He was camped outside the fire station like a fucking stalker. Damn it. Why was it so hard to be a normal human being? Why couldn't he just stay at home and cook a pan of pasta like any other stay-at-home—

"What are you thinking so hard about?"

"Pasta." Jodi turned to face Rupert's warm grin, and all his worries faded away. "I was thinking I should've stayed at home and cooked it for you."

"You do make the best spag bol. The only thing better to come home to is your beautiful smile." Rupert's grin widened.

Jodi laughed. "Did you read that in the lonely hearts ads?"

"Nope. Made it up myself. Shoulda been a poet, eh?"

"Erm . . ."

"Don't answer that." Rupert brushed Jodi's hair out of his eyes. "Seriously, though. What brings you here? I thought your appointment was at two. You haven't been waiting out here all this time, have you?"

"No, I saw Ken, then I went to Sainsbury's, then I came back."

"Ah, you bought milk?"

"Yup. And bread and butter. Check me out."

"Awesome," Rupert said. "Did you take it home?"

"No, it's right—" Jodi looked down at his empty hands. "Shit. I left it on the Tube."

Rupert bit his lip, but it didn't contain the throaty chuckle that washed away Jodi's irritation at his own stupidity. "Don't worry about it. Who needs milk anyway?"

"You do. For your tea."

"So we'll get some more. Fuck it."

Rupert slipped his arm around Jodi's waist, and they started walking back the way Jodi had come. Jodi leaned into Rupert and absorbed his warmth, trying not to wonder if Rupert was touching him because he wanted to, or simply holding him up. Did it even matter? For a little while, Jodi convinced himself that it didn't. Everything else was either falling into place or carving itself a new one. Why would this be any different?

"Jodi?"

"Hmm?"

Rupert stopped walking and put his hands on Jodi's shoulders. "Can I try something?"

"Try something?"

"Yeah. It's probably something we should do at home, but everything seems so . . ." Rupert winced. "It gets so heavy there, you know? I just want to . . . Fuck it. I just want to kiss you in a place where you can run for the hills if you need to, and still have a home."

"You want to kiss me?"

Rupert grinned nervously. "I do. Is that okay?"

It was *very* okay, but Jodi couldn't quite find the words to say so. He covered Rupert's hands with his own and leaned forward, stretching his neck to reach Rupert's lips. He kissed Rupert once, twice, three times—light, gentle kisses—and then something changed. The air shifted, and Jodi needed more, much more, and he needed it *now*.

He released Rupert's hands and put his palms flat on Rupert's strong chest, shoving him back into the wall of a nearby bank. Rupert let out a surprised grunt, then he gripped Jodi's jacket and pulled him tight against him. "Don't play with me. I haven't got it in me to lose you again."

"You're not going to lose me." Jodi kissed Rupert harder this time, like he could drive Rupert's doubts away with clashing teeth and bruised lips. "I want this, Rupe. I want you, and that's never going to change. It's part of me. I can feel it."

"I can feel it too."

It took Jodi a moment to cotton on to what Rupert meant. Then he felt it: the mind-blowing sensation of Rupert's hard dick against his own. "Oh wow."

Rupert grinned, though Jodi didn't miss the flash of relief in his gaze. "Yeah. Wow. We still got it."

"'Still'? This crazy heat isn't new?"

"Not for me," Rupert said. "You're the only bloke I've ever been with, but you blew my mind from the start. It's always been incredible between us. Couldn't ask for more."

"You blew my mind." The echo of Jodi's own thoughts left him dizzy, but the good kind of dizzy: the heady, giddy kind that made him feel lighter than air until a growl from his stomach interrupted a chain of thought that was about to get *way* out of hand.

Rupert chuckled. "Jesus. I felt that too. Hungry, are ya?"

"Guess I must be. Does that mean we have to go home?"

"Do you want to go home?"

Jodi shrugged. There was nothing he wanted more than to hustle home with Rupert and let the chips fall where they may, but something—perhaps his own raging boner—told him they both needed to cool off before they hit the ground—the bed—running and fucked everything up all over again. "Can we eat somewhere else?"

"Sure. Got anywhere in mind?"

Of course he hadn't. Jodi hadn't eaten out in years—five to be exact if his sieve-like brain had its way. *Fuck it.* He pointed across the street to the first restaurant he saw.

"You want Moroccan barbecue?"

"Erm, yeah?"

Rupert laughed. "That's good enough for me. Let's go."

Chapter
EIGHTEEN

The restaurant was dark and warm, and the food spicy and rich. Rupert had never eaten anything like the fruity meat stew that had appeared after he'd pointed at the first word he'd recognised on the menu—"couscous," as it happened—and he hadn't had a beer in months.

"Go on," Jodi said. "Just have one. Fuck it, right?"

"Fuck it" seemed to be the mantra of the day. Rupert ordered a beer to go with the water he already had, and a bottle of dubious Moroccan lager turned up a few moments later. With the waiter gone, Rupert leaned forward and swiped some chicken from Jodi's plate. "Is it good?"

"It's lush," Jodi said. "Can I have some of yours?"

In answer, Rupert filled his fork and held it out, trying not to drool as Jodi wrapped his lips and tongue around it, all the while wondering how the most boring day in the world had morphed into a day where he couldn't stop smiling, or thinking about sex.

He blamed Jodi for that.

Still, Rupert couldn't help pinching himself. He'd come to accept Jodi would never be the same, but it seemed to matter less with each day that passed, and tonight? Watching Jodi inhale his food like he actually wanted to eat it while his kiss lingered on Rupert's lips? Yup. Had to be a dream.

"Can I smell your beer?"

"What?"

Jodi picked up Rupert's bottle of Casablanca. "I want to smell it. See if I miss it."

Sadness threatened Rupert's bubble of cumin-scented happiness. Jodi had been told that he'd never be able to safely drink again, that his brain would forever be sensitive to anything he ingested—booze, over-the-counter drugs, heavy doses of caffeine. They hadn't exactly partied the past four years away, but Rupert would miss the late nights sat on the kitchen floor, drinking whiskey, while Jodi ate Nutella from the jar with Indie's dippy egg spoon. And the morning cuppas, snatched before Rupert left for work, or stretched out on the couch when he came home from a night shift. He'd miss it all. Missed it already.

But he craved Jodi more than he could ever miss him, especially when Jodi was right there, sniffing Rupert's beer with a bemused frown that made Rupert want to climb across the table and kiss the shit out of him.

"I don't get it." Jodi put the bottle down. "It smells like piss."

"You must remember drinking it before you met me."

Jodi shrugged. "I do, but none of that seems real anymore. It used to feel like it had all just happened yesterday, but now it doesn't even feel like me. I'm not that interested in what I used to do."

"Yeah? Then why the sniff test?"

"To see if I'm really not that interested, or wallowing in denial."

Rupert didn't dare ask what Jodi had concluded by sticking a beer bottle up his nose. Sometimes, it was better for his sanity if he didn't know every little thing that filtered through Jodi's recovering brain. "Okay, so if we're leaving the past alone and staying in the present, how am I going to answer all the questions you want to ask me about our sex life?"

"I have a loophole."

"Which is?"

"Haven't thought of it yet. Fuck it. Tell me everything."

Jodi set his fork down. Rupert wanted to coax him into eating a bit more, but the truth was, now that the conversation had returned to sex, he didn't feel much like eating either.

Rupert pushed his plate away and swigged his beer. "I don't know where to start. You'll have to help me out."

"Who's the lube for?"

"What?" Rupert choked on gassy lager. "What lube?"

"The lube in the bedside table. The arse lube."

"Erm, it's for both of us, I s'pose, but that's not what you're really asking, is it?"

"Not exactly."

Rupert kind of wanted Jodi to spell it out so he knew for sure he wasn't about to jam his foot in his mouth, but this wasn't the time to be coy. If they wanted to move forward, those days were over. "The lube's for you, boyo. Always."

"We don't switch?"

"Never."

Jodi flushed. "That scares me."

"It would scare me too. In fact, it did—it all did, until you taught me how to do it right."

"Taught you?"

"I've never wanted to bottom, and for a long time, even after I left Jen and came out, I thought that made me, I don't know, not gay enough to call myself gay, or some shite, but you showed me otherwise. You showed me how loving a bloke was about far more than who put what where."

Jodi traced a pattern Rupert couldn't decipher on the jade-green tablecloth. "I've been trying not to think about that bit. I think I knew, on some level, that I was . . . that you . . . Fuck's sake. I knew I was the bottom. I just couldn't handle what I thought it meant."

Rupert raised an eyebrow. "What did you think it meant?"

"Probably everything I taught you it didn't. Or maybe I was scared. You've got a big dick, haven't you?"

As ever, Jodi's ability to swing a conversation like a waltzer made Rupert's head spin. "I guess you'll find out, soon enough, if you ever want to, but it doesn't matter. I'd never hurt you like that, or any other way. You have to know that."

"I do," Jodi said. "I'm still scared of it, but I want to do it, if you want to?"

They'd barely kissed. Talking about fucking felt surreal. Rupert reached across the table and took Jodi's hand, absorbing his tremble. "How about we just go home and share a bed? Sleep. Breathe. Be together. The rest will come in its own time."

Jodi nodded slowly. "Yeah. Let's do that. Let's go home to bed. You'll stay with me, won't you? Like you said?"

"Every night till you ask me not to."

Rupert took Jodi home with every intention of coaxing him into bed, tucking him up, then watching over him while he fell asleep. And perhaps Jodi let most of it happen with the same good intentions, but like everything recently, things changed in the blink of an eye. A rustle of clean sheets and a heated gaze. A brush of lips and bare skin on bare skin. Then clothes disappeared and suddenly Rupert found himself half-naked and on top of Jodi, on the verge of doing all the things he'd told himself he wouldn't do.

"Stop thinking." Jodi gripped Rupert's face and kissed him fiercely. "Just let it happen."

Rupert kissed Jodi back, pressing him deep into the mattress. "What do you want?"

"I don't know . . . I don't care. Please, I don't want to stop."

Rupert didn't want to stop either. Couldn't, even if he'd tried. He rolled over, taking Jodi with him so Jodi was above him, and raised his arms over his head, gripping the headboard and ceding control. Jodi met his gaze. Rupert nodded. *Take what you need. I'm yours.*

Jodi ran his hands over Rupert's bare chest. "I don't know what to do. I mean, I know what I'd do if you were a woman, but I haven't got a clue where to start with you."

"Maybe it's the same." Rupert drove his hips up gently. "Just do what feels good, like you taught me."

In answer, Jodi leaned down and blew warm air over Rupert's chest, then closed his lips around Rupert's nipple.

Rupert gasped and threw his head back. Jodi had always had a way with his lips and tongue and—*fuck*—his teeth. Closing his eyes, Rupert groaned, long and loud, thankful he'd seen the downstairs neighbours head out for a night at the bingo earlier.

Jodi moved down Rupert's body, exploring and reacquainting himself with Rupert's sensitive spots. He found every one with no guidance from Rupert—his ribs, his appendix scar. Then he reached

Rupert's waistband and froze briefly, before he fumbled with the button of Rupert's jeans.

He pulled them over Rupert's hips, taking Rupert's underwear with them. "Wow."

Heat flooded Rupert's cheeks. It felt like he'd had a perpetual boner ever since Jodi had first let slip that sex was on his mind, but he'd done everything he could to ignore it—cold showers, thinking of his bloody mother. He'd even gone as far as to pretend he didn't have a dick at all, and he hadn't had a wank in . . . damn. He couldn't remember. Since the accident, pleasuring himself had been the last thing on his mind, and before . . . Jodi had always done that shit for him.

And done it so well just the sketchy, surreal memories of those heady encounters were enough to make his cock jump.

Jodi jumped too. "Jesus. It's fucking huge."

"Piss off." Rupert hooked his hands under Jodi's shoulders and pulled him up the bed in one smooth movement. "Leave my dick alone if it scares you so much. We don't have to do anything—"

Jodi silenced him with another bruising kiss. Rupert took the hint and reached for Jodi's jeans, undoing them and sliding them over Jodi's slim hips. He left Jodi's boxers in place, but Jodi had other ideas.

"Fuck that," he said. "I want to be like you."

Rupert snorted. "No, you don't."

"I do."

"Why?"

Jodi wriggled out of his remaining clothes, then fixed Rupert with a shrewd stare. "Because you're a good man."

What that had to do with getting naked, Rupert had no idea, but coming from Jodi, a man Rupert had idolised as much as he'd loved . . . Jesus fecking Christ, could they do nothing without Rupert wanting to bawl his eyes out?

Apparently not, but Jodi straddled Rupert's chest before Rupert could dwell on it.

"I wouldn't do this to a woman," Jodi said. "Unless she asked me to."

Rupert eyed Jodi's cock as it carved a gentle rut in his chest. "Perhaps she would. I can't imagine anyone not wanting this."

"Yeah?"

"Yeah. How does it feel? Do you like it?"

Jodi sucked in a breath. "Fuck yeah. It feels amazing. Can't believe I forgot about something like this. How does that happen?"

Rupert could picture how it happened all too well, but it wasn't the time for morbid imaginings. This was beyond what he'd dared hope for, and he wasn't going to let the shadows chase it away. He closed his fist around Jodi's cock, squeezing, lightly at first, but then harder as Jodi's eyes widened and rolled into the back of his head.

"Oh God, yeah." Jodi thrust his hips forward. "Don't stop, don't stop."

Rupert gave into Jodi's whispered plea, for a while, at least. He'd missed this side of Jodi—the uninhibited, sexual side of him— untamed, and a little wild. From the very first time he'd laid a hand on Jodi, he'd been enthralled by the way he moved his body, the sounds he made. Jodi was beautiful.

But eventually, as Jodi's thighs trembled and his gasps caught in his chest, Rupert pushed his luck and pulled Jodi closer . . . close enough to flick his tongue over Jodi's dick.

Jodi's eyes flew open. "*Shit.*"

"Is that a good 'shit'?"

"What the fuck do you think?"

Rupert grinned. "I think you want more."

Jodi shuffled forward on his knees and pushed his cock into Rupert's mouth. "Then give me more."

As if Rupert could say no. As if he wanted to. He'd always got off on giving Jodi head. Perhaps it had been the power—the control it gave him over this beautiful man who Rupert felt so plain beside . . . but Rupert didn't feel like that anymore. Hadn't in years. Jodi had taught him to feel nothing but pleasure when they were laid bare to each other like this.

He took Jodi deep, scraping him against the roof of his mouth and down his throat. Jodi, perhaps expecting Rupert to ease him in gently, cried out, jerking violently. Rupert held him still, controlling the pace initially. Then he relented and let Jodi fuck his mouth, slowly at first, but then faster and harder, until Jodi yelled out a curse and shot down his throat.

For a long moment, Jodi gasped and clung to the headboard. His arms shook and his legs quivered. He stared at Rupert, his mouth opening and closing, but nothing intelligible came out. Alarmed, Rupert wriggled from beneath him and pried his hands from the bed frame, easing him onto his back.

"Jodi? Talk to me. You all right?"

For a long, anxious moment, Jodi didn't answer, then he burst out laughing and yanked Rupert down to lie on top of him. "All right? I feel like I've just done a bloody skydive."

"Landed on your feet, I hope."

"I landed on the fucking moon."

Jodi laughed some more, and his euphoric humour was infectious. Rupert wrapped his arms around him and held him tight, smiling so hard his cheeks ached. "Are you ready to come back to earth and go to sleep?"

"Sleep?" Jodi sunk his teeth into Rupert's shoulder. "But what about you? I want you to feel like I do—if I can do it half as well as you can. I want—"

It was Rupert's turn to kill the conversation. He kissed Jodi gently, warmly, with barely a tickle of the heat that had just exploded between them. "We've got all the time in the world to fuck about. Come and sleep with me? Please?"

Jodi tried to scowl, but a tired, sheepish smile won out. He crawled under the covers and held up the duvet. Rupert slipped in beside him and rolled onto his side to spoon him from behind, the way they'd always slept before the accident, even in the heat of summer. It took him a moment to realise what he'd done, and for the umpteenth time, the magnitude of how far they'd come in a matter of weeks threatened to overwhelm him.

Then Jodi wriggled backward, pressing his warm body against Rupert's, and reached for Rupert's arms, tugging them around him. He kissed Rupert's palm and let out a sleepy sigh. "I'm not obsessed with sex, Rupe, I promise. I just really fucking love you."

Chapter
NINETEEN

J odi writhed beneath Rupert, revelling in the weight of the body pinning him down. Rupert kissed him roughly and pulled at his T-shirt. "Off."

Breathless, Jodi raised his arms. Rupert yanked the offending shirt over Jodi's head and tossed it away. "Up. Turn around. Hands on the headboard."

Jodi obeyed with a healthy shot of nerves. In the last week, being intimate with Rupert had proved as natural as breathing, but with no memory of the sex life they'd shared before the accident, Jodi had often felt exposed and laid bare by his ignorance. Ignorance that was equal parts embarrassing and *hot* as hell as they learned—relearned—how to pleasure each other: the handjobs, the blowjobs. The grinding together until Jodi was sure he'd combust. Somehow, Jodi knew they'd barely scratched the surface.

Cool air hit his back. He shivered and dropped his head. Rupert soothed him with warm hands, rubbing circles into the base of his spine. "Relax."

Jodi tried, then gave up. He didn't want to relax, because then he might fall asleep. And he didn't want to sleep. He wanted to absorb Rupert's every touch and commit them to his sketchy memory in permanent ink. "What are you going to do to me?"

"Do you really want me to tell you?"

"No." Jodi already had a pretty good idea what Rupert had in mind. He remembered rimming from his relationship with Sophie— her gentle tongue, and her soft skin against his. He'd loved it, and the thought of Rupert doing that to him— "*Fuck!*"

Rupert's tongue was far from gentle, and the scruff of his stubble scratched Jodi's thighs in just the right way, taking him to that dangerous precipice between pleasure and pain.

Jodi chose pain, and then pleasure, losing himself to the toe-curling sweep of Rupert's tongue. Dear God, it was nothing like he remembered with Sophie. This wasn't playful and naughty—a drunken fumble they wouldn't talk about in the morning. This *was* the morning. Rupert meant this, and Jodi could hardly bear it.

Too soon, Rupert pulled away and kissed a path up Jodi's back, stopping at his neck where he sunk his teeth in, biting down until Jodi wriggled free and threw himself at Rupert, sending them both tumbling to the mattress, pillows scattering onto the floor. "That was amazing."

"Yeah?" Rupert grinned. "I like it too, both ways. Drives me up the feckin' wall when you do it to me."

Up the wall. Yup, that made sense. "I couldn't come from it, but that's what makes it so hot. It's like torture."

"The best kind," Rupert said. "It's good for, um, prep too."

"Prep?"

Rupert smirked.

"Oh." Jodi pictured the lube still hidden away in the drawer. "You mean for fucking?"

"Aye. I'm no expert on how it feels to bottom, but you've told me before that a little, er, rimming action gets you to just the right point between relaxed and—"

"Gagging for it?"

Rupert snorted. "Something like that."

Jodi bit his lip. The old him hadn't been wrong, but alongside the thrill of anticipation, and a desperate yearning for Rupert he could hardly contain, he was still fucking terrified. Rupert's tongue was *lush*, but his dick? Jesus. How was it even possible?

The rational side of him knew exactly how it was possible, but that didn't stop his stomach flipping as he imagined how it would feel to have Rupert sliding inside him, stretching him, fucking him. How it was *going* to feel when it happened.

Which wasn't today. Jodi wanted Rupert to fuck him as much as he wanted just about anything, but he didn't quite have the balls yet. Besides, there was something else he had to do first. Something he'd been dreaming about since his attraction to Rupert had shown its hand. Something he knew was going to be the most beautiful thing he'd ever seen, or at least, could remember seeing.

He sat up and leaned back, eyeing Rupert's cock. He'd yet to put his hands or mouth on it, because somehow Rupert had managed to make their every sexual encounter about Jodi: about teaching him to enjoy Rupert's touch again, slowly, carefully, when Jodi let him and didn't come like a train in five seconds flat, which had happened more times in the last week than Jodi cared to admit.

Rupert squeezed Jodi's thighs. "What are you thinking?"

"I'm thinking about how I can make you come."

"You don't have to do that."

"I know. I want to. Do you want me to?"

"Now there's a question." With the early-morning sun filtering through the gap in the curtains, Rupert's soft smile was dazzling. "Do you really not know the answer?"

Jodi knew. Despite Rupert's softly-softly approach, he hadn't hidden how much he wanted Jodi. Couldn't, with his dick digging into Jodi with every grind and roll. "I don't know how to do it."

"Yes, you do."

"No, seriously, I don't. I mean, I know *what* to do, I just don't know how to make it good."

"Ah, see I thought that too when we first met. Thought I'd put your dick in my mouth and start chewing it by mistake, I was so feckin' nervous."

Jodi laughed, couldn't help it. Rupert's way with words was something else. "So what did you do? 'Cause I'm sure even I would remember someone taking a bite out of my dick."

"Very funny," Rupert deadpanned. "If you must know, you told me to treat your dick like my own, and you were right. Once I'd got myself in that mind-set, it wasn't as alien and terrifying as I thought, and it all kinda clicked."

Treat it like my own. Jodi closed his eyes and called on the clandestine occasions he'd pleasured himself in the weeks before he'd come to realise his desire for Rupert was everything he was missing. Pictured every squeeze, every twist, and combined the memories with the more recent ones he had of Rupert doing it for him—his strong, warm grip and devilish tongue. *I can do this.*

Jodi opened his eyes and moved down Rupert's body, absorbing Rupert's sharp gasp. *Here goes nothing . . .*

A few days and *many* mutual orgasms later, Jodi found himself home alone. Rupert was on his mind, as ever, but with him at work until morning, Jodi was trying to keep busy.

For the most part, he'd succeeded, but it was early evening now. He'd been to his appointments, done all his exercises, and run out of things to clean. He'd even managed to reheat the curry he and Rupert had cooked together the day before without burning the place down, though it had crossed his mind that such a thing would bring Rupert home quicker than the end of his shift.

Idiot.

Jodi closed the dishwasher with a thump. Though eating as much as Rupert wanted him to was hard going, making dinner with him had become one of Jodi's favourite things to do. By all accounts he'd used to be good at cooking, and these days, muddling through, using every pan in the kitchen to make chicken madras, was almost as much fun as relearning some of the other skills he'd forgotten.

Skills. Ha. Heat bloomed in Jodi's gut. He drifted to the living room, recalling Rupert's gravelly moan when he'd come from Jodi's touch that morning, and the night before, and the night before that. Treating Rupert's dick like his own had turned out to be easier than he'd imagined, and making Rupert come? Watching him, entranced by him, absorbing every breath and groan? Damn. Beautiful didn't quite cut it anymore. Who knew having another man's cock in his mouth could be so fucking magical?

Rupert, apparently—

Stop thinking about sex.

In an effort to distract himself, Jodi bypassed the couch and the nap he could've done with and went into the office. He sat in front of the iMac and tapped the keyboard to activate it. Like his laptop, the screen flashed to life with a photograph of Rupert, this time sitting on a wall in full fire gear, helmet and all, smeared in soot and grime, drinking from a grubby mug while he spoke with another firefighter whose face Jodi couldn't see. It was obvious neither man had been aware of the photograph being taken, and Jodi wondered how the image had come to be on his computer. The logical answer, that he'd taken it himself, was equal parts embarrassing and amusing.

Looks like I really was the creepy one.

Jodi launched the web design software he'd been trying to reacquaint himself with, and Rupert and his mystery friend were swallowed up by toolbars and coding widgets. He studied the project he'd been working on—a contract Sophie had told him he'd lost when he'd dropped off the map after the accident. The brief, as far as Jodi could tell, had been to build an innovative site for the company's new line of pop-up tents. The brand was aimed at children, and Jodi's initial take on the project, started nearly a year ago, had been a minimalist black-and-white effort with few avenues for users to do more than add products to baskets and pay.

It hadn't struck Jodi as very innovative, or imaginative. He didn't know much about children, but he thought of Indie and his mind filled with colour, possibility, and light. Question was, how did he translate that into a functional website without giving himself a migraine?

He spent a few hours trying to find out, until he ran into a coding wall he couldn't guess his way around. It happened from time to time, and he'd learned the only solution was to admit defeat and look it up.

Didn't make it any less frustrating, though. He pushed his chair back from the computer and scanned the shelves behind him, searching for the book he'd apparently once told Rupert was his tech bible. It wasn't where he thought he remembered putting it. He searched the shelf below and the one above, but came up blank. Then his gaze fell on a flowery book that was so drastically out of place with the tech magazines and software manuals lining the shelves, Jodi couldn't believe he hadn't noticed it before.

He plucked the book from the shelf and turned it over in his hands. It appeared to be a photo album. He flipped through a few pages. Images of Rupert and him stared back at him. Jodi sat, turning to the beginning. A child's—Indie's—scrawl covered the page.

Dear Daddy and Jodi,

Here is your anniversary present. Auntie Sophie helped me make it. Daddy, you need to smile bigger. Jodi is beating you. Lots of love and crunchy cuddles, Indie (and Auntie Sophie) xxx

"Crunchy cuddles"? Jodi was officially mystified, but that was quickly forgotten as a snap of him and Rupert, taken somewhere in the city—Hyde Park, according to Indie—caught his attention. The photo was dated June 2010, six months after he and Rupert had met, and given how they were stretched out on the grass with their arms around each other, it was clear they'd already been madly in love.

Jodi turned a page, and another, and another, and discovered a timeline of images that plainly showed the love and life he and Rupert had shared. His chest tightened, and he thought he would cry, but instead of tears came laughter, and a smile so wide he thought his face might split. He'd loved Rupert then, and he loved him still. The remnants of their broken dreams lay scattered all around, and were laid bare on the glossy pages of the photo album, but what remained was something beautiful, and for the first time he could remember, he felt proud of who they'd been then, and who they were now.

We really are going to be okay.

Jodi shut the album with a yawn that made his jaw pop. He checked the time. It was after midnight. Shit, how had that happened? He stood up. The room tilted a little, like it often did when he was overtired, and the warning throb of an impending headache buzzed down the side of his face. *Great.* Time for bed and a handful of codeine.

He took the drugs and went to the bedroom, scanning the shelves for any other errant photo albums he hadn't yet noticed. There were none. He tried under the bed, remembering a large plastic box that, in his haste to hoover like a madman a few weeks ago, he'd forgotten to open. The box rattled as he pulled it toward him. Intrigued, he lifted the lid. A traffic cone–sized dildo, amongst other . . . things, greeted him.

Startled, Jodi dropped the lid and shoved the box under the bed. Jesus. Was that his? Rupert's? And what the fuck was it for? Like he didn't know. But the trouble was, he didn't. In theory, Jodi knew who put what where, but as he pictured Rupert's cock, and the giant dildo, he couldn't imagine enjoying having either one crammed inside him.

But, for once, sex wasn't what he wanted to think about. He pushed the box to the back of the "Rupert Files" and crawled into bed. His vision was too blurry to watch TV, so he turned off the lamp and closed his eyes, ignoring the strange falling sensation that made the bed feel like a magic carpet. He blocked out the album and tried to make peace with the bewilderment that accompanied the joy warming his veins. The album documented the entire five years he was missing—where they'd been, what they'd done, and how they felt. Undeniable love and laughter seeped out of every page, which left him with just one question: why the hell hadn't anyone shown him the album before?

Chapter
TWENTY

Rupert had never finished a night shift in such a good mood. He emerged from the station to a haze of dawn sunshine, and could hardly bear to head straight underground to the Tube.

Feeling reckless, he ditched it at Highbury and jogged the remaining five miles home. It took longer than a Tube ride, but running cleared his head of the long night's work, and running home to Jodi's arms seemed somehow fitting. If Jodi was awake, at least.

Rupert hoped he was. He'd grown indulgently used to finding Jodi waiting for him in the kitchen, greeting him with a sleepy smile and a cup of the terrible concoction Jodi called tea. All this time, he'd thought he'd known what he was missing, but now that he had some of it back, it was clear his own memories had done Jodi's way of loving him no justice. Far from being a token gesture of their old life, this brave new world felt somehow more real.

He let himself into the flat. It was dark and still, with no sign of Jodi being up just yet. Rupert swallowed his disappointment and went to the kitchen, flipping the kettle on. A cuppa while curled up beside a sleeping Jodi sounded like heaven, then perhaps he'd get a few hours shut-eye too. They had all day in the world to fuck around, right?

Rupert brewed his tea with a smirk. Rebuilding their physical relationship was becoming less terrifying by the day, and he wondered if today would be the day fate gave them the green light to move on.

His mind still in the gutter, he took his tea into the bedroom. Jodi was hunched up under the covers, the duvet over his head. Rupert set his mug down. "Morning, boyo."

The greeting was whispered, but it was usually enough to bring Jodi round.

Jodi didn't move. Rupert leaned over the bed and gently drew the covers back. "Jodi?"

"Rupe?" Jodi moaned and hid his eyes.

Rupert grasped his shoulder. Despite the heavy duvet, Jodi's skin was clammy and cold. "I'm here. What's the matter? Can you look at me a sec?"

Jodi raised his head and gazed at Rupert with one eye, the other half-closed and drooping, pulling the left side of Jodi's face with it.

Rupert's stomach dropped through the floor. *Jesus. He's had a fucking stroke.* "Jodi? I need you to tell me what's happened, okay?"

"Head hurts," Jodi slurred. "Can't see you."

"What about your arms and legs? Can you move them?"

Jodi clumsily shifted his right arm, covering his face with his hand, and mumbled something nonsensical, until he broke off with a groan so full of pain it was like a bullet to Rupert's heart.

He covered Jodi with the duvet again and retrieved his phone from his pocket, dialling 999 with his thumb. The operator connected him to the ambulance control room. "He has a TBI," Rupert explained after listing Jodi's symptoms. "I'm a firefighter with Green Watch at Brixton, and I think he might've had a stroke."

The operator dispatched help and stayed on the line. "Try not to panic. It might look worse than it is."

"We ain't that lucky."

"Come on now. Check his breathing again."

Rupert obeyed, following her instructions until he heard sirens outside. "They're here."

He dashed to the hall and buzzed the paramedics in. He bid the operator good-bye, then listed Jodi's history and symptoms as they moved swiftly to the bedroom. The younger ambulance technician took one glance at Jodi and disappeared to fetch the stretcher, and the frown on the remaining paramedic did little to quell Rupert's fears.

"Has anything like this happened before?" the paramedic asked.

"No." Rupert eyed the ECG monitor, though he had no idea what he was looking for. "He's had some seizures and headaches, some muscle spasms and dizziness, but nothing like this."

"We'll take him to King's," the paramedic said. "They've got his history and better TBI facilities. How long was he home alone for?"

"All night. He could've been like this all fucking night—" Rupert clapped a hand over his mouth.

The paramedic grasped his shoulder. "We don't know that for sure. This could've happened ten minutes before you walked in. We'll get him to King's as fast as we can. If this is a stroke, there's every chance they can reverse it."

Easy for him to say, but as Jodi stared blankly at Rupert with his one working eye, Rupert knew the dash to King's was his only chance. "Okay. Let's go."

The ambulance crew hooked Jodi up to an oxygen machine and loaded him onto a stretcher. Jodi reacted little until they got outside into the bright sunshine, then he cried out and lurched off the side of the stretcher. Rupert caught him. "Easy, boyo."

"Hurts, Rupe . . . please."

"I can't. I'm sorry. They'll give you something as soon as we get to the hospital. Please, Jodi. You need to let us get you there, okay?"

Rupert shielded Jodi from the sun as the crew loaded him into the ambulance. Inside, he knelt by the stretcher. Jodi curled into the foetal position and reached out his right hand. Rupert took it in his own shaking grasp, squeezed it tight, and brushed Jodi's sweat-dampened hair out of his face. "I've got you. I promise."

The paramedic touched Rupert's shoulder. "You need to sit down and put a seat belt on."

Rupert shook his head. "No. I'm staying here."

"Sir—"

"No!"

The paramedic let it go. Rupert wondered briefly if he'd come across this crew before, but London was a big city with thousands of paramedics working the streets. Rupert had forgotten more of them than he actually knew. He squeezed Jodi's hand again. "Just hold on, boyo. Everything's going to be okay."

Jodi curled tighter into a ball and pressed his head into Rupert's chest. Rupert rubbed his neck and flinched. Though cold to the touch, the tension in Jodi's body was terrifying. Was that a stroke symptom? Rupert had no idea, and the ingrained professional calm he'd called on to get this far abruptly evaporated, and blind panic set in. Was this it? Was everything they'd been through not enough? Had the past few weeks been nothing but a cruel trick? For a moment, nausea overwhelmed him, but as the ambulance rumbled to life and hit the road, burning around corners, sirens blaring, the task of keeping himself upright became all-consuming.

The ambulance made the twenty-five-minute drive in eighteen. A team of A & E doctors and nurses were ready, and Rupert was pushed aside. He backed into the wall, trying to keep out of the way until the paramedic took his arm and led him out into the corridor.

"They won't let you stay in there. Here you go . . ." The paramedic opened a door to an empty waiting room. "Wait here. A doctor will come with news as soon as they can."

He left. Rupert fell into a chair and put his head in his hands. He couldn't do this, not again. He couldn't sit in this damn fucking chair and wait to be told there was little left of the man who'd carried his heart from the moment they'd met. *Sophie. I need Sophie.* Rupert pulled his phone from his pocket, but it wasn't his phone. In his panic as they'd left the flat, he'd grabbed Jodi's instead. Rupert tapped in Jodi's passcode, hoping Jodi hadn't changed it since the accident. The phone lit up. Rupert found Sophie's number and waited for her to answer. She didn't, so Rupert killed the call. He couldn't leave her a voice mail like this. Not again.

He shoved the phone back in his pocket and got up, drifting to the window. Outside, Camberwell was already alive—buzzing with the colourful chaos that was unique to South London. An Afro-Caribbean man crossed the road with an elderly dog. He stopped and shared a few words with a younger, Eastern European girl. They parted with a laugh and wave, and Rupert envied them so much his bones hurt. He'd forgotten what it was like to smile without a care in the world.

"Are you with Jodi Peters?"

Rupert spun around. A young doctor stood in the doorway, dressed in purple scrubs, a startling pink stethoscope around her neck. Rupert blinked. For some reason, he'd expected a middle-aged man. "Yes. I'm his partner, Rupert O'Neil."

"Good. I'm Dr. Stanton. I've been looking after Jodi since he came in. I've taken bloods, and given him something for the pain and some precautionary antibiotics. The stroke team are with him now. They're running a few extra tests, and then he'll be going up for a CT scan."

"A brain scan?"

"Yes."

"Did he have a stroke?"

Dr. Stanton ventured further into the room and sat down, gesturing for Rupert to do the same. "We don't know at this stage. The slurred speech and one-sided paralysis are classic indicators of a stroke, but are also symptomatic of many other things—meningitis, haemorrhage, seizures—especially with a TBI as recent as Jodi's."

Recent. Rupert felt sick again. With all that had happened since, the accident often seemed like it had occurred years ago, and the reality that Jodi had a lifetime of consequences to live with had always been tough to stomach. "When will you know?"

"Quickly. The stroke team works fast and we should have their assessment within the hour."

An hour seemed an unbearable amount of time to wait, but there was little Rupert could do but thank the doctor. "What do *you* think?"

Dr. Stanton paused in the doorway. "I think we should wait for the test results. Nothing is certain until then."

She left Rupert alone with his thoughts, and it wasn't long before hopelessness overwhelmed him. This was bad . . . It had to be, because even if it wasn't a stroke, it was bound to be something equally debilitating and horrid, because that was how shit worked for them now, how it worked for Jodi. His brain injury and everything that came with it was permanent, and no amount of fumbling blowjobs could change the fact that he'd been condemned to a life of pain and suffering.

How fucking stupid had they been to think—to believe—it could be any other way?

Too stupid for Rupert to contemplate. He put his head in his hands and didn't move until Sophie appeared fifteen minutes later.

Rupert stared at her. "How did you know?"

"Pat and Ron downstairs saw the ambulance. I was in Pimlico when they called me."

The elderly downstairs neighbours were a pair of busybodies who spent most of their time twitching curtains, but as Sophie dropped into the chair beside him and her familiar, comforting scent surrounded him, Rupert had never been more glad of their nosiness. "It could be a stroke, Soph. We might have lost him all over again."

"You don't know that. What have the doctors said?"

"Not much. They're waiting on tests."

"Tests for what?"

Rupert shrugged. "I don't really know. Stroke, meningitis, a fucking brain bleed. Does it matter? He's fucked."

"Stop it." Sophie gripped Rupert's face and forced him to meet her gaze. "It's okay to be scared, but you have to give him a chance. Don't write him off."

"I'm not writing him off. I'm just being realistic."

"You're thinking too fast."

Whatever. Rupert lost the will to argue. He dropped his head into his hands again and stayed that way, taking little comfort from Sophie's gentle hand on his back, until footsteps roused him sometime later.

"Mr. O'Neil?"

Rupert jumped. It seemed like he'd been waiting a week for Dr. Stanton to return. "Do you know what it is? Did he have a stroke?"

Dr. Stanton held her hands up. "We're still waiting on results. I came to see if you wanted to sit with him."

It was a daft question. Rupert left Sophie in the waiting room and followed Dr. Stanton to the curtained bay where Jodi's bed was. Jodi was curled on his side in much the same way Rupert had left him, except the oxygen mask had been swapped for nasal tubes, and a cannula had been inserted into the back of his hand.

Rupert bent over the bed rail. Jodi appeared asleep, but he wasn't convinced. "All right down there, boyo?"

Jodi groaned and cracked an eye open. "Rupe?"

"I'm here. How're you doing? Do you feel better?"

"I can move my tongue."

Rupert smiled in spite of the dull terror putting up shelves in his insides. "That's good. How's the head?"

"Dunno."

Not so good, though Rupert knew Jodi well enough to know whatever drugs were dripping through his IV must have at least taken the edge off the pain. "Hang in there. We'll know what's going on soon."

"I'm okay . . . Don't get worried. I love you."

It was a little late for Rupert not to get worried. Worry had been his constant companion from the moment the police had ferried him to Jodi's bedside all those months ago, but Jodi's sentiment now—so different from the long weeks of nothing after the accident—went a long way. "I love you more. Can I do anything for you?"

"Warm me up? Bloody . . . freezing."

Jodi was already huddled beneath two blankets. Rupert searched around the bed space, but could find no more, so he pulled the curtain back, looking for a nurse. Jodi caught his hand.

"Lie with me?"

"Lie with you?" Rupert let Jodi draw him closer. "You're in hospital. We can't do that here."

Jodi opened both eyes, though one still drooped. "Please?"

Rupert had never been able to refuse Jodi, even when whatever he wanted was beyond what Rupert could give. But he could give him this. There was room enough for both of them on the bed, and who knew when they'd get to lie together again if Dr. Stanton returned with bad news.

It took some manoeuvring, but with Rupert's help, Jodi was able to shuffle over so Rupert could lie down beside him. Then, he pressed himself into Rupert's body and lay his head on his chest. Rupert tucked the blankets around him and held him close. It felt a little surreal. If he shut his eyes, he could almost pretend they were at home.

Almost.

A while later, Dr. Stanton appeared with another doctor in tow— Dr. Nevis, Jodi's neurologist.

Rupert's heart sank. He started to get up, but Dr. Stanton shook her head. "Stay where you are. He's fast asleep. Do you want me to get your friend from the waiting room?"

"Please."

Dr. Stanton ghosted away and returned with Sophie before Rupert could blink. Sophie took her place at Jodi's other side, reached over, and squeezed Rupert's hand. Her smile was encouraging. *She's fucking deluded.*

"It's good news," Dr. Stanton said.

Rupert blinked. He'd heard her wrong, or maybe her definition of good was already warped by the short time she'd spent on the job.

Perhaps sensing his cynicism, Dr. Nevis took a step forward. "The stroke team have ruled out any stroke activity, and Jodi's brain scans look clear. Nothing has changed since we scanned him last month. His blood results are clear, and everything else is coming back normal, or at least what we'd expect from someone at Jodi's stage of TBI recovery. Taking his symptoms into account, I'd say the most likely diagnosis at this stage is a hemiplegic migraine. They're quite common in people who've had a significant head injury."

Significant. Rupert hated that word. "What does 'hemiplegic' mean?"

"Hemiplegic means one-sided paralysis," Dr. Stanton said. "Temporary numbness and weakness in one side of the body, blurred vision, and difficulty speaking. The accompanying headache is pretty brutal too. It's one of the worse migraine variants."

"But the good news is they're not dangerous," Dr. Nevis said. "Or progressive. We can manage them if they become a long-term side effect of the TBI."

"But . . ." Rupert shook his head slightly.

The doctors waited, but Rupert didn't know what he was trying to say. His every nerve had been braced for the worst possible news, hearing the opposite had stunned him mute.

Sophie squeezed his hand. "What happens now?"

"We'll send him to a ward to be monitored," Dr. Stanton said. "Certainly for the rest of the day and possibly overnight, depending on how he does."

"Then what?" Rupert asked.

Dr. Stanton raised an eyebrow. "Then you take him home."

"Home?" Jodi suddenly stirred. He opened his eyes and met Rupert's with a sleepy gaze. "Can I go home?"

Rupert cupped Jodi's face and stroked his scruffy cheek with the pad of his thumb. "Not just yet. They want to keep an eye on you for a little while."

Jodi fought Rupert's hold on him and sat up. Rupert tensed, ready to catch him if he swayed, but Jodi held firm. "I don't want to stay here."

Dr. Nevis took a step forward. "How are you feeling?"

"Pukey," Jodi said. "Like you fed me full of that morphine shit again."

"Headache?"

"A bit. Not like before though. This one feels like a hangover."

Dr. Nevis asked Jodi a few more questions and conducted an examination, then he exchanged a glance with Dr. Stanton, who nodded. "We can monitor you down here for an hour or so, and if you feel up to it, discharge you this afternoon under the condition that you come straight back if anything changes. That's my best offer. Do we have a deal?"

Of course he had a deal. The doctors ghosted away. Rupert reclaimed his place at Jodi's side and gently punched his arm. "I don't know what the bloody hell just happened."

"It's good news," Sophie said. "I've heard of those migraines. A girl at work had them. They're bloody horrible, but it's better than a stroke, eh?"

Jodi looked bemused. "Who had a stroke?"

"We thought you had," Rupert said. "But it was a migraine. You remember what Dr. Nevis told you when he examined you a minute ago?"

"Hemiplegic migraine." Jodi shuddered. "God, it hurt so much I thought my head was going to explode. I'm sorry, Rupe. I could see how scared you were, but I couldn't get my tongue to work."

Rupert laughed, exhaustion and relief merging together into a hysteria he could barely contain. Jodi shot him a quizzical glance, then shoved his hands in his pyjama pockets. "Where the fuck is my phone?"

"I've got it. Why?"

Rupert handed it over. Jodi took it and pressed a few buttons. "Because I'm setting the timer. An hour, he said. I'm not staying a bloody minute longer."

"You have to stay until they're sure you're all right," Sophie said. "Don't be a dick."

Jodi rolled his eyes, then rubbed his head. "I'm not being a dick. I just want to go home. This place is bad for Rupert. Look at him. He's aged a hundred years in the last ten minutes."

"Hey!" Rupert glared. "Don't take the piss out of me. We thought you'd had a fucking stroke."

"Well, I didn't. I know it's shit, Rupe, but this is what my life is like now. We can't change that, but we don't have to let it define us. I don't want to spend every day waiting to die. I just want to go home . . . with you and look at the photo album I found in the office. Can we do that? Please?"

How could Rupert refuse? Since the accident, pessimism had become his baseline, invading his soul like the old Jodi had never chased it away all those years ago, but this new Jodi—fuck, this *was* Jodi, and Rupert loved him as much as he always had. Perhaps more.

For the first time in as long as he could remember, the future looked as bright as it had ever been.

Chapter
TWENTY-ONE

"I'm okay, Rupe, honestly. You don't have to follow me around."
Jodi wrapped a towel around his waist and left the bathroom
with Rupert trailing behind him.

"I'm not following you around."

"No? So why sit on the bog the whole time I'm in the shower,
then?"

Rupert shrugged. "Because you're naked?"

"Nice try." Jodi turned away and tried to maintain his irritation
as he flipped through his stack of colour-sorted T-shirts. Despite the
hospital's assurances that his brief stay with them had been nothing
more than a blip, Rupert had been his shadow ever since they'd come
home. "I'm fine. I'd tell you if I wasn't."

"I know."

And so it went on. It was 2 p.m. when Jodi finally ran out of
patience. He went out into the hall and found Rupert's shoes, then
took them back to the living room and threw them at Rupert's chest.
"I'm hungry. Let's go."

They left the flat. Rupert started to turn right. Jodi tugged his
arm. "Let's go this way."

Rupert frowned. "Are you sure?"

"Why wouldn't I be?"

Rupert didn't seem to have an answer, so they turned left, away
from the Tube station and toward the open-air market. Jodi sniffed
the air. "Can we get some of that falafel shit from the Israeli dude?"

"Hmm?"

"Falafel," Jodi said. "I don't want to sound too much like a hipster
in a quinoa shop, 'cause I know you hate that shit, but I kinda feel like
hummus."

"What are you talking about?"

"Lunch." Jodi glanced at Rupert. He'd had a thing for Middle Eastern food since their Moroccan dinner, and judging by the number of spicy flatbreads Rupert had brought home since, he had too. "Aren't you hungry?"

"Jodi."

Rupert's tone stopped Jodi in his tracks. "What?"

Silence.

Jodi frowned. He hated it when people did this—left big gaps in conversations and expected him to catch up. When would they learn? He wasn't asking for an easy life, only for people to just tell him when he missed something really fucking important. "Rupe, please. I'm not going to guess, because I don't know how."

Rupert closed his eyes briefly. When he opened them again, his gaze was so tortured that Jodi's heart skipped a beat. "I never walk this way."

"This way?" Jodi glanced around. "What do you mean 'this way'?"

More silence. Jodi surveyed his surroundings again, taking it all in—the betting shop, bakery, and Halal butchers. The people, cars, zebra crossing. *Shit. The zebra crossing.* "Is that the place?"

Rupert nodded. "Didn't you know?"

"Nope." Jodi hadn't given much thought to where the accident happened, and it had never occurred to him to avoid the scene. He'd crossed the road at the very same crossing just yesterday. "Are you all right?"

Rupert shrugged and looked away. Jodi caught his face in his hand. "Don't hide from me. It's okay to be upset. I sort of wish I was too."

"It doesn't bother you?"

"Not really. It's just a road. The accident could've happened anywhere."

"You're right." Rupert pried Jodi's hand from his face. "It's . . . I don't know. I see people going about their business without a care in the world, and I kinda want to scream at them. Tell them how dangerous it is. Then I picture you doing the same thing, back then, and now, and I want to scream at you too."

"Scream at me?"

"Or at least wrap myself around you so nothing ever hurts you again."

"Nothing's going to hurt me. Come on. Let me cross the road and show you."

"No."

"Rupert."

Rupert shook his head. "No. I can't do it."

"Yes, you can. Don't take that day and make it everything. There's so much more to us than that. Do you trust me?"

"Of course I do."

Jodi held out his hand. "Then let's go."

Later that day, Jodi persuaded Rupert to go the gym. They'd made it across the road unscathed, but Rupert had been on edge afterward—distracted and jumpy. He'd needed a break from the flat, from Jodi, from everything. He would never have said it, but Jodi knew. How could he not? Besides, Rupert's absence gave Jodi a chance to do something he probably should've done weeks ago.

He stood at the kitchen window and waited for Rupert to disappear into the Tube station, then went to the office and shut the door, like the barrier between him and the rest of the flat somehow contained the embarrassment of what he was about to do. *Daft twat.*

Since the accident, and especially since he'd been left alone more, the internet had become his best friend. He'd googled everything from how to cook scrambled eggs without them sticking to the saucepan, to the correct way to load the dishwasher. So far, providing he stuck to legit sites, it hadn't let him down, but this . . . Yeah. This was something else.

The search engine filled the wide screen of his iMac. Jodi hesitated. Would there be pictures? He hoped so . . . or did he? Would seeing it on screen be better than the images he'd conjured in his mind?

Jodi took a deep breath and typed *anal sex* into the search engine. A barrage of pornography and sites aimed at women came back. He forced himself not to look at the porn, and considered the *Cosmopolitan* article. It had been written for women thinking of trying anal sex for the first time, but it was all the same, right? A year ago, he'd have known. *Like that matters now.* Jodi silenced his demons and scrolled past the article.

It took some searching, but eventually, he found a blog post that seemed to have been written just for him. He scanned the article, taking in the hints and tips on preparation. One word stood out—*relax.* Was he relaxed? Naked with Rupert, he felt a million times the opposite, but there was no doubt in Jodi's mind that he was ready for Rupert to fuck him.

A tasteful diagram caught his attention. Heat crept over him, warm and slow, like lava oozing down a mountain, and he resisted the urge to shove his hand down his jeans. He hadn't had a wank since he and Rupert had started building new bonds where old ones had been swallowed up by the accident. It had almost seemed like the promise of what was to come had been enough, that glimmer of hope . . . a future to replace the past he'd lost. Wanking over that felt a little wrong, but as he read the article a second time, picturing Rupert's fingers, and then his dick, easing inside him as he got lost in Rupert's gaze—Jesus. Was there anything hotter?

Jodi didn't reckon so, and getting tied up in Rupert-laced knots didn't bode well for the relaxation the article said he'd need if getting fucked by Rupert wasn't going to hurt like hell and be a disaster for all involved.

Relax. Another deep breath. Jodi memorised the preparation tips, then tore himself from the computer and went to the bedroom. The lube bottle was still in the drawer, and a rummage under the bed revealed the plastic box he'd stumbled across the day the hemiplegic migraine had knocked him for six last week. A box he wished he'd found months ago, when the possibility of hot man sex with Rupert had first entered his mind.

Jodi lifted the lid from the box. The dildo and a vast array of other sex toys stared back at him in much the same way they had when he'd first found them. He picked up a big purple dick with a pump attached to it. Knowing he'd been the bottom in his and Rupert's sexual past, there was only one place these things had been.

Perhaps they're new? Jodi snorted. As if. Who kept a stash of unused sex toys under the bed?

He put the giant purple cock down and rummaged around for something smaller. The article had said preparation was key, and with nothing bigger than Rupert's crazy-hot tongue paving the way in recent memory, he needed to start with something smaller. Except, it seemed the old Jodi had been far braver than Jodi felt now. A thorough search revealed nothing smaller than a butt plug that made his eyes water.

Then his gaze fell on what looked like some kind of torch. He picked up and pressed the button, but instead of light, came vibration . . . a deep, low buzz that travelled right through him. A click he hadn't heard in ages sounded in his brain. It was a probe, he was sure of it, and though a memory of using one eluded him, he was suddenly certain that this toy was *good*.

So what now? Jodi stared at the toy. Having a wank was one thing, but did he really have the nerve to press that thing into—

The front door opened. Jodi jumped a mile and threw the probe back in the box, jammed the lid on, and shoved it under the bed. What the fuck was Rupert doing home already? Jodi scrambled to his feet, stumbled, and fell to his knees again just as Rupert appeared in the bedroom doorway.

Rupert sighed. "Seriously? Will you stop tidying?"

Jodi got, carefully this time, to his feet. "I'm not tidying. I was, er, looking for something. And what the fuck are you doing here anyway? You left, like, ten minutes ago."

"Twenty-five, actually. Just enough to get all the way to the gym and realise I'd forgotten my bag."

"Oh."

"'Oh'?" Rupert raised an eyebrow. "I know you shoved me out the door, but I figured you wouldn't be that upset to see me."

"I'm not upset." Jodi tried to push crossly past Rupert, but Rupert caught him in a grip strong enough to make Jodi weak at the knees. *I like that.*

"Why are you all flushed?" Rupert put his hand to Jodi's forehead. "Are you feeling okay?"

"I'm fine! Fuck's sake. Stop treating me like I'm breakable."

Rupert let Jodi go. Jodi didn't move, guilt warring with an emotion he couldn't quite name. Rupert seemed pissed and frustrated, like he was ready to blow, and Jodi was lost in it, snared, and couldn't look away.

"What were you doing when I came in?"

"Nothing."

"Liar."

Jodi swallowed. "I was going through the box."

"What box?"

Jodi couldn't answer, but it didn't matter. Comprehension dawned on Rupert's face, and it was his turn to have colour in his cheeks.

"What were you looking in there for?"

Jodi shrugged. "I don't know. I guess I just thought I needed to do something . . . you know, to be ready for you, I'm so scared I'm going to do it wrong, but that box is full of massive dildos, and then I found this probe thing and—"

Rupert ended Jodi's embarrassed ramble with a kiss that drove every emotion he'd ever felt from his soul, all except the desire and love Rupert had never hidden from him, even when Jodi hadn't had a clue what it meant. "Boyo, if you taught me anything, it's that you don't need nothing but two boys that love each other to make this good. Will you let me show you what you showed me?"

Rupert walked Jodi slowly to the bed and pushed him down. He'd been waiting for this, yearning for it. For weeks, Jodi had claimed to be ready, but Rupert's heart had said no, and so Rupert had said no too, distracting Jodi with other things . . . other ways to come, all the while waiting for the final knot of fear in his gut to give way. Fear of his own failure and of Jodi's relapse. Fear of losing everything they had—old and new—all over again.

He couldn't quite say what had changed. Maybe it had been seeing Jodi stroll through the scene of the accident without a care in the world. Like he hadn't left his—and Rupert's—whole life in bits at the side of the road. Like the event itself really had ceased to matter.

Or perhaps it had been observing Jodi as he'd stared at the toys in the box, unaware of Rupert watching him from the doorway. Anyone else would've just seen a young man kneeling on the floor, looking into a nondescript box, but Rupert knew all too well what Jodi had been staring so hard at. That probe. Rupert shivered. Jesus, they'd had some fun with that.

But he pushed the toy box from his mind. The time for play would come later. For now, it was all about Jodi, and him, together, like they'd always been, even when they'd been so far apart Rupert had truly believed they'd never find their way back.

He kissed Jodi with all he had, and covered him with his body, feeling their contours mould together like they had been one and the same to begin with. Jodi shuddered. Rupert opened his eyes to find Jodi gazing at him with a healthy mix of love, arousal, and apprehension that made Rupert's heart swell, healing the many cracks it'd suffered since the accident. The old Jodi was gone, and Rupert would mourn him forever, but this Jodi . . . Rupert loved him more than he would ever have believed possible, and despite the pain that had brought them to this point, part of him wouldn't change a thing. Wouldn't give up this moment.

Rupert stripped Jodi's clothes, peeling back the layers of pain and heartache until there was nothing but Jodi—his long limbs and bare skin. Rupert kissed every inch of him, rolled him over and kissed him again and again, burying his face in him, breathing him in, saturating himself in all that was Jodi, as Jodi writhed beneath him.

Jodi gasped. "Please, Rupe, please. I can't."

"Can't what? What do you want?"

"You. I need you."

It had been a while since those words had last turned Rupert inside out. He scrambled out of his own clothes and tossed them aside. He grasped Jodi's hips and yanked him back, grinding his cock along where Jodi needed him most. "This what you want? Like this? You want it like this?"

"I don't care. Just fuck me. Please. Don't make me beg."

As if. Rupert had never made Jodi beg for anything, but taking Jodi on all fours when he hadn't been fucked for months was probably a bad idea, especially when there was no guarantee that Jodi's body would remember Rupert's dick any more than Jodi did.

He rolled Jodi onto his side and fumbled in the bedside drawer for condoms and lube. Then he lay behind Jodi, hooking his arm loosely around Jodi's neck so he could grip his hand, for his own benefit as much as Jodi's, needing something—anything—to ground him.

Jodi's shoulders trembled. Rupert kissed his cheek. "Don't be scared, boyo. I've got you. I promise."

"I know. I've always known."

That was enough for Rupert. He rolled a condom on and lubed up, then turned his attention to Jodi, gently rubbing lube into him with a slick finger.

Jodi groaned. "Damn. I like that even more than I thought I would."

"Yeah?" Rupert twisted his finger, then added a second, slowly, trying not to get lost in the wet heat of Jodi's body tightening around him. "What about this?"

He scissored his fingers, stretching Jodi out. Jodi gasped and moaned again, before it was muffled by the pillow he shoved his face into. "Rupert, *please.*"

Rupert played Jodi for as long as he could stand, resisting the urge to touch himself, or grind his dick into Jodi's back, but as Jodi writhed and groaned, clearly on the point of release, suddenly, he couldn't wait. He needed this as much as Jodi.

And he needed it now.

He withdrew his fingers and aligned his body with Jodi's. Then he pushed forward, easing himself inside Jodi, inch by inch, following the natural cues of Jodi's body like they'd done this just yesterday, and the day before that, and before that. Like they'd never stopped. Jodi's body consumed him, squeezing him tight. Rupert's eyes rolled, but he fought for control, watching Jodi, listening to every breath and moan, searching for any sign of distress.

Jodi let out a pained gasp. Rupert froze and squeezed Jodi's hand. "Want to stop?"

"No . . . God, no. I just need a minute."

Rupert waited, his face buried in Jodi's neck, counting the speeding thrum of Jodi's pulse beneath his lips. Jodi remained silent and still for so long that Rupert wondered if this was it, if it was over until the next time Jodi told him the moment was right to try again. There was no rush. They had all the time in the world.

Then Jodi moved, so slightly at first Rupert thought he'd imagined it. He pushed his hips back again and again, circling in a slow rhythm that almost had Rupert coming before they'd got started. "Jesus. That feels amazing."

"Yeah." Jodi released a shaky breath. "Like that, like that. Fuck me, Rupert. I'm okay, I promise."

Rupert lifted Jodi's leg and thrust gently. Jodi threw his head back. Rupert cupped his face and kissed his throat, feeling Jodi's near-silent moan against his lips. God, he remembered this. The sensation of Jodi falling apart in his arms, entangled in a warm web of love and desire, nothing in the world but each other.

He scraped Jodi's neck with his teeth. Withdrew from Jodi, then pushed back in, harder than before. Jodi cried out and punched the bed. He arched his spine, opening himself more to Rupert. "Shit, yeah."

Rupert groaned. He'd been so afraid of hurting Jodi or sending them both careening twenty steps back, he hadn't considered how to handle the crazy heat sweeping over him, even hotter than he could remember. He shifted, pushing Jodi onto his front, pressing his face into the pillow, fucking him harder and harder, until his hips were slapping Jodi's with so much force that the bed hit the wall.

"I'm going to come." Jodi gripped the headboard and raised himself up, defying the weight of Rupert pinning him down. "Oh God, oh God, I'm going to come."

Then Jodi yelled out, screaming, long and loud, like he used to. Rupert thrust again, once, twice, three times, then coherent thought abandoned him, and he came hard, collapsing on Jodi's back, absorbing every jolt and judder of Jodi beneath him.

For a long moment, he was lost in that white, misty place where there was nothing but the release of his dick still pulsing inside Jodi, the wet warmth of their sweat-slicked bodies pressed together, and the smell of sex hanging over them like a haze of all that was right with the world.

Then reality set in, and not much changed. He pushed Jodi's damp hair away from his face. "Okay?"

Jodi grunted. "I'm fucked."

"Sounds about right. Can you move?"

"Not with you sitting on top of me."

Rupert carefully withdrew and rolled away.

Jodi caught his hand. "Don't go too far. I'm not done with you yet."

Rupert chuckled. "Yeah?"

"Maybe. Can you help me up?"

Rupert helped Jodi roll over and sit up, then he sat back on his heels and took in Jodi's flushed cheeks and dazed grin. "You really are okay, aren't you?"

"Rupert, I'm happy. I don't know what else there is."

There was nothing else. Rupert found the duvet that had somehow ended up on the floor and the toy box caught his eye. He lifted the lid and retrieved the probe. "This was our favourite. We used it all the time."

"I thought it looked interesting."

Jodi smirked, but it was overtaken by a yawn. Rupert chuckled and tossed the probe in the box. He laid the duvet over Jodi, then drifted to the bathroom to clean up. On the way back, the door to Jodi's office called to him. He padded inside and scanned the shelves until he found the photo album Jodi had asked about in the hospital. *There it is.* Despite Jodi's request, they'd yet to get round to looking at it.

He took it into the bedroom and held it out. "I'd forgotten about this. You always said there was no point having physical albums anymore when everything was stored on our phones and computers. We only have the photos in the living room up because Indie made us."

"That's sad . . . and I was wrong. I wish I'd seen this a long time ago." Jodi took the album and flipped to a photo of him and Rupert lying on the grass in Hyde Park, enjoying a hazy summer afternoon of London sun. "There's no way I could've denied this."

"I'm sorry."

Jodi glanced up. "Don't be. It all worked out in the end, didn't it?"

"I guess so."

"You know so." Jodi held out his hand and beckoned Rupert closer, then tugged him into the bed to lie beside him. "This whole thing has been a nightmare for both of us, but I'm happy now, Rupe, I really am."

"Then I'm happy too. I still don't understand, though."

Jodi shrugged. "Neither do I, but I don't care. I reckon there will always be a part of my brain out there, waiting for me to catch up, but I'm in no hurry to find it. Here and now, you and me, it's enough for me."

It made as much sense as anything ever had. Rupert pulled Jodi close and kissed his head. "It's more than enough, boyo. It's everything."

Epilogue

Indie clutched Jodi's hand and pressed her face to the glass window. "Can we have the white one?"

Jodi followed her mesmerised gaze and regretfully shook his head. "No kittens, remember? Daddy said."

"Daddy said no pets, ever, actually."

She had a point, but Jodi was hoping Rupert hadn't truly meant the words he'd uttered so forcefully when Jodi had asked if he could bring Indie to the rescue home half a mile from the flat. "I'm sure he'll change his mind if we find the right one. A grown-up cat who doesn't make a mess."

"But I don't know which one to choose," she wailed. "There's so many. I want them all."

"Okay, how about we go and get a drink and have a think about it?"

It took a while to coax Indie from the kitten ward of the rescue home, but eventually they found themselves in the café, Indie drinking a lurid pink Slush Puppie that would make Rupert's hair curl when he found out about it, and Jodi fumbling with the cap on a bottle of water.

Indie took the bottle from him and removed the cap. "Jodi?"

"Yeah?"

"Will your hands always shake?"

He resisted the urge to sit on his offending hands. He'd grown so used to the random tremors that he often didn't notice them, but Indie did. Indie saw everything. "Only when I'm trying to make them do something they've forgotten how to do."

"Ah." She nodded sagely. "Have your eyes forgotten how to see your computer too?"

He chuckled. "A little bit, but it's all right, because I've got me some Clark Kent glasses to help."

"Daddy likes those glasses."

"Does he?"

"Yes, I heard him telling Aunt Sophie they make him want to—"

"Okaaaay." He cut her off before she could repeat something she was far too young to be saying. "Back to business. Are you sure you want a cat? We could get a dog, maybe?"

She shook her head. "Dogs smell."

"So do cats when they live indoors with a litter tray."

"You won't let it smell," she said confidently. "You make even Daddy's socks smell nice."

It was nice of her to say, though Jodi couldn't remember a time Rupert had ever smelt anything less than amazing. And, in a world where so much had apparently changed, Indie's faith in his age-old cleaning obsession was oddly reassuring. "So, a cat it is. You're going to have to choose one, you know. Or let one choose you."

"How would I do that?"

Good question. "How about we go back inside and ask the nice lady if we can sit with a couple? See if any of them take a liking to you?"

"But not the kittens?"

"Not the kittens."

They finished their drinks and went back inside. A friendly member of staff showed them to a "socialisation" room, which was attached to one of the many compartments that held multiple cats.

"We're running out of room," the woman explained. "Ideally, they'd all have their own pod."

It was on the tip of Jodi's tongue to ask what would happen when the centre reached full capacity, but he stopped himself just in time, remembering Indie's innocent ears.

"What happens when you're full?" Indie asked.

Jodi cringed and tried to catch the woman's eye, but she ignored him and fixed Indie with a steady gaze. "Some of the older animals, and the ones with health problems that are least likely to be adopted, will be put to sleep."

Indie's eyes widened. "You mean, they'll die?"

"I'm afraid so."

Jodi glared at the woman, ready to give her a piece of his mind, but Indie slid into his lap before he could speak.

"We have to get a disabled one, Jodi. Can we? Can we, please?"

It broke Jodi's heart that Indie had spent the last year—like they all had—learning what being disabled truly meant—the limitations and restrictions, the pain and heartache—even though most folk would look at Jodi and have no idea that he woke up some mornings unable to remember how to dress himself.

Don't be so dramatic. Okay, so shit like that was rare these days, but there was no denying Jodi's accident had irrevocably changed the lives of everyone he loved, Indie included.

The woman opened the plastic window separating them from the cats, and Indie instantly lost interest in anything Jodi had to say, her gaze fixed on the window. For a long moment, nothing happened, then, as fate would have it, a three-legged cat hopped through the gap straight into Indie's reaching arms, and Jodi was more certain than he'd ever been of anything that Rupert was going to *kill* him.

Rupert stared at the black bundle of fur making itself at home on top of the fridge. "What the bejesus is that?"

"It's a cat," Jodi deadpanned, staring at Rupert like he was the world's biggest idiot.

"That's not a cat."

"Yes, it is."

"It's got no legs."

"It's got three."

"Okay, so it's half a cat. What the hell is it doing in here?"

Jodi rolled his eyes. "Like you don't know."

"I want to hear you say it."

"Why?"

"So I can tell you you're a dickhead without any fucking loopholes."

"Aw, come on now." Jodi slid off his stool and came to Rupert's side. "You're not really cross."

"Aren't I?" Rupert fought to maintain his glare as Jodi slipped his arms around Rupert's waist and brushed a featherlight kiss to his cheek. "'Cause I'm pretty sure I told you—and Indie—that if you brought a cat back here, I was off to live at the station."

"Didn't mean it, though, did you?"

Of course he hadn't. He'd known full well how Indie and Jodi's trip to the animal shelter a week ago would end. "When did it get here? Don't tell me it's been here all week and I haven't noticed?"

Jodi chuckled. "No. The woman from Apple Wood came by yesterday to inspect the flat, and I picked the cat up this morning. It took you ten seconds to spot Forrest when you came home."

"Forrest?"

"Forrest Stump."

"Forrest Stump?" Dear God. Rupert had craved Jodi's ridiculous sense of humour while it had been missing in action, and somehow he'd forgotten how terrible it could be. "You called half a cat Forrest Stump?"

"It's not half a cat."

"It ain't a whole one."

"Would you say that if she had half a brain?"

"What? No, of course I wouldn't . . ." The penny dropped even as Jodi's arms slackened from their loose embrace. "Jodi—"

"Don't," Jodi said. "It's okay, honest. I know you didn't mean anything by it, but that's the point, isn't it? Forrest had been at Apple Wood for six months. Her time was up next week, and you know what would've happened, don't you?"

Rupert knew. "Jodi, that doesn't happen to humans."

"Not anymore. If I'd had that accident a hundred—Christ, even fifty—years ago, I wouldn't have made it this far."

The jump from stray cat to grown man was vast, but Rupert heard Jodi loud and clear, and the thought of him being cast aside for the sake of a disability most people would never notice hurt his heart.

Rupert caught Jodi as he turned away, and pulled him back into his arms, laying his hand over the steady beat of Jodi's heart. "Boyo, you've got everything you'll ever need right here."

A little while later, Rupert found Jodi in his office, working on whatever he was working on, like he did around this time every day now that his business was cautiously up and running again. After many false starts, they'd figured out that routine was one of the best ways to keep Jodi on track. It didn't pan out every day, mainly because what remained of the old Jodi objected so fiercely to such a structured life, but today was a good day. At least, it had been until Rupert stuck his foot in his mouth.

Rupert dropped Forrest on Jodi's desk, grinning as she sashayed straight across the keyboard, blocking Jodi's view of the screen. "We made friends."

Jodi smiled too and nuzzled Forrest's face. "Yeah? Hello, girl. Told you he was all right really."

"'All right,' really?"

"Yeah," Jodi said. "You're all right, you know. I'd shag ya."

"I'll bear that in mind." Rupert did his best to look miffed, and failed, because it was hard to be truly annoyed when Jodi was smiling. "We can fuck later, though. We've got shit to do first."

"We have?"

"Yup." Rupert brandished the real reason he'd sought Jodi out—the flowery photo album they did their best to update every week. "Have you picked your photo yet?"

Jodi shook his head and retrieved his phone from the windowsill behind him, plugging it into the computer and bringing up the photo application. "I took loads this week. I don't know how I'm going to choose."

"So choose a couple."

"That's against the rules."

"Our rules, so who gives a fuck?"

Jodi laughed. "True. Oooh, what about this one?"

Rupert peered over Jodi's shoulder at the screen, dodging Forrest's tail as she swiped it over his face. The image was of Jodi and Indie, sitting at the top of the slide in the nearby park, grinning like idiots and squinting in the summer sun. "That's lovely. When did you take that?"

"Thursday. We went to the park when you were in the shower, remember?"

Rupert shrugged and mussed Jodi's hair. "I don't remember everything, boyo."

Consternation flashed in Jodi's gaze. Too often he did expect Rupert to remember *everything*, like he'd forgotten that even without a brain injury life just wasn't like that. "You know I really appreciate you letting me take Indie out, don't you?"

"I reckon you appreciate it as much as I love that you want to."

Jodi shot Rupert a quizzical glance. "Why wouldn't I?"

Rupert shrugged again. "Your relationship with Indie was one of the things I loved most about you."

"You mean . . . before?"

"Aye. I never gave up on you, boyo, but there was some shit I convinced myself I'd never see again. You and Indie against the world was one of them."

For a moment, Jodi looked upset, but his gaze quickly cleared. As his recovery had progressed, he'd got better at handling negative emotions. He clicked through a few more images, finishing on a selfie he'd taken of him and Rupert outside the fire station a couple of nights ago when Jodi had met him after work. "I like this one too."

Rupert studied the photo. At first glance it seemed like nothing out of the ordinary, then he remembered that had been the day Jodi had come into the station and shown his face to a station full of men he hadn't seen since the accident—men he had no memory of. He had spent the week leading up to his visit learning their names and histories so they'd never know it. "I love you."

Jodi lolled his head on Rupert's shoulder. "I love you too. Shall I print these out?"

"Aye."

The printer in the corner flashed to life, filling the room with the whirring Rupert had always found strangely calming. He waited until it was finished and then replaced Jodi's phone with his own as Jodi took the already printed photographs and set about sticking them into the last few pages of the album.

"We need a new one," Jodi remarked.

Rupert nodded absently as he printed the photo he'd picked out to be the final image in the album. Jodi appeared at his shoulder as he pulled it from the printer.

"Our mortgage agreement? Are you fucking serious?"

"Deadly." Rupert trimmed the edges of the photo so it would fit in the small album. "It's kinda crass, but I want to remember this."

"You're not likely to forget we're moving house, mate."

"No . . . but I might forget there was a time when we didn't think we'd ever be able to."

Jodi said nothing, his gaze suddenly distant as he clearly searched his patchy memories for ones that matched what Rupert meant. "It never bothered me that this place was mine, even before. I never felt like you owed me or some shit. You know that, don't you? It wasn't my home until you and Indie came."

"I know, boyo, I know. If it's any consolation, I never felt like a kept man, but this . . . ." Rupert gestured at the photograph that documented the joint mortgage that would finance their exodus from the bustling big smoke of the city. "Moving away with you and Indie, to a house I can put my name to . . . Fuck, I don't know. I guess I just feel like I've finally given you both what you deserve."

"Indie deserves the world, Rupe. Me? I'm happy with a jar of Nutella and a wank job."

Trust Jodi to lower the tone. Rupert took a halfhearted swipe at him, but Forrest intercepted his hand, leaping onto Jodi's shoulder with a low growl that told Rupert as much as he needed to know about whose cat she was going to be.

As if he'd expected anything less. Jodi had been irresistible to *him* from the day they'd met, and despite what life had thrown at them, nothing had changed—nothing, and everything.

"Do you think Jen will ever want Indie back?"

"Hmm?" Rupert glanced down at Jodi. "Oh, shit . . . I don't know. I'm still getting used to the fact that she gave her up in the first place."

Jodi grunted. He hadn't seemed at all surprised when Jen had appeared one evening a few months ago, bearing the good news that she was emigrating to Brazil with her new boyfriend. *"Face it, mate. She's a selfish twat."*

Indeed, and her loss was Rupert's gain. He wasn't going to let her invade another moment of his life, not even this one . . . especially not this one. Rupert pulled Jodi close again and squeezed him as tight as he dared. The accident had nearly killed them both—in different ways—but what they had now was as imperfectly perfect as it had ever been, and he wouldn't change a thing. "I fucking love you, boyo, you know that?"

Jodi looked up and grinned. "Course I do, knobhead. That's why I made it this far."

"Knobhead?"

"Yeah . . . knobhead, my whole fucking world, whatever I call you, it all means the same, 'cause I love you too, Rupe. More than you'll ever know."

Dear Reader,

Thank you for reading Garrett Leigh's *What Remains*!

We know your time is precious and you have many, many entertainment options, so it means a lot that you've chosen to spend your time reading. We really hope you enjoyed it.

We'd be honored if you'd consider posting a review—good or bad—on sites like **Amazon, Barnes & Noble, Kobo, Goodreads, Twitter, Facebook, Tumblr,** and your blog or website. We'd also be honored if you told your friends and family about this book. Word of mouth is a book's lifeblood!

For more information on upcoming releases, author interviews, blog tours, contests, giveaways, and more, please sign up for our weekly, spam-free newsletter and visit us around the web:

Newsletter: tinyurl.com/RiptideSignup
Twitter: twitter.com/RiptideBooks
Facebook: facebook.com/RiptidePublishing
Goodreads: tinyurl.com/RiptideOnGoodreads
Tumblr: riptidepublishing.tumblr.com

Thank you so much for Reading the Rainbow!

RiptidePublishing.com

Also by
GARRETT LEIGH

Misfits
Between Ghosts

The Roads Series
Slide
Marked
Rare
Freed

Blue Boy Series
Bullet
Bones
Bold

Heart

Only Love Series
Only Love
Awake and Alive

Heated Beat Series
My Mate Jack
Lucky Man

More Than Life
Shadow Bound

Coming Soon
Rented Heart

About the AUTHOR

Garrett Leigh is a British writer and book designer, currently working for Dreamspinner Press, Loose Id, Riptide Publishing, and Black Jazz Press. Her protagonists will always be tortured, crippled, broken, and deeply flawed. Throw in a tale of enduring true love, some stubbly facial hair, and a bunch of tattoos, and you've got yourself a Garrett special.

When not writing, Garrett can generally be found procrastinating on Twitter, cooking up a storm, or sitting on her behind doing as little as possible. That, and dreaming up new ways to torture her characters. Garrett believes in happy endings; she just likes to make her boys work for it.

Garrett also works as a freelance cover artist for various publishing houses and independent authors. For cover art info, please visit blackjazzdesign.com.

Website: garrettleigh.com
Facebook: facebook.com/garrettleighbooks
Twitter: twitter.com/Garrett_Leigh
Instagram: instagram.com/garrett_leigh

Enjoy more stories like
What Remains
at RiptidePublishing.com!

58340213R00149

Made in the USA
Charleston, SC
07 July 2016